The Complete Esoteric Wisdom Collection (Vol 1)

The Kybalion, Corpus Hermeticum, The Emerald Tablet & The Virgin of the World — Foundations of Hermetic Philosophy

A Modern Translation

Adapted for the Contemporary Reader

The Three Initiates | Hermes Trismegistus

Translated by Tim Zengerink

Table Of Contents

Preface - Message to the Reader

What If You Could Help Rebuild the Greatest Library in Human History?

Thousands of years ago, the Library of Alexandria stood as the crown jewel of human achievement — a sanctuary where the collected wisdom of every known civilization was gathered, preserved, and shared freely.

And then, it was lost.

Through fire, conquest, and the slow erosion of time, humanity lost not just books — but ideas, dreams, discoveries, and stories that could have changed the world forever.

Today, the Library of Alexandria lives again — and you are invited to be a part of its restoration.

Our mission is simple yet profound:

To rebuild the greatest library the world has ever known, and to translate all timeless works into every language and dialect, so that no seeker of knowledge is ever left behind again.

By joining our movement to rebuild the modern Library of Alexandria, you become part of an unprecedented mission:

- **Unlimited Access to the Greatest Audiobooks & eBooks Ever Written:**

  Instantly explore thousands of legendary works—Plato, Shakespeare, Jane Austen, Leo Tolstoy, and countless more. All instantly available to read or listen, placing a complete literary universe at your fingertips.

- **Beautiful Paperback & Deluxe Editions at Printing Cost**

  Own any title as an elegant paperback, deluxe hardcover, or stunning collectible boxset—offered to you at true printing cost, delivered straight to your door. Build your personal Library of Alexandria, crafted for beauty, built for durability, and worthy of proud display.

- **Fresh Translations for Modern Readers—in Every Language & Dialect**

  Enjoy timeless masterpieces reimagined in clear, contemporary language—no more outdated phrases or obscure references. Alongside the original versions, we're tirelessly translating these classics into every language and dialect imaginable, ensuring accessibility and understanding across cultures and generations.

- **Join a Global Renaissance of Literature & Knowledge**

  You directly support expanding our library, publishing deluxe editions at true cost, translating works into all global languages, and bringing humanity's greatest stories to people everywhere. By joining today, you're not just preserving a legacy of masterpieces; you set in motion a powerful wave of literary accessibility.

Become a Torchbearer of Knowledge.

Join us for free now at **LibraryofAlexandria.com**

Together, we will ensure that the light of human wisdom never fades again.

With gratitude and a shared love of knowledge,
The Modern Library of Alexandria Team

Visit:

www.libraryofalexandria.com

Or scan the code below:

Introduction

The Hidden Teachings of Hermes:
Light from the Dawn of Time

In the mysterious borderlands between ancient philosophy, mystical revelation, and occult science lies a tradition of thought that has endured for millennia—one that has inspired sages, alchemists, mystics, and philosophers from every era. This is the Hermetic tradition: a body of wisdom said to originate from the legendary figure Hermes Trismegistus, the "thrice-great" sage who was revered as a god of wisdom, a prophet of the divine, and a synthesizer of Egyptian, Greek, and cosmic insight.

The Complete Esoteric Wisdom Collection (Vol. 1) brings together four foundational texts of this tradition: The Kybalion by the mysterious "Three Initiates," and three classic Hermetic writings attributed to Hermes Trismegistus—The Corpus Hermeticum, The Emerald Tablet, and The Virgin of the World. These works do not offer theology in the dogmatic sense, nor philosophy in the academic sense. Instead, they present a spiritual science—an intuitive, symbolic, and deeply experiential guide to the nature of the universe, the soul, and the divine mind that binds all things.

These are not easy texts. They are not meant to be read once, but studied, reflected upon, and experienced inwardly. They speak a symbolic language that must be deciphered not only by intellect, but by the imagination and the spirit. Yet for those who persist, they offer a vision of existence that transcends ordinary perception: a cosmos that is mental, energetic, hierarchical, purposeful, and sacred.

This introduction will offer a map through this esoteric terrain, beginning with the modern synthesis of The Kybalion, then turning to the ancient voice of Hermes himself in The Corpus Hermeticum, The

Emerald Tablet, and The Virgin of the World. Along the way, we will explore the key Hermetic doctrines—mentalism, correspondence, vibration, polarity, rhythm, cause and effect, and gender—and the metaphysical vision that underpins them. We will also see how these teachings influenced later developments in Neoplatonism, Gnosticism, alchemy, Renaissance thought, and modern esotericism.

The Kybalion:
Seven Principles of the Hermetic Mind

Published in 1908 by the enigmatic "Three Initiates," The Kybalion represents a revival of Hermetic wisdom in the modern era. Drawing on ancient ideas but couched in a clear, instructional tone, it lays out seven principles that, according to the text, govern all reality. These principles are not merely metaphysical concepts—they are laws of consciousness, modes of perception, and tools of transformation.

1. The Principle of Mentalism: "All is Mind; the Universe is Mental." This principle asserts that everything begins and ends in consciousness. Reality is not a collection of dead matter, but a living thought in the mind of the All. This view anticipates both idealist philosophy and quantum metaphysics.

2. The Principle of Correspondence: "As above, so below; as below, so above." This ancient maxim expresses the unity of all levels of reality—macrocosm and microcosm reflect each other. It invites the student to read the world symbolically and understand hidden truths through analogy.

3. The Principle of Vibration: "Nothing rests; everything moves." All phenomena are states of vibration—whether physical, mental, or spiritual. Understanding vibration allows the initiate to attune to higher frequencies and shift states of consciousness.

4. The Principle of Polarity: "Everything is dual; everything has poles." Opposites are actually extremes of the same thing. Love and hate, hot and cold, light and dark—each exists on a continuum. The adept learns to reconcile opposites through

transmutation.

5. The Principle of Rhythm: "Everything flows, out and in." All events move in cycles. The pendulum swings, tides rise and fall. Knowing rhythm allows one to ride the waves of change rather than be overwhelmed by them.

6. The Principle of Cause and Effect: "Every cause has its effect." Nothing happens by chance. The wise student seeks to operate from the level of causes rather than be pushed around by effects.

7. The Principle of Gender: "Gender is in everything." Masculine and feminine principles exist not only biologically but metaphysically, as creative forces in all planes of existence. True mastery comes from their harmonious integration.

These principles form the basis of Hermetic practice and worldview. They are not beliefs but keys—tools that allow the initiate to reframe their experience, reclaim their agency, and work in harmony with the laws of the universe.

The Kybalion draws from ancient wisdom but speaks to modern seekers. It teaches that we are not victims of fate, but co-creators in a living cosmos. Its tone is both mystical and practical, its message both empowering and humbling. In many ways, it prepares the reader for the deeper, more poetic voice of Hermes Trismegistus.

The Corpus Hermeticum, The Emerald Tablet, and The Virgin of the World

The three classic Hermetic texts in this volume come from a tradition that flourished in the early centuries of the Common Era. Though rooted in earlier Egyptian and Hellenistic sources, the Hermetic writings were likely composed between the 1st and 4th centuries CE, during a time of intense cultural syncretism, religious experimentation, and philosophical exploration in the Greco-Roman world.

The Corpus Hermeticum is the heart of Hermetic literature. It consists of philosophical dialogues between Hermes and his student, often named Tat or Asclepius. These writings blend Platonism, Egyptian mythology, Stoicism, and Gnostic themes into a unified spiritual cosmology. The central themes include:

- The nature of the divine mind (Nous) and the All.
- The origin of the cosmos through emanation rather than creation.
- The role of the human being as a microcosm and intermediary.
- The concept of gnosis—inner, direct knowledge of the divine.
- The fall and redemption of the soul through rebirth into spiritual awareness.

The tone of these dialogues is visionary, initiatory, and poetic. They describe mystical experiences, cosmic visions, and the journey of the soul through various states of being. Hermes speaks not as a theologian or logician but as a spiritual guide awakening the student to their divine origins.

The Emerald Tablet, though brief, has had an outsized impact on Western esotericism. Attributed to Hermes and inscribed in cryptic poetic verse, the Tablet encapsulates the entire Hermetic worldview in just a few lines. Its famous axiom—"That which is below is like that which is above, and that which is above is like that which is below"—captures the principle of correspondence.

The Tablet describes the creation of the cosmos through the union of opposites, the transformation of elements, and the ascent of spirit through matter. It is an alchemical text in the deepest sense—not only about metals but about the soul's purification and integration. It has been quoted, glossed, and revered by alchemists, Rosicrucians, and magicians for centuries.

The Virgin of the World, another Hermetic text, presents a more mythological and cosmological tone. It speaks of the mysteries of Isis and Osiris, the sacred feminine, and the transmission of esoteric wisdom from divine beings to early humanity. It integrates Egyptian religious motifs with Greek philosophical reflection and reflects the initiatory character of ancient temples.

This text emphasizes the divine nature of true knowledge, the sacredness of the world, and the need for purity of heart in the seeker. It stands as a reminder that Hermeticism is not just a set of doctrines, but a sacred path—a lineage of initiation into the mysteries of existence.

Hermeticism in the Modern World: Legacy and Living Practice

The Hermetic tradition has never been static. From the Renaissance magi to 19th-century occult orders to 21st-century seekers, its core teachings have been rediscovered, reinterpreted, and reactivated across the centuries. Its influence can be seen in alchemy, Kabbalah, Rosicrucianism, Gnosticism, Theosophy, Jungian psychology, and the modern mindfulness movement.

Why does Hermeticism endure?

Because it speaks to the deepest longing of the human soul: to understand the cosmos, to awaken divine potential, to bridge the visible and invisible. It offers a map of the inner world that resonates with ancient intuition and modern insight. It teaches that the universe is alive, that we are not separate from it, and that knowledge is not memorization but transformation.

These texts are not relics. They are invitations. They do not demand belief; they invite exploration. They are not commandments but whispers—guiding the soul toward its source, helping it remember what it already knows.

To read this volume is to step into a temple of wisdom—not built of stone, but woven from the subtle threads of symbol, myth, vision, and law. It is to sit at the feet of Hermes, the messenger of the gods, and listen to truths spoken not in human language alone, but in the secret language of the spirit.

Welcome to The Complete Esoteric Wisdom Collection (Vol. 1). May its teachings inspire your inquiry, deepen your awareness, and awaken in you the memory of the divine spark you carry within.

The Kybalion

The Three Initiates

Introduction

We are pleased to present this little book to students and seekers of the Secret Doctrines, based on the ancient Hermetic teachings. Even though many writings on occultism refer to these teachings, surprisingly little has been written about them directly. For this reason, we believe that those who are eager to uncover hidden truths will welcome the release of this volume.

The goal of this book is not to promote a specific philosophy or doctrine. Instead, it aims to provide students with a clear understanding of the Truth, helping them connect and make sense of the different pieces of occult knowledge they may have encountered. These bits of knowledge can often seem to contradict each other, discouraging beginners. We are not trying to build a new "Temple of Knowledge" with this book. Rather, we offer it as a "Master-Key" that will help students unlock the many doors within the Temple of Mystery they have already entered.

Throughout history, no part of the world's occult knowledge has been as closely guarded as the Hermetic teachings. These teachings have been carefully passed down for thousands of years from their founder, Hermes Trismegistus, known as the "scribe of the gods." He lived in ancient Egypt at a time when humanity was still in its early stages. Legend has it that Hermes not only lived during the time of Abraham but also taught the wise sage himself. Hermes has always been seen as a guiding light in occultism, illuminating many teachings that have spread through the centuries. Many of the core ideas found in the mystical teachings of various cultures can be traced back to Hermes. Even the oldest teachings from India seem to have their roots in Hermetic thought.

It is said that many advanced spiritual seekers from India traveled to Egypt to learn from Hermes himself. These travelers gained the "Master-Key" from him, which helped them understand and connect their different beliefs. In this way, the Secret Doctrine became well established. People from many lands considered Hermes the "Master of Masters," and his influence was so powerful that even after centuries of changes, similarities remain in the spiritual ideas taught by different cultures today. Students of religion can see traces of Hermetic teachings in every significant religion, whether ancient or modern. Despite the differences between various beliefs, the Hermetic teachings act as a bridge, uniting them.

Hermes' mission was not to create a school of thought that would dominate the world's ideas. Instead, he planted the seeds of truth, allowing them to grow in many forms. Throughout history, a few dedicated individuals have preserved the original purity of his teachings. These individuals refused to share the teachings widely, reserving them for the few who were ready to understand them. These truths were passed down quietly, from teacher to student, by word of mouth. In every generation, in different parts of the world, there have been a few Initiates who kept the sacred flame of Hermetic wisdom alive. These guardians of the truth have always been willing to share their light to rekindle the lamps of those whose understanding had grown dim. They faithfully tended the "Perpetual Lamp of Wisdom," ensuring that it never went out, just as a poet once wrote: "O, let not the flame die out! Cherished age after age in its dark cavern—in its holy temples cherished. Fed by pure ministers of love—let not the flame die out!"

These dedicated teachers were never interested in gaining approval from the public or gathering large followings. They understood that only a few people in each generation would be ready to receive the truth or recognize it when presented. They kept the deeper teachings— what they called the "strong meat"—for the few who could handle it, while others received simpler lessons—"milk for babes." They saved their most valuable teachings for those who truly appreciated them, rather than sharing them with those who would not understand and instead treat them with contempt. However, these teachers always followed the teachings of Hermes, who said, "Where fall the footsteps of the Master, the ears of those ready for his Teaching open wide." They also lived by the saying, "When the ears of the student are ready to hear, then cometh the lips to fill them with wisdom." Still, their wisdom was kept hidden, as expressed in another Hermetic teaching: "The lips of Wisdom are closed, except to the ears of Understanding."

Some have criticized the Hermetic approach, saying that their secrecy was unhelpful. But history shows the wisdom of the Masters, who knew it was pointless to teach what the world was not prepared to accept. The Hermetists did not try to become martyrs. Instead, they chose to stay silent, watching patiently as others were persecuted and misunderstood for trying to share advanced truths with those who were not ready. Even now, persecution continues, and there are still parts of the Hermetic teachings that, if shared openly, would provoke hostility and scorn from the masses, just as in the past when people cried, "Crucify! Crucify!"

In this book, we aim to introduce the key ideas of The Kybalion, focusing on practical principles that you can apply yourself. Rather than offering all the details, we leave it to the true student to explore and use these teachings. If you are genuinely ready to learn, you will discover how to apply these principles. If not, you will need to grow into the kind of person who can understand them. Otherwise, the Hermetic teachings will be nothing more than "words, words, words" to you.

Chapter I

Hermetic Philosophy. "The lips of wisdom are closed, except to the ears of Understanding."—The Kybalion.

The foundational esoteric and mystical teachings that have influenced the philosophies of nations and cultures for thousands of years originated in ancient Egypt. Egypt, known for the Pyramids and the Sphinx, was the birthplace of hidden wisdom and spiritual teachings. Many nations borrowed from its Secret Doctrine. Countries such as India, Persia, Chaldea, Medea, China, Japan, Assyria, Greece, Rome, and others benefited greatly from the knowledge offered by the wise teachers and masters of Egypt to those prepared to receive it.

In ancient Egypt lived great masters and adepts who have rarely been equaled, much less surpassed, throughout history. The greatest of all mystical schools was located in Egypt, and the students who entered its temples later became masters and teachers themselves, spreading this sacred knowledge to different parts of the world. All serious students of the occult acknowledge the wisdom they owe to these ancient masters of Egypt.

Among these remarkable masters was one called "The Master of Masters." This figure, Hermes Trismegistus, lived in Egypt in ancient times. He is recognized as the founder of occult wisdom, the creator of astrology, and the discoverer of alchemy. His life story has been lost over the centuries, though various countries have argued over which one could claim to be his birthplace, thousands of years ago. No one knows the exact time of his final presence in Egypt, but scholars place it during the earliest dynasties—long before the time of Moses. Some believe he lived during the time of Abraham, and certain traditions suggest that Abraham learned some of his mystical knowledge from Hermes himself.

According to tradition, Hermes lived for 300 years. After his death, the Egyptians honored him as a god, calling him Thoth. Many years later, the Greeks also worshipped him as a god, referring to him as Hermes, the god of wisdom. The Egyptians revered him for countless centuries, calling him "the scribe of the gods" and giving him the title "Trismegistus," meaning "the thrice-great," a name that reflected his unmatched greatness. Throughout the ancient world, the name Hermes Trismegistus became synonymous with the source of wisdom.

Even today, the word "hermetic" refers to something secret or tightly sealed, a nod to the fact that Hermes' followers kept their teachings hidden. They followed the principle that wisdom should not be shared with those unprepared to understand it, summarizing this idea with the phrase "milk for babes, meat for strong men." This principle, though familiar in Christian texts, was used by the Egyptians long before Christianity.

This careful sharing of knowledge has always defined the Hermetic tradition, and it continues to do so today. Hermetic teachings exist in many religions and countries but have never been tied to any specific place or religious group. The ancient teachers warned against turning these teachings into rigid beliefs. History shows the wisdom of this caution. The mystical knowledge of ancient India and Persia faded because religious leaders blended it with theology, burying it under superstition and dogma. The same happened in ancient Greece and Rome. Similarly, the Hermetic teachings of the Gnostics and early Christians were lost during the time of Constantine, when philosophy was replaced with theology. The Christian Church lost much of its original spirit and had to search for centuries to reconnect with its ancient beliefs. Now, in the twentieth century, it seems the Church is once again striving to rediscover these ancient mystical truths.

However, some faithful individuals have always kept the flame of truth alive. These devoted souls carefully guarded this knowledge, ensuring it was never lost. Thanks to their dedication, we still have access to these teachings today. But they are not widely available in books. Instead, this wisdom has been passed down directly from master to student. Even when it was written, the meaning was hidden in the language of alchemy and astrology, so only those with the right understanding could grasp it. This secrecy was necessary to protect the teachings from religious persecution during the Middle Ages when the truth was often met with fire, torture, and execution. Even now, few reliable books on Hermetic philosophy exist, though references to it can be found in many writings on occult subjects. However, Hermetic philosophy remains the "Master-Key" that can unlock all occult teachings.

In the early days, a collection of essential Hermetic teachings was compiled and passed from teacher to student. This collection was called "The Kybalion," though the meaning of the title has been lost over time. These teachings have been transmitted orally through the generations. They consist of maxims, axioms, and principles that are not clear to outsiders but become understandable to students once explained by Hermetic initiates. These teachings form the foundation of "The Art of Hermetic Alchemy," which focuses on mastering mental forces rather than manipulating physical materials. The legend of the "Philosopher's Stone," said to turn base metals into gold, is actually an allegory about transforming mental energy, understood by true students of Hermeticism.

In this book, which serves as the first lesson, we invite students to explore the teachings of The Kybalion. These teachings are explained here by us, humble students of the tradition, who still learn from the wisdom of Hermes, the Master. We present many of the maxims, axioms, and principles from The Kybalion, accompanied by explanations and examples to make the ideas easier to understand for modern readers, as the original text is intentionally written in complex terms.

The original sayings from The Kybalion appear in quotation marks, with proper credit given. Our explanations are integrated into the main text. We hope that this book will be as valuable to today's students as it has been to those who have walked this path before, following the teachings of Hermes Trismegistus—the greatest of all masters. As The Kybalion says: "Where fall the footsteps of the Master, the ears of those ready for his Teaching open wide." And, "When the ears of the student are ready to hear, then cometh the lips to fill them with Wisdom."

According to these teachings, this book will reach those who are ready to receive its lessons. Likewise, when a student is ready for the truth, the necessary book or teacher will appear. This reflects the Hermetic Principle of Cause and Effect, also known as The Law of

Attraction, which brings together students and teachers at the right time. So it is, and so it shall be!

Chapter II

The Seven Hermetic Principles. "There are seven Principles of Truth. Anyone who truly understands them holds the Magic Key that opens all the Doors of the Temple." — The Kybalion. The Seven Hermetic Principles, which form the foundation of the entire Hermetic Philosophy, are: I. The Principle of Mentalism. II. The Principle of Correspondence. III. The Principle of Vibration. IV. The Principle of Polarity. V. The Principle of Rhythm. VI. The Principle of Cause and Effect. VII. The Principle of Gender. These Seven Principles will be discussed and explained throughout these lessons. But first, here's a brief explanation of each one.

The Principle of Mentalism. "THE ALL is MIND; The Universe is Mental." — The Kybalion. This Principle teaches that "All is Mind." It explains that THE ALL (the true reality behind everything we see and experience as "The Material Universe," "Life," "Matter," "Energy," and all that we perceive with our physical senses) is actually SPIRIT. This spirit, while beyond our full understanding or ability to define, can be thought of as an Infinite, Universal, Living Mind. It also teaches that the whole universe, as well as everything within it, exists in the Mind of THE ALL and follows the Laws of Created Things. We "live and move and have our being" within this Mind. By understanding this, we can explain all the mental and psychic phenomena that grab so much public attention, which otherwise seem impossible to understand through science. Knowing this great Hermetic Principle of Mentalism helps people to easily understand the rules of the Mental Universe and use them to improve their lives. The Hermetic Student can then wisely apply the great Mental Laws, instead of just using them randomly. With this Master-Key in hand, the student can unlock many doors in the mental and psychic temple of knowledge, and walk through them with understanding. This Principle also explains the true nature of "Energy," "Power," and "Matter," and shows why and how they are all controlled by the Mastery of Mind. One of the ancient Hermetic Masters wrote long ago, "He who understands the truth about the Mental Nature of the Universe is well on his way to Mastery." These words are just as true today as they were back then. Without this Master-Key, Mastery is impossible, and the student will knock in vain on the many doors of The Temple.

The Principle of Correspondence. "As above, so below; as below, so above." — The Kybalion. This Principle teaches that there is always a relationship between the laws and events on different planes of Being and Life. The old Hermetic saying goes, "As above, so below; as below, so above." Understanding this Principle gives people the ability to solve many puzzles and unlock hidden secrets of Nature. There are planes beyond our understanding, but by using the Principle of Correspondence, we can comprehend much more than we otherwise could. This Principle applies universally to all levels of the material, mental, and spiritual universe—it is a Universal Law. The ancient Hermeticists considered this Principle one of the most important mental tools for clearing away the barriers hiding the Unknown. Using this Principle could even lift the Veil of Isis, allowing a glimpse of the goddess's face. Just as knowledge of Geometry allows people to measure distant stars while sitting in their observatories, knowledge of the Principle of Correspondence lets them reason from the Known to the Unknown. By studying the smallest things, they can understand the greatest.

The Principle of Vibration. "Nothing rests; everything moves; everything vibrates." — The Kybalion. This Principle teaches that "everything is in motion"; "everything vibrates"; "nothing stays still." These facts are supported by modern science, and every new discovery further confirms them. But this Hermetic Principle was known thousands of years ago by the Ancient Egyptian Masters. It explains that the differences between various manifestations of Matter, Energy,

Mind, and even Spirit are mainly caused by different rates of vibration. From THE ALL, which is Pure Spirit, down to the grossest form of Matter, everything vibrates—the higher the vibration, the higher the position on the scale. The vibration of Spirit is so incredibly fast that it seems motionless—just like how a rapidly spinning wheel can appear to stand still. At the other end of the scale, there are forms of matter whose vibrations are so slow that they appear to be at rest. Between these extremes are countless degrees of vibration. From tiny particles like electrons and atoms to planets and galaxies, everything is moving and vibrating. This is true not just in the material world, but also on the levels of energy, force, and the mind, where different states depend on vibration, and even on spiritual levels. Understanding this Principle, along with the right methods, allows Hermetic students to control their own mental vibrations and even influence those of others. The Masters use this Principle to control Nature's phenomena in various ways. "He who understands the Principle of Vibration holds the sceptre of power," one ancient writer said.

The Principle of Polarity. "Everything is dual; everything has poles; everything has its pair of opposites. Things that seem alike can be different, and things that seem opposite are really connected in nature, just differing in degree. Extremes meet. All truths are only half-truths, and every paradox can be solved." — The Kybalion. This principle teaches that everything has two sides or two poles. Every aspect of life has a pair of opposites, a concept rooted in ancient Hermetic teachings. It also clarifies many puzzling contradictions like "Thesis and antithesis are identical but differ in degree," "Opposites are the same, just varying in degree," and "All opposites can be harmonized." It reveals how two sides that seem far apart are, in fact, just the outermost ends of the same thing, with many degrees between them. For example, heat and cold are considered opposites, but they are simply different degrees of the same thing. If you look at a thermometer, there's no clear point where heat ends and cold begins. There's no such thing as absolute heat or cold—just varying levels of temperature, which are expressions of vibration. In this way, heat and cold are just two extremes of what we call "temperature."

This principle also applies to light and darkness, which are different degrees of the same thing. Where does darkness end and light begin? What's the difference between big and small, hard and soft, or loud and quiet? These are just shifts in degree between two poles. Even love and hate—two emotions that seem completely opposite—are connected by a spectrum, with feelings like "liking" or "disliking" in the middle. You might find yourself not knowing whether you like or dislike something because both are just different points on the same emotional scale. This idea also explains how feelings can shift quickly. Many people have experienced a sudden change from love to hate or hate to love. These changes happen naturally, but Hermetic teachings show that you can intentionally change these feelings by using your willpower and specific methods. Good and evil are also two ends of the same thing. Hermetic practitioners know how to turn negative emotions into positive ones by using the Principle of Polarity. This practice, called "Mental Alchemy," is a key part of the ancient and modern Hermetic tradition. Anyone who masters this principle can change their emotional state and even influence others if they put in the necessary time and effort.

The Principle of Rhythm. "Everything flows in and out, like tides. Everything rises and falls. The swing of a pendulum happens in all things. The distance it swings to one side will be matched by the distance it swings to the other. Rhythm balances everything." — The Kybalion. This principle teaches that everything in life moves like a pendulum, with a back-and-forth motion, like the ebb and flow of tides. This rhythmic motion happens between the two poles of everything, as described by the Principle of Polarity. There is always a flow forward and a pullback, an advance and a retreat, and a rise followed by a fall. This rhythm can be seen in all areas of life: the creation and destruction of worlds, the rise and fall of nations, and the lives of people, animals, and even thoughts. Hermetic students find this principle especially important in understanding how their minds work. They've discovered ways to lessen the effects of rhythm on their thoughts by applying specific methods and mental exercises. Although it's impossible to stop rhythm from happening, they've learned how to avoid being controlled by it. Instead, they consciously use it to their advantage.

The Hermetic masters can position themselves at the emotional or mental state they prefer and neutralize the natural swing of the pendulum that would pull them to the opposite side. Many people unknowingly resist these shifts to some degree, but masters do it deliberately and with focused willpower. This gives them a sense of stability and peace that may seem unbelievable to others, who are often tossed around by their emotions like a swinging pendulum. Hermeticists have studied the principles of polarity and rhythm closely and have developed ways to counteract their effects. Learning to control these natural forces is a core part of what Hermetics call "Mental Alchemy."

The Principle of Cause and Effect. "Every cause has its effect, and every effect has its cause. Everything happens according to laws. What people call 'chance' is just a law that hasn't been recognized yet. There are many levels of causation, but nothing escapes the law." — The Kybalion. This principle states that everything that happens has a cause, and every cause produces an effect. Nothing happens randomly; everything follows a set of laws. Even events that seem like chance are simply the result of laws that people don't understand. While there are many levels of cause and effect, with higher causes influencing lower ones, nothing escapes this universal law.

Hermetic practitioners have learned how to rise above the normal cycle of cause and effect by moving their minds to a higher plane. By doing this, they become the ones causing events, rather than being affected by them. Most people are controlled by external causes—like their environment, other people's wills, or their own habits and emotions—without realizing it. They are like pieces on a chessboard, moved by outside forces. However, those who understand this principle become players in the game of life. They take control of their thoughts, emotions, and actions, and they shape their environment instead of being shaped by it. While even the masters must follow the laws of higher planes, they learn to take charge of their lives on their own level.

The Principle of Gender. "Gender is in everything. Everything has both masculine and feminine principles, which are present on every level of existence." — The Kybalion. This principle teaches that gender exists in everything. Masculine and feminine energies are always at work, not only in the physical world but also on mental and spiritual levels. In the physical world, this principle appears as biological sex, but on higher levels, it takes different forms. No creation—whether physical, mental, or spiritual—can happen without both masculine and feminine principles working together. Understanding how these principles work sheds light on many of life's mysteries.

Every person and every thing contains both masculine and feminine qualities. For example, even men have feminine traits, and women have masculine traits. To fully understand mental and spiritual creation, you must study and understand this principle. It holds the answers to many puzzles about life. However, Hermetic teachings warn against mistaking this principle for the immoral ideas promoted by some groups. These distorted beliefs, which focus on indulgence and misuse of natural principles, have no place in Hermetic philosophy. The Hermetic tradition strongly condemns such practices, which only harm the mind, body, and soul. Hermetic teachings are pure, and those who seek base or corrupt ideas must look elsewhere. As the saying goes, "To the pure, all things are pure; to the corrupt, all things are corrupt.

Chapter III

Mental Transmutation "Mind, just like metals and elements, can be changed from one state to another, from one degree to the next, from one condition to another, from one extreme to the opposite, and from one kind of vibration to another. True Hermetic Transmutation is a Mental Art."—The Kybalion.

As mentioned before, the Hermetists were the first alchemists, astrologers, and psychologists, with Hermes being the founder of these fields of thought. Modern astronomy evolved from astrology, modern chemistry grew from alchemy, and modern psychology developed from the mystical psychology of the ancients. However, it would be wrong to assume that the ancient people were unaware of the knowledge that modern schools believe to be their unique discovery. Ancient Egyptian records carved in stone clearly show that they had a deep understanding of astronomy, with the design of the Pyramids reflecting their knowledge of the science. They were also familiar with chemistry since fragments of their writings reveal they understood the chemical properties of materials. In fact, many ancient ideas about physics are now being confirmed by new scientific discoveries, particularly in areas related to the structure of matter. Furthermore, the ancient Egyptians were highly skilled in psychology, especially in aspects that are often overlooked by modern science. Today, these overlooked areas are being rediscovered under the term "psychic science," which has puzzled modern psychologists and made them reluctantly admit that there might be some truth to it.

The truth is that beyond material chemistry, astronomy, and psychology—meaning psychology in terms of how the brain works—the ancients possessed knowledge of a higher form of each subject. They studied astrology, which is a deeper form of astronomy; alchemy, which is a deeper form of chemistry; and mystic psychology, which goes beyond the surface level of modern psychology. They had both inner knowledge, which modern scientists lack, and outer knowledge, which is the only kind of understanding most modern scientists possess. Among the many secret skills of the Hermetists was something called Mental Transmutation, which is the focus of this lesson.

"Transmutation" generally refers to the ancient practice of changing metals—especially turning base metals into gold. According to Webster's dictionary, "to transmute" means "to change the nature, form, or substance of something into another." In the same way, "Mental Transmutation" is about transforming mental states, forms, and conditions into different ones. You could call it "Mental Chemistry" if that helps—a kind of practical mystic psychology.

But there is more to Mental Transmutation than it might seem at first. Transmutation, whether we talk about alchemy, chemistry, or mental work, is powerful enough by itself. Even if it stopped at just changing thoughts, it would still be one of the most important areas of study. But this is just the beginning—let's explore why.

The first of the Seven Hermetic Principles is the Principle of Mentalism, which states: "THE ALL is Mind; the Universe is Mental." This means that the true nature of everything in the Universe is the Mind, and that the entire Universe exists within the Mind of THE ALL. We will explore this principle in more detail later, but for now, let's think about what happens if this principle is true.

If the entire Universe is made of Mind, then Mental Transmutation is the art of changing the Universe itself through mental effort. This means transforming things related to matter, energy, and thought. Mental Transmutation is what the ancient mystics referred to as "Magic," although they provided few practical instructions on how to do it. If everything is fundamentally mental, then mastering the ability to change mental conditions gives a person control over both mental and material conditions.

Only the most advanced Mental Alchemists have reached the level of mastery needed to control physical forces, such as influencing the elements of nature, stopping storms, or even causing or preventing earthquakes and other powerful events. While these abilities may sound unbelievable, many experienced occultists believe that people with these abilities—called Masters—have existed and still exist today.

Reliable teachers assure their students of this, based on personal experiences that support these claims. These Masters do not show off their powers in public but prefer to live in seclusion, focusing on their personal growth along the Path of Attainment. We mention them here to highlight that their powers are purely mental, working according to the Hermetic Principle of Mentalism. "The Universe is Mental"—The Kybalion.

Even though not everyone reaches the level of a Master, many Initiates and Teachers can work effectively on the Mental Plane, practicing Mental Transmutation. In fact, all forms of "psychic phenomena," "mental influence," "mental science," and "new-thought" practices operate on the same principle, regardless of what they are called.

Students and practitioners of Mental Transmutation work within the Mental Plane, transforming mental states and conditions according to specific methods. These methods include various "treatments," "affirmations," and "denials" used by schools of mental science. However, most of these methods are imperfect and lack the deep understanding possessed by the ancient masters. Modern practitioners often work without knowing the true principles that underlie their efforts.

Using Hermetic methods, a person can not only change their own mental states but also influence the mental states of others, sometimes without even realizing it. In many cases, this influence happens consciously, especially when the person affected does not know how to protect themselves mentally. Furthermore, as many practitioners of modern mental science know, people's thoughts and desires can even change the external conditions of their lives, as long as those conditions are connected to the minds of other people.

Since the public is already familiar with these ideas, we won't go into them in detail. Instead, we want to show how the Hermetic Principle of Polarity is at work in all these practices, whether they are used for good or bad purposes. The same mental force can be directed in opposite ways, depending on how it is applied.

This little book will outline the key principles of Mental Transmutation so that anyone who reads it can understand the core ideas and use them as a master key to unlock many aspects of the Principle of Polarity.

We will now move on to the first of the Hermetic Seven Principles: the Principle of Mentalism, which teaches that "THE ALL is Mind; the Universe is Mental," as written in The Kybalion. We ask readers to pay close attention and study this principle carefully because it is the foundation of the entire Hermetic philosophy and the Mental Art of Transmutation.

Chapter IV

The All "Behind the Universe of Time, Space, and Change, there is always the Substantial Reality—the Fundamental Truth."—The Kybalion.

"Substance" refers to what lies beneath all outward appearances—it is the essence, the core reality, the thing itself. "Substantial" means something that truly exists, that is essential and real. "Reality" refers to the state of being real—something that lasts, remains true, and holds firm.

Behind everything we see and experience, there must be a Substantial Reality. This is the law. When a person reflects on the Universe, of which they are a part, they see nothing but constant change—matter changes, forces change, and even mental states change. Nothing simply stays as it is; everything is always in the process of becoming something else. Nothing remains still—everything is born, grows, and eventually dies. The moment something reaches its peak, it begins to decline. This constant rise and fall follow the law of rhythm. Nothing remains the same; everything shifts and transforms. Creation and destruction, birth, growth, and death are always happening in cycles.

A thoughtful person will eventually realize that all these changing things must be mere appearances or expressions of a deeper force—some kind of Substantial Reality that lies beneath them all. Throughout history, across different cultures and eras, thinkers have acknowledged the need to recognize this Substantial Reality. Every philosophy that has earned respect has been based on this idea. People have called this Reality by many names. Some have referred to it as God, using various titles. Others have called it the Infinite and Eternal Energy, while some have tried to name it Matter. Regardless of the name, all these thinkers have agreed that this Reality exists. Its existence is obvious and requires no proof.

In these lessons, we follow the example of great thinkers, both ancient and modern—especially the Hermetic Masters—by calling this Substantial Reality "THE ALL." We believe this term is the best way to refer to what is beyond names and descriptions. We accept the teachings of these wise thinkers and those enlightened beings who have reached higher levels of understanding. They have all said that the true nature of THE ALL is unknowable. Only THE ALL can fully understand itself.

The Hermetists teach that THE ALL, in its essence, must always remain unknowable. They see all the attempts by theologians and philosophers to define or describe the nature of THE ALL as the limited efforts of human minds trying to grasp the infinite. These efforts always fail and will continue to fail, given the nature of the task. People who pursue such inquiries get lost in endless thoughts, leading them nowhere and leaving them unprepared for the practical challenges of life. They are like a squirrel running in circles on a wheel, going nowhere and ending up where they started—still trapped.

Even worse are those who try to assign human traits, emotions, or qualities to THE ALL. They imagine it has the same emotions as people, including jealousy or the desire for praise and offerings. Such ideas reflect the childish thinking of early humanity and are now being abandoned by mature minds.

It's important to clarify the difference between Religion and Theology, as well as Philosophy and Metaphysics. Religion, to us, is the personal realization of THE ALL's existence and a person's relationship with it. Theology, on the other hand, involves people assigning personal qualities and desires to THE ALL and acting as intermediaries between it and others. Philosophy is the pursuit of knowledge within the realm of the knowable, while Metaphysics tries to explore what is beyond understanding—much like theology. In our view, Religion and Philosophy are grounded in reality, while Theology and Metaphysics are shaky, offering no real support for the human mind or soul. We don't demand that our students agree with these definitions but offer them to clarify our position. You won't hear much about Theology or Metaphysics in these lessons.

While the true nature of THE ALL is beyond our understanding, there are certain truths about its existence that our minds must accept. These truths align with the insights of enlightened beings from higher levels of awareness, and they are worth exploring. We now invite you to join us in this exploration.

"The Fundamental Truth—the Substantial Reality—cannot be named, but wise people call it THE ALL."—The Kybalion.

"In its essence, THE ALL is unknowable."—The Kybalion.

"Still, reason's insights must be accepted and respected."—The Kybalion.

Human reason gives us certain truths about THE ALL that we must accept if we are to think clearly, even though these truths do not remove the mystery surrounding THE ALL.

THE ALL must be everything that truly exists. Nothing can exist outside of it, or else THE ALL would not be complete. THE ALL must be infinite because nothing exists to limit, define, or restrict it. It must be infinite in time, meaning eternal, since there is nothing else that could have created it. Something cannot come from nothing, and if THE ALL had ever not existed, it would not exist now. It must continue to exist forever, as nothing can destroy it. THE ALL must also be infinite in space, meaning it must be everywhere, without interruption or separation. There is nothing outside of it to break its continuity. It must also be infinite in power, or absolute, as nothing exists to limit or challenge it. THE ALL is subject to no other power because no other power exists.

THE ALL must be unchangeable because there is nothing to cause it to change. There is nothing into which it could transform and nothing from which it could have transformed. It cannot gain or lose anything and cannot become more or less than it already is. THE ALL has always been and will always remain exactly as it is. Nothing else exists for it to become.

Because THE ALL is infinite, eternal, and unchangeable, anything that is temporary or limited cannot truly be THE ALL. Since nothing exists outside of THE ALL, all finite things must ultimately amount to nothing. Don't be alarmed by this idea. We are not leading you toward the teachings of Christian Science under the cover of Hermetic Philosophy. There is a way to resolve these seemingly conflicting ideas, and we will get to it soon.

We observe what we call "matter," which serves as the foundation for all physical forms. But is THE ALL simply matter? No, because matter cannot give rise to life or mind. Since life and mind are present in the Universe, THE ALL cannot be merely matter. Nothing can rise higher than its source. An effect cannot contain more than what is present in its cause. Also, modern science tells us that matter is not truly solid but is energy or force vibrating at a low frequency. As one modern thinker said, "Matter has melted into mystery." Science now rests on the idea of energy, not matter.

But is THE ALL just energy or force? No, because energy and force, as defined by materialists, are mechanical and lifeless. Life and mind cannot come from something without life or intelligence. As we said earlier, nothing can rise higher than its source. Since life and mind exist, THE ALL cannot be only energy or force. We know this to be true because we are alive and capable of thinking about this question, as are those who argue that energy is everything.

What, then, is greater than matter or energy? Life and mind, in all their many forms, stand above them. But is THE ALL simply life and mind as we know them? Yes and no. THE ALL is not life or mind in the way we experience them. Instead, it is something far greater—something the enlightened call "Spirit." THE ALL is Infinite Living Mind, as far beyond our understanding of life and mind as life and mind are beyond mechanical forces or matter. It is what the illumined refer to when they say the word "SPIRIT."

THE ALL is Infinite Living Mind—what the enlightened call SPIRIT.

Chapter V

The Mental Universe "The Universe is Mental—held in the Mind of THE ALL."—The Kybalion.

THE ALL is SPIRIT. But what exactly is Spirit? It's hard to define Spirit because it is essentially the same as THE ALL, which cannot be explained or fully understood. Spirit is just a name people use to describe the highest idea of Infinite Living Mind. It refers to the Real Essence—Living Mind that is far beyond the life and mind we know, just as life and mind are superior to mechanical energy and matter. Spirit is something beyond what we can fully grasp, and we use the word only to help us think and talk about THE ALL. For the sake of understanding, we can think of Spirit as Infinite Living Mind, even though we admit that we can't truly understand it. We must either approach it in this way or stop thinking about it altogether.

Now let's consider the nature of the Universe, both as a whole and in its individual parts. What is the Universe? We know that nothing can exist outside of THE ALL. But does that mean the Universe is the same as THE ALL? No, because the Universe is made up of many things, is constantly changing, and doesn't fit the characteristics we know to be true about THE ALL. If the Universe is not THE ALL, does that mean it is nothing? That idea doesn't feel right either, because we know the Universe exists in some way. If the Universe is neither THE ALL nor nothing, what can it be? Let's explore this more carefully.

If the Universe exists, it must have come from THE ALL, since something cannot come from nothing. But how could THE ALL create the Universe? Some philosophers say that THE ALL made the Universe out of itself, from its own being. But this idea doesn't work, because THE ALL cannot be divided or reduced. Also, if every part of the Universe were a piece of THE ALL, each part would have to know it was THE ALL, and THE ALL could not forget its own nature and become a simple object or creature. Some people, realizing that THE ALL is everything, have claimed that they are identical to THE ALL, declaring, "I AM GOD," much to the amusement of ordinary people and the concern of wise thinkers. This claim would be as strange as a tiny cell in your body shouting, "I am the entire human being!"

So, if the Universe is not THE ALL and wasn't made by dividing THE ALL, what else could it be? The answer lies in the "Principle of Correspondence." This principle says that what happens on one level of existence mirrors what happens on other levels. The Hermetic saying, "As above, so below," applies here. Let's try to understand how THE ALL might create by looking at how we create things in our own experience.

On our level, humans can create things in two main ways. First, we can make something by using materials from the outside world. But this cannot apply to THE ALL, because there is nothing outside of it to use. Second, we reproduce by creating new life, passing part of ourselves to our offspring. But this also cannot apply to THE ALL, since it cannot give away or divide any part of itself, nor can it multiply or increase. This leaves only one other way to create: through thought. Humans create mental images and ideas without using physical materials or reproducing themselves, yet these mental creations are still real within their own minds.

Following the Principle of Correspondence, we can say that THE ALL creates the Universe in a similar way—mentally. Just as humans create thoughts and images in their minds, THE ALL creates the Universe within its Infinite Mind. This idea agrees with the teachings of the wise and enlightened throughout history. THE ALL creates everything mentally, without using materials or dividing itself. There is no other way it could create.

Just as you, as a person, can create a world of thoughts within your mind, THE ALL creates many Universes within its own Mind. However, your mind is limited, while THE ALL's Mind is infinite. The two are alike in nature but different in scale. As we continue, we will explore the process of creation in more detail. But for now, keep this in mind: the Universe and everything in it is a Mental Creation of THE ALL. In truth, everything is Mind!

"THE ALL creates countless Universes in its Infinite Mind. To THE ALL, the birth, growth, and end of millions of Universes is as brief as the blink of an eye."—The Kybalion. "The Infinite Mind of THE ALL is the womb of Universes."—The Kybalion.

The Principle of Gender applies to everything, whether physical, mental, or spiritual. But gender, in this sense, is not the same as biological sex. Instead, gender refers to the concept of creation and generation. Wherever anything is created, the Principle of Gender is at work, including in the creation of Universes.

It's important not to misunderstand this teaching. We are not saying that there is a male and female God or Creator. That idea is just a distorted version of older teachings. The truth is that THE ALL is beyond gender, just as it is beyond all other laws, including time and space. THE ALL is the source of all laws but is not bound by them. However, when THE ALL creates on a lower level of existence, it follows the laws and principles of that level, including the Principle of Gender. On the mental plane, this principle appears as two aspects: the Masculine and the Feminine.

This may sound surprising at first, but you already accept this idea without realizing it. People talk about God as the Father and Nature as the Mother. They refer to the Divine Father and the Universal Mother, instinctively recognizing the Principle of Gender in the Universe.

However, the Hermetic teaching does not imply that there are two separate beings. THE ALL is One. The two aspects—Masculine and Feminine—are just different ways that THE ALL expresses itself. The Masculine aspect represents the Will of THE ALL, which directs and sets things in motion. The Feminine aspect, which we might call Nature, carries out the work of creation and evolution, developing everything from simple forms to human beings and beyond, all according to natural laws. You can think of the Masculine aspect as the Divine Father and the Feminine aspect as the Universal Mother, from whom all things are born. But remember, these are only metaphors to help us understand the process. The truth is that the entire Universe is created and exists within the Infinite Mind of THE ALL.

You can better understand this idea by applying the Law of Correspondence to yourself. In your mind, there is a part of you that observes your thoughts and mental images—the part you call "I." There is also the part that generates those thoughts, which you might call "Me." Just as you witness your own mental creations, THE ALL creates and observes the Universe within its Mind.

It's no wonder that people feel a natural sense of reverence toward THE ALL. This feeling is what we call "religion"—a deep respect for the Father Mind. And when we look at the wonders of Nature, we are filled with awe, sensing a connection to the Mother Mind, just as a child feels safe and comforted in a parent's embrace.

Don't make the mistake of thinking that the world you see around you—the Earth, which is just a tiny speck in the vast Universe—is the whole of existence. There are countless other worlds, some far greater than ours, and many Universes exist within the Infinite Mind of THE ALL. Even within our solar system, there are levels of life far higher than our own. Compared to the beings that exist on these higher levels, we are like the simple creatures that live at the bottom of the ocean compared to humans. Yet these higher beings were once like us, and we too will evolve and rise to even greater heights, for that is the destiny of humanity, as the wise have taught.

Death is not an end but a transition into a new life. You will continue to grow, rising to higher and higher levels of existence over endless ages. The Universe is your home, and you will explore its farthest reaches long before the end of time. You are a part of the Infinite Mind of THE ALL, and your possibilities are limitless in both time and space.

When the grand cycle of existence eventually draws to a close, and THE ALL reabsorbs all its creations, you will return willingly, for you will finally understand the full truth of being one with THE ALL. This is what the enlightened have seen and shared with us.

Until then, rest assured that you are safe, protected by the infinite power of the Father-Mother Mind.

"Within the Father-Mother Mind, mortal children are at home."—The Kybalion. "There is no one in the Universe without a Father or a Mother."—The Kybalion.

Chapter VI

The Divine Paradox. The half-wise, noticing that the Universe isn't completely real, think they can ignore its laws. These people are arrogant and foolish, and they end up suffering because of it, like someone being thrown against rocks and torn apart by the forces of nature. The truly wise, however, understand how the Universe works and know how to use higher laws to overcome lower ones. They master the art of Alchemy, transforming bad things into good ones, and through this skill, they succeed. True mastery isn't about strange dreams, wild visions, or unrealistic ideas. It's about using higher forces to rise above the lower ones, freeing yourself from the hardships of the lower planes by living at a higher level. The real tool of the Master is transformation, not denial or arrogance.

This is the Paradox of the Universe, which appears because of the Principle of Polarity. This principle is at work when THE ALL begins to create. It teaches us the difference between half-wisdom and real wisdom. While the Infinite ALL sees the Universe and everything in it as something like a dream or a meditation, to all things that are finite, the Universe must be treated as real. Life, actions, and thoughts should follow the rules of the Universe, even as we remember the higher truth behind it. Everything must work according to its own plane and laws. If THE ALL were to believe the Universe was fully real, there would be no way for anything to rise to a higher level. The Universe would stop growing, and progress would end. Similarly, if a person, through half-wisdom, acts as though the Universe is only a dream, like one of their own dreams, they will get stuck. They'll wander aimlessly, making no real progress, until the natural laws they ignored force them awake, leaving them hurt and confused. Keep your mind focused on your goals, but also watch where you step, or you'll trip while looking upward. Remember the Divine Paradox: while the Universe isn't truly real, it still exists. Always keep in mind the two sides of truth—the Absolute and the Relative—and be careful of accepting only half-truths.

The Hermetic teaching called the Law of Paradox is tied to the Principle of Polarity. Hermetic writings often refer to this paradox when discussing life and existence. Teachers frequently warn students not to overlook the "other side" of any topic. This warning is especially important when thinking about the Absolute and the Relative, which can confuse many students and lead them away from common sense. Students are reminded to understand the Divine Paradox between the Absolute and the Relative, or they may get lost in half-truths. This lesson is meant to make this concept clear. Read it carefully.

The first thought that comes to someone who learns that the Universe is a mental creation of THE ALL is that everything in the Universe is just an illusion, a dream. This idea can be hard to accept. However, like all great truths, it needs to be understood from both the Absolute and the Relative perspectives. From the Absolute point of view, the Universe is like a dream, something fleeting and unreal compared to THE ALL. We see hints of this idea in everyday life when we talk about the world as temporary, always changing, with things coming and going. All philosophers, scientists, and religious thinkers agree that anything created must be temporary and imperfect compared to the infinite nature of THE ALL. This idea isn't unique to Hermetic teachings—it can be found in many different schools of thought.

The Hermetic teachings don't claim the Universe is unreal any more than other philosophies do, though their way of presenting the idea may sound more surprising. Anything with a beginning and an end is, in some sense, unreal, and all philosophies agree on this point. From the Absolute view, only THE ALL is truly real. Whether the Universe is made of matter or is a mental creation in THE ALL's mind, it is temporary and ever-changing. It's important to understand this before judging the Hermetic idea that the Universe is a mental creation. Think about other ideas and see if they don't also align with this truth.

But focusing only on the Absolute view shows only one side of things. The Relative view also matters. Absolute Truth means seeing things as THE ALL sees them, while Relative Truth means seeing things as humans understand them. While THE ALL may view the Universe as just a dream, for the finite beings within it, the Universe feels real and must be treated as such. Although we know the Universe isn't the ultimate reality, we still have to live and act as though it is. We aren't THE ALL, after all.

For example, we know that matter seems real to our senses, even though science tells us it's made up of atoms and particles of energy in constant motion. If we kick a stone, it feels solid, even though we understand it's just a collection of vibrating particles. But remember, our foot and brain are also made of these particles, and without our mind, we wouldn't even be aware of the stone or the foot at all.

Similarly, an artist's idea or a writer's characters feel real to them, even though they only exist in their minds. If this is true for humans, how much more real must the mental images in THE ALL's mind feel? To us, this mental Universe is the only reality we can know, no matter how high we rise in understanding. As we move closer to understanding THE ALL, we begin to see how temporary things are. But only when THE ALL brings us fully into itself will the illusion completely disappear.

So, instead of worrying about whether the Universe is an illusion, we should focus on understanding and using its mental laws. These laws are just as real and unchangeable as any physical laws, and we are all bound by them. Everything except THE ALL must follow these laws, because THE ALL is the source of all laws. No being, no matter how powerful, can escape the laws. Even the most advanced Masters, who seem like gods to us, must obey the laws of the Universe. If these high beings must follow the laws, it's foolish for ordinary people to think they can ignore them just because they understand the Universe is mental in nature.

The Hermetic Principle of Mentalism explains that everything in the Universe is mental in nature, but it doesn't change scientific ideas about the Universe, life, or evolution. In fact, science supports the Hermetic teachings. The only difference is that science calls the foundation of the Universe "energy," while Hermeticism calls it "mind." The philosopher Herbert Spencer's idea of "infinite and eternal energy" aligns closely with Hermetic thought, though Hermetic teachings add that this energy is part of THE ALL's mind.

Students of Hermeticism don't have to abandon their scientific beliefs. They only need to understand that "THE ALL is Mind, and the Universe is mental." The other six Hermetic principles will fit naturally with scientific knowledge, helping to clarify complex ideas. This alignment shouldn't be surprising since Hermetic thought influenced the early Greek philosophers, whose ideas form the foundation of modern science. The main difference between science and Hermeticism lies in the acceptance of the Principle of Mentalism, but science is slowly moving toward this understanding.

This lesson aims to show that the Universe, its laws, and its phenomena are just as real to us as they would be under other philosophical systems, even though everything is always changing and temporary. Regardless of what we believe, we must live as though these things are real. The difference with Mentalism is that it recognizes mental power as the greatest force, which can transform life for those who understand and use it.

Students must learn the advantages of Mentalism and apply its laws. But they should avoid the mistake of thinking the world isn't real and ignoring their responsibilities, as the half-wise do. Those who make this mistake end up suffering because of their foolishness. Instead, students should follow the example of the wise, using higher laws to overcome lower ones and transforming negative things into positive ones. As the Kybalion teaches, mastery lies not in strange dreams or fantasies, but in using higher forces to overcome lower ones, escaping pain by rising to a higher level. Always remember: transformation, not denial, is the key tool of the Master.

We don't live in a dream world, but in a Universe that feels real and demands our effort. Our goal isn't to deny the Universe, but to live fully, using its laws to rise higher and higher. Life's meaning may be beyond our understanding, but the wisest advice is to live according to the best in us and follow the Universe's upward path, no matter how things appear. We are all on a journey, with resting places along the way. Read the Kybalion carefully, and follow the example of the wise, avoiding the mistakes of the half-wise, who suffer because of their ignorance.

Chapter VII

"The All" in All. "While All is in THE ALL, it is equally true that THE ALL is in All. To the one who truly understands this truth, great knowledge has come."—The Kybalion. Many people have often heard the idea that their God (called by many names) is "All in All," but very few have realized the deeper, hidden truth behind these words, which are usually spoken without much thought. This common phrase is actually a remnant of the ancient Hermetic teaching quoted above. As the Kybalion says: "To the one who truly understands this truth, great knowledge has come." Since this is the case, let us search for this truth, because understanding it holds great importance. This Hermetic principle hides one of the most powerful truths in philosophy, science, and religion.

We have already explained the Hermetic teaching that the nature of the Universe is mental—that "the Universe is Mental, existing within the Mind of THE ALL." As the Kybalion says in the passage we just quoted: "All is in THE ALL." But there is also a related truth that must not be overlooked: "It is equally true that THE ALL is in All." Though these two ideas might seem to contradict each other, they actually make sense when viewed through the Law of Paradox. This law helps us understand the relationship between THE ALL and the mental universe it creates. We've talked about how "All is in THE ALL." Now, let's explore what it means that "THE ALL is in All."

Hermetic teachings tell us that THE ALL is present within its creation—it exists in every part, particle, and combination in the Universe. This idea is often explained using the Principle of

Correspondence. Teachers encourage students to imagine something in their minds, such as a person, an idea, or a character. A writer or playwright, for example, might picture their characters, just as a painter or sculptor imagines what they want to create. In each case, the mental image exists only within the creator's mind. At the same time, the creator is also present within the image they form. In other words, the life, spirit, and meaning of the mental image come from the mind of the person who created it. Think about this idea carefully until you fully understand it.

To make this clearer, let's use Shakespeare's characters as an example. At the time Shakespeare imagined Othello, Iago, Hamlet, or King Lear, these characters only existed in his mind. Yet, Shakespeare was also "inside" each of these characters, giving them their personality, life, and purpose. Similarly, when we think about characters like Micawber, Oliver Twist, or Uriah Heep, we might ask: Are these characters separate, independent beings, or are they extensions of Dickens, their creator? Do famous sculptures or paintings, like the Venus of Medici or the Sistine Madonna, have spirits of their own, or do they reflect the creative power of their artists? According to the Law of Paradox, both ideas are true depending on how we look at them. Micawber is both Micawber and, at the same time, part of Dickens. But although we can say Micawber reflects Dickens, they are not exactly the same.

In the same way, a person might say: "The spirit of my creator is within me, but I am not my creator." This view is very different from the mistaken belief that some people loudly claim when they say, "I am God!" Imagine how strange it would sound if Micawber or the sneaky Uriah Heep declared, "I am Dickens!" Or if some of Shakespeare's lowly characters proudly announced, "I am Shakespeare!" THE ALL exists in the earthworm, but the earthworm is not THE ALL. Yet the mystery remains: Even though the earthworm is just a small part of the creation, living entirely within the Mind of THE ALL, THE ALL is still present within the earthworm and within every particle that makes it. Is there any greater mystery than this idea: "All in THE ALL, and THE ALL in All"?

Of course, these examples are limited and cannot fully capture this idea, since they describe the creation of mental images by finite human minds, while the Universe is the creation of an Infinite Mind. The difference between these two types of creation is vast. Yet, the same principle applies to both. The Principle of Correspondence shows that what is true on one level is also true on another—"As above, so below; as below, so above."

The more a person becomes aware of the spirit that exists within them, the higher they will rise in their spiritual development. This awareness, recognition, and expression of the spirit within us is the true meaning of spiritual growth. Remember this: Spiritual development is the recognition, realization, and manifestation of the spirit within us. This is the essence of true religion.

There are many levels of existence in the Universe, ranging from the lowest forms of matter to the highest forms of spirit, which are very close to the essence of THE ALL. Everything in the Universe is constantly moving upward on this scale of life. Even though things might seem to move in different directions at times, everything is ultimately progressing toward THE ALL. This upward movement is a journey of returning home, and no matter how things may appear, all progress leads back to THE ALL. This is the message of enlightened teachings.

The Hermetic teachings explain that the Universe was created mentally by THE ALL. At the start of creation, THE ALL, in its state of "Being," directed its Will toward "Becoming," and this is how the creative process began. This process involves lowering the level of vibration until it reaches a point where the densest form of matter appears. This phase is known as Involution, during which THE ALL becomes deeply connected with its creation. Hermetic teachings compare this to the way an artist or writer becomes so absorbed in their work that they almost forget themselves, living entirely within their creation. If we replace the word "wrapped" with "rapt," it may help us better understand this concept.

This first stage of creation is sometimes called the "Outpouring" of divine energy, while the next stage, Evolution, is called the "Indrawing." At the furthest point of the Outpouring, the vibrations are at their lowest, and this is the point furthest from THE ALL. When the Evolution stage begins, the pendulum of Rhythm starts swinging back toward home. Hermetic teachings describe this as a return journey.

During the Outpouring, creation is unified and whole. But as Evolution begins, the Law of Individualization takes over. This means that creation begins to separate into individual units of force. What started as unformed energy returns to THE ALL as countless developed life forms that have grown through physical, mental, and spiritual evolution. These beings rise higher and higher along the scale of life, becoming more advanced as they move closer to their source.

The ancient Hermetists often use the word "Meditation" to describe how the Universe was created mentally in the Mind of THE ALL. They also sometimes use the word "Contemplation." But what they really seem to mean is the use of Divine Attention. The word "Attention" comes from a Latin root meaning "to reach out" or "to stretch out," so paying attention is like mentally stretching out or extending your mind's energy. Once you understand the real meaning of "Attention," this idea becomes much clearer.

The Hermetic Teachings about Evolution say that THE ALL began the process of Creation by meditating on the Universe. In doing so, it set the foundations of the material world and brought it into existence through thought. After this, THE ALL gradually awakens from its Meditation, and this awakening sparks the beginning of Evolution. This process unfolds step by step on the material, mental, and spiritual levels. Everything begins to move toward the spiritual.

Matter becomes less heavy, new forms of life start appearing, and combinations of elements form. Life grows and shows itself in higher forms, and Mind becomes more visible as the vibrations rise higher and higher. The entire Evolution process moves forward following the laws of the "Indrawing" phase. This whole process takes countless ages, each lasting millions of years, but the Illumined tell us that the entire creation—both Involution and Evolution—is only like the blink of an eye to THE ALL.

When these endless cycles of time finally come to an end, THE ALL pulls back its Attention, Contemplation, and Meditation from the Universe because the Great Work is complete. At that point, everything returns to THE ALL, where it first came from. Yet, the mystery remains: even though all things return to THE ALL, the spirit of each soul is not destroyed—it expands infinitely. The Creator and the Created become one. This is what the Illumined tell us.

This example of THE ALL meditating and then awakening is only an attempt by teachers to explain something infinite using a simple idea. Even so, "As Below, so Above" applies. The difference is only in degree. Just as THE ALL wakes up from its meditation on the Universe, people also stop focusing on the material world over time and instead turn more toward the Spirit within, which is "The Divine Ego."

There is another point we want to mention, even though it touches on metaphysical ideas, which we usually avoid because such thoughts often lead nowhere. But it's important to address a question that everyone who seeks truth eventually asks: "Why does THE ALL create Universes?" This question takes different forms, but it all comes down to this same curiosity.

Many people have tried to answer this, but no answer fully explains it. Some suggest that THE ALL creates to gain something, but that makes no sense since THE ALL already has everything. Others think THE ALL created the Universe to have something to love or for amusement, or maybe because it felt lonely or wanted to show its power. These are all childish ideas from an immature way of thinking.

Some thinkers suggest that THE ALL creates because it feels an inner need or instinct to create. While this idea is more advanced than others, it still has a flaw. If THE ALL were forced to act by its own nature or creative instinct, then that instinct would be more powerful than THE ALL, and that makes no sense. However, THE ALL does create, and it seems to experience some kind of satisfaction in doing so. It's hard to avoid the conclusion that THE ALL might have something similar to an inner nature, a creative instinct like humans, but on an infinite scale, with infinite desire and will. It wouldn't act unless it wanted to, and it wouldn't want to unless it found satisfaction in acting. This inner nature can be understood through the Law of Correspondence.

Even with that said, it is better to think of THE ALL as acting completely freely, without any internal or external force influencing it. This is the heart of the problem—and the challenge of understanding it.

In truth, there is no "reason" why THE ALL acts, because having a reason would suggest a cause. And THE ALL is beyond the law of cause and effect, except when it decides to set that law into motion. In the end, the nature of THE ALL is impossible to fully understand— just as THE ALL itself is unknowable. We can only say that "THE ALL acts because it acts." THE ALL is its own reason, law, and action, all at once. THE ALL, its reason, its law, and its action are all the same thing—just different ways of naming the same truth.

The teachers sharing these ideas believe that the answer to this mystery is hidden deep within THE ALL, along with the secret of its existence. The Law of Correspondence helps us understand only part of THE ALL, the part connected to "Becoming." Beyond that lies the aspect of "Being," where all laws dissolve into one Law, and all principles merge into one Principle. In that state, THE ALL, Principle, and Being are one and the same. This is why trying to explain these things through metaphysics is pointless. We mention this only to acknowledge the question and show that the usual answers from metaphysics and theology are inadequate.

Some ancient and modern Hermetic teachers have leaned toward the idea that THE ALL has an inner nature, following the Law of Correspondence. However, the legends say that when advanced students asked Hermes, the Great, about this mystery, he pressed his lips together and stayed silent, showing that there is no answer. Perhaps he was applying the saying, "The lips of Wisdom are closed, except to the ears of Understanding," meaning even his advanced students didn't yet have the understanding needed for the answer. If Hermes knew the secret, he didn't share it. And if Hermes remained silent, what ordinary person would dare to teach it?

Whatever the answer may be—if there even is one—the truth remains: "While All is in THE ALL, it is equally true that THE ALL is in All." This teaching is essential. And we can add one final reminder: "To the one who truly understands this truth, great knowledge has come.

Chapter VIII

The Planes of Correspondence. "As above, so below; as below, so above."—The Kybalion. The second great Hermetic principle explains that there is harmony, agreement, and connection between all the different levels of life, existence, and reality. This truth is fundamental because everything in the Universe comes from the same source, and the same laws, principles, and qualities apply to every unit and every combination of forces as they operate on their respective levels of existence.

For easier understanding, Hermetic philosophy divides the Universe into three main types of phenomena, known as the Three Great Planes: The Great Physical Plane, the Great Mental Plane, and the Great Spiritual Plane. These divisions are not absolute but are more like steps along the continuous scale of life, starting from the lowest form of undifferentiated matter and rising to the highest point, which is pure spirit. The boundaries between these planes blend into one another, so it is difficult to clearly separate the higher forms of the physical from the lower forms of the mental, or the higher mental from the lower spiritual.

In short, the Three Great Planes are like broad categories representing different levels of how life manifests. Although we won't go into deep detail about these planes here, it is useful to give a general description to help with understanding.

One question that beginners often ask is: "What exactly is a plane?" This word has been used a lot in occult writings, but it is not always clearly explained. People often wonder if a plane is a physical place with size and dimensions or if it's just a state of mind or condition. The answer is that it is neither a place nor simply a condition. It is more like a degree or level in a scale that can be measured, but not in the usual sense of dimensions like length, width, and height. This concept may seem strange at first, but let's explore it further.

In everyday life, a "dimension" refers to measurements such as length, width, and height—or sometimes thickness or circumference. However, occultists and some scientists recognize another dimension beyond these physical ones. This extra dimension is often referred to as the "Fourth Dimension," which is used to measure the different degrees or levels of existence, called "planes."

This Fourth Dimension could be described as the Dimension of Vibration. Both modern science and Hermetic teachings recognize that everything in the Universe is constantly moving and vibrating— nothing ever stays still. Every object and form, from the lowest to the highest, vibrates at a specific rate. These vibrations differ not only in speed but also in the way they move and behave. The degree of vibration determines the level, or plane, on which something exists.

The higher the vibration, the higher the plane and the more advanced the form of life on that plane. So, even though a plane is not a physical location or a simple state of being, it shares qualities with both.

It's important to keep in mind that the Three Great Planes are not actual separations within the Universe but are used by Hermetic thinkers to help us study and understand the different levels and forms of life. Whether it's an atom, a force, the mind of a human, or the being of an angel, all are different levels within the same system. The only difference between them is the degree of their vibration, and everything in the Universe is a creation of THE ALL, existing within the Infinite Mind of THE ALL.

Each of the Three Great Planes is further divided into Seven Minor Planes, and each Minor Plane is again divided into seven sub-planes. These divisions are not strict and rigid; instead, they smoothly transition into one another. They are mainly used to help us study and understand the complex activities and forces at work in the Universe.

The Great Physical Plane and its Seven Minor Planes cover all things related to physical matter and energy. This includes everything we recognize as material objects, forces, and physical energy. However, the Hermetic teachings emphasize that matter is not a separate thing by itself. Matter is just one form of energy, vibrating at a very low frequency. Hermetic teachings classify matter under the category of energy, assigning three of the Seven Minor Planes of the Physical Plane to it.

The Seven Minor Physical Planes are: The Plane of Matter (A), the Plane of Matter (B), the Plane of Matter (C), the Plane of Ethereal Substance, the Plane of Energy (A), the Plane of Energy (B), and the Plane of Energy (C).

The Plane of Matter (A) includes the forms of matter we are familiar with—solids, liquids, and gases—as described in physics textbooks. The Plane of Matter (B) contains higher, more refined forms of matter, which science is only beginning to understand, such as the energy associated with radioactive elements like radium. The Plane of Matter (C) holds the most subtle and delicate forms of matter, which modern science has not yet discovered.

The Plane of Ethereal Substance includes what scientists call "the Ether," a highly flexible and nearly weightless substance that fills all space. This ether acts as a medium for transmitting energy waves like light, heat, and electricity. It serves as a link between matter and energy because it shares qualities with both. According to Hermetic teachings, this plane is further divided into seven sub-levels. In fact, there are seven types of ether, not just one.

Above the Plane of Ethereal Substance is the Plane of Energy (A). This plane consists of the ordinary forms of energy that science recognizes, with seven sub-planes: Heat, Light, Magnetism, Electricity, and Attraction (including forces like Gravity, Cohesion, and Chemical Affinity). There are also other kinds of energy that scientific experiments have detected, though they have not yet been named or classified. The Plane of Energy (B) consists of seven sub-planes of more advanced energy forms, which science has yet to discover. These forces are sometimes called "Nature's Finer Forces," and they are involved in mental phenomena, making such events possible. The Plane of Energy (C) contains seven sub-planes of energy that are so advanced they resemble life itself. However, this energy is beyond what ordinary human minds can understand. It is only accessible to beings from the Spiritual Plane, and it can be thought of as a kind of divine power. These beings, compared to the most advanced humans, seem like gods.

The Great Mental Plane includes all living beings we know, along with other types that are less familiar to most people but are known to occultists. The seven minor planes of the Mental Plane can be described as follows, though this classification is somewhat simplified and not meant to be fully detailed here.

The Plane of Mineral Mind involves the states and conditions of the entities that give life to minerals and chemicals. These entities are not the same as the molecules, atoms, or particles that make up minerals. Instead, they are like the souls that animate these physical forms, just as a human body is not the same as the soul that inhabits it. These entities have low levels of life, mind, and development—just slightly more advanced than the energy units found on the higher physical planes. Most people don't think that minerals have mind, soul, or life, but occultists know they do, and modern science is starting to agree. Molecules, atoms, and particles show behaviors that could be described as attraction, repulsion, love, and dislike. Some modern scientists even believe that the emotions and desires of atoms are just a simpler version of those found in humans.

The Plane of Elemental Mind (A) includes the mental and vital development of beings that are unknown to most people but are recognized by occultists. These entities are invisible to ordinary human senses, but they play important roles in the Universe. Their intelligence is between that of minerals and plants.

The Plane of Plant Mind consists of the mental and life states of the beings that make up the plant world. The idea that plants have life, mind, and even souls is becoming more accepted, with recent scientific studies showing new insights into how plants live and think.

The Plane of Elemental Mind (B) involves more advanced elemental beings that are part of the natural order. They exist between the mental levels of plants and animals and share characteristics of both.

The Plane of Animal Mind includes the mental states of beings that animate animals, which are familiar to us all. There's no need to describe this level further, as the world of animals is well-known.

The Plane of Elemental Mind (C) consists of beings that are still invisible but have qualities that blend both animal and human traits. The most advanced of these beings have intelligence that is nearly human.

The Plane of Human Mind contains all the mental and life experiences of human beings, divided into seven levels. Most people today exist on the fourth level, and only the most intelligent have reached the fifth. It has taken humanity millions of years to reach this point, and it will take many more years to reach the sixth and seventh levels. However, earlier civilizations have already moved through these levels and advanced to higher planes. Some people today have already reached the sixth and seventh levels and gone beyond. Those who reach the sixth level will be like "Super-Men," while those on the seventh will be "Over-Men."

While we've mentioned the Elementary Planes briefly, we won't go into too much detail here, as it's beyond the scope of this discussion. These planes serve a similar role to the black keys on a piano, which complement the white keys. While the white keys alone can create music, the black keys are essential for certain scales and harmonies. In the same way, the Elementary Planes connect the other planes and allow for transitions between them. Some forms of evolution happen on these planes, and those who understand these ideas can gain new insights into how life moves from one kingdom to another. The great elemental beings are well-known to all occultists, and their presence is mentioned throughout esoteric writings. Readers of stories like Bulwer's Zanoni will recognize the kinds of beings that inhabit these planes of life.

Moving from the Great Mental Plane to the Great Spiritual Plane, how can we describe these higher states of Being, Life, and Mind? It is hard to explain them to minds that are not yet ready to understand even the deeper levels of the Human Mind. It is like trying to describe light to someone born blind, sweetness to someone who has never tasted anything sweet, or harmony to someone born deaf. We can only speak about them in very general terms.

The seven minor planes of the Great Spiritual Plane, each with its seven sub-divisions, are home to beings whose Life, Mind, and Forms are far beyond anything we can imagine. These beings are as advanced beyond today's humans as humans are beyond earthworms, minerals, or even certain forms of energy or matter. Their lives are so far above ours that we cannot fully grasp the details. Their minds are so far ahead of ours that, to them, our thinking seems more like a mechanical process. The matter that makes up their forms belongs to the highest planes, and some are even said to be made of pure energy. What can we say about such beings?

On these seven minor planes exist beings that we might call Angels, Archangels, and Demi-Gods. On the lower levels are great souls known as Masters and Adepts. Above them are the vast Angelic Hosts, beings so advanced that they are beyond human imagination. Higher still are beings so great that they can be called "gods" without disrespect, for their intelligence, power, and existence resemble what humans imagine when thinking of Deity. These divine beings, as well as the Angelic Hosts, take a deep interest in the Universe and play a major role in guiding evolution and cosmic progress. Their influence can be seen throughout human history, inspiring many legends, religions, and traditions. Over time, they have shared their knowledge and power with the world, always following the laws of THE ALL.

Even though these advanced beings are extraordinary, they are still creations within the Mind of THE ALL. They follow the same cosmic laws and processes as everything else in the Universe. They are mortal beings. We may call them "gods," but they are really like older siblings to humanity—souls who have grown far beyond the rest of us and have chosen to delay their union with THE ALL so they can help others on their journey along the Path. However, these beings still belong to the Universe and are subject to its rules. They are not Absolute Spirit.

Only the most advanced Hermetists can understand the deeper teachings about the powers and experiences of the Spiritual Planes. These ideas are so advanced that they can easily confuse anyone without years of study in Hermetic philosophy. Those who understand these teachings are often souls who have carried knowledge from previous lifetimes. Much of this wisdom is considered too sacred and powerful to share openly, as it can be dangerous if misunderstood. Those who study Hermeticism will recognize that the word "Spirit," in this context, means something much deeper than religious or holy ideas. For Hermetists, "Spirit" refers to the Animating Principle, the force that gives life and energy, similar to living power or inner essence.

This power can be used for both good and evil purposes, following the Principle of Polarity. Many religions recognize this dual nature in their ideas of the Devil, Satan, or fallen angels. Because of this danger, knowledge of the Spiritual Planes is kept secret within the inner circles of esoteric and occult orders. Those who misuse spiritual power face a terrible fate. The law of Rhythm will pull them back to the lowest levels of material existence, where they must slowly make their way back toward Spirit. These fallen souls are burdened by the memory of the heights they once reached and lost. The legends of fallen angels are based on real events, as advanced occultists know. Any attempt to gain power selfishly on the Spiritual Planes will cause a soul to lose balance and fall, no matter how far they had risen. However, even these fallen souls are given the chance to return, though they must face the consequences of their actions and work their way back according to the universal laws.

We must always remember that the Principle of Correspondence applies to every plane of existence. "As Above, so Below; as Below, so Above." All seven Hermetic principles are active on every level—physical, mental, and spiritual. The Principle of Mental Substance applies to all planes, as everything exists within the Mind of THE ALL. The Principle of Correspondence reveals the harmony between different planes. The Principle of Vibration explains the differences between planes, since everything vibrates at a unique rate. The Principle of Polarity shows that all things exist in pairs of opposites. The Principle of Rhythm is seen in the rise and fall of events on every plane. The Principle of Cause and Effect teaches that every cause creates an effect, and every effect has a cause. The Principle of Gender is always present, with creative energy expressing both masculine and feminine qualities.

"As Above, so Below; as Below, so Above." This ancient Hermetic truth explains how the same principles apply at every level of existence. As we explore the remaining principles, we will see even more clearly how this great principle of Correspondence connects everything in the Universe.

Chapter IX

Vibration. "Nothing rests; everything moves; everything vibrates."— The Kybalion. The third great Hermetic principle, the Principle of Vibration, teaches that everything in the Universe is in motion. Nothing stays still—everything moves, vibrates, and revolves. Some early Greek philosophers understood this truth and included it in their teachings, but it was later forgotten by most thinkers outside of Hermetic circles. In the 19th century, physical science rediscovered this principle, and discoveries in the 20th century provided even more proof that this ancient teaching was correct.

The Hermetic teachings say that not only does everything move and vibrate constantly, but the differences between all forms of energy and matter exist because of their varying rates and types of vibration. Even THE ALL vibrates, though it does so at such a high intensity and speed that it appears to be perfectly still—just like a spinning wheel can seem motionless when it spins fast enough. According to these teachings, Spirit exists at one extreme of the vibration scale, and at the other extreme are the densest forms of matter. Between these two ends, there are countless levels of vibration, each creating a different form of existence.

Modern science now agrees that everything we think of as matter and energy is just different forms of vibratory motion. Some scientists are even beginning to explore the idea that mental processes might also be forms of vibration. Let's look at what science says about vibration in matter and energy.

Science shows that all matter vibrates to some degree, with these vibrations tied to heat. Whether an object is cold or hot, it vibrates at a certain rate, meaning it is always in motion. Every part of the Universe is in motion, from the smallest particles to the largest celestial bodies. Planets orbit around stars, many spinning on their axes, while stars revolve around larger centers. These centers, in turn, may revolve around even greater ones, continuing infinitely. On a smaller scale, molecules within matter are constantly moving, vibrating around and against each other. Molecules are made up of atoms, which also move and vibrate. Atoms contain even smaller parts—called electrons, ions, or corpuscles—which orbit each other and vibrate rapidly. All forms of matter, from the smallest to the largest, follow the Principle of Vibration.

The same principle applies to all forms of energy. Light, heat, magnetism, and electricity are all forms of vibratory motion, likely originating from the ether. While science does not fully understand forces like cohesion (which holds molecules together), chemical attraction (which binds atoms), or gravity (which draws all matter together), Hermetic teachings suggest that these forces are also forms of vibratory energy. Hermetists have taught this idea for ages, even though science is only beginning to explore it.

The ether, which science describes but does not yet fully understand, is considered by Hermetists to be a higher form of matter. They call it the "Ethereal Substance," believing it is made of matter vibrating at a higher rate. This substance is incredibly fine and elastic, filling all of space and serving as a medium for transmitting energy, such as light, heat, and electricity. It acts as a bridge between matter and energy, possessing its own unique vibrations.

Scientists often use the example of a spinning wheel, top, or cylinder to illustrate how increased vibration affects an object. Imagine a wheel spinning slowly. At first, it is easy to see, and you hear no sound from it. As the speed increases, you start to hear a low hum or growl. As it spins even faster, the sound becomes a musical note that rises higher on the scale with each increase in speed. Eventually, it reaches a point where the sound becomes too high for human ears to hear, and silence returns.

If the wheel's speed keeps increasing, it will start to glow red. As the vibration rises, the red turns to orange, then yellow, and continues through green, blue, indigo, and violet. Beyond violet, the colors disappear, as the human eye can no longer register them. Yet, even though we can't see them, the object continues to emit rays—like those used in photography—and eventually gives off X-rays and other powerful forms of energy. When it reaches the correct vibration, it also begins to release electricity and magnetism.

If the wheel continues to accelerate, its molecules will break apart, turning into their original atoms. These atoms will then separate into their smaller components, such as electrons or corpuscles, following the Principle of Vibration. Eventually, even these particles will dissolve, and the wheel will no longer be made of matter—it will have become Ethereal Substance. At this point, science can no longer follow the process, but Hermetic teachings say that if vibration keeps increasing, the object will go through higher stages of existence. It will rise beyond material form, moving through mental and spiritual levels, until it finally returns to THE ALL, the source of all things.

Though the wheel will have stopped being an "object" long before reaching the level of Ethereal Substance, the example still helps us understand the effect of increasing vibration. It's also important to remember that when the object emits light, heat, or other energies, it is not actually turning into those forms of energy. Instead, it reaches a vibration that allows these energies, which were trapped within it, to be released. These forms of energy are usually confined within material objects because energy interacts with and becomes entangled in material forms. This process of creation—where the force that creates something becomes wrapped up within the creation—is something that happens on all levels of existence.

The Hermetic teachings go far beyond what modern science teaches. They explain that every thought, emotion, reason, will, or desire—any mental state—creates vibrations. Some of these vibrations are released and can affect the minds of other people through a process called "induction." This is the principle behind phenomena like telepathy, mental influence, and other ways one mind can affect another. Today, these ideas are becoming more familiar to the public, thanks to the spread of occult knowledge by various schools, teachers, and movements.

Every thought, emotion, or mental state has a specific rate and pattern of vibration. With enough focus and effort, a person can reproduce these mental states, just as a musical note can be recreated by making an instrument vibrate at the right frequency or as a specific color can appear when vibrations match. By understanding how the Principle of Vibration applies to mental processes, a person can adjust their mind to any state they desire, gaining control over their thoughts, moods, and emotions. This same understanding also allows them to influence the minds of others, creating specific mental states in those around them. In a way, this is like producing mental vibrations at will, just as science produces physical vibrations. However, mastering this power requires proper instruction, practice, and effort. This ability is part of what Hermetists call Mental Transmutation, which is a branch of the Hermetic Arts.

Thinking carefully about these ideas reveals that the Principle of Vibration is at the heart of the abilities shown by Masters and Adepts. These advanced individuals appear to bypass the laws of nature, but in reality, they are simply using one natural law to counteract another. They achieve their extraordinary results by changing the vibrations of physical objects or forms of energy, which leads to what many people call "miracles."

As one of the old Hermetic writers wisely said, "He who understands the Principle of Vibration has grasped the scepter of Power."

Chapter X

Polarity. "Everything is dual; everything has poles; everything has its pair of opposites; like and unlike are the same; opposites are identical in nature, but different in degree; extremes meet; all truths are but half-truths; all paradoxes may be reconciled."—The Kybalion. The fourth Hermetic principle, the Principle of Polarity, explains that everything in existence has two sides, two aspects, or two poles. Each thing has a pair of opposites, with many degrees in between the two extremes. The old paradoxes that have confused people for ages can be explained by understanding this principle. People have always noticed something similar to this idea and have expressed it through sayings such as, "Everything is and isn't at the same time," "All truths are only half-truths," "Every truth contains some falsehood," and "There are two sides to everything."

The Hermetic teachings explain that the differences between things that seem completely opposite are only differences in degree. They show that opposites can be reconciled and that "thesis" and "antithesis" are the same in nature, only varying in degree. Understanding this principle makes it possible to see how opposites can come together as part of the same truth. For example, Spirit and Matter are just two poles of the same thing, with many stages of vibration in between. The ALL and the Many are also the same, with the difference being a matter of mental manifestation. Likewise, Law and laws, Principle and principles, and Infinite Mind and finite minds are opposite poles of the same concept.

On the physical level, we can see this principle in action with temperature. Heat and cold are not completely different things but are two ends of the same scale. A thermometer shows different degrees of temperature, with one end labeled as "cold" and the other as "hot." Between these two extremes are many degrees of warmth, and the same measurement can be called either "hotter" or "colder" depending on your perspective. There is no absolute point where heat ends, and cold begins—it is all just a matter of higher or lower vibration. The terms "high" and "low" are also relative and are just two sides of the same thing.

This principle applies to many other areas as well. If you travel east far enough, you will eventually find yourself going west, and the same is true if you travel north or south. Light and darkness are two ends of the same spectrum, with many levels between them. In music, the scale is made up of notes that rise until they repeat in a higher octave, showing how one thing flows into another. The same is true with colors, which are just different vibrations—red being a lower vibration and violet a higher one. Size is also relative, with large and small being two ends of the same concept. Noise and quiet, hard and soft, sharp and dull—each of these are poles of the same thing with many degrees in between.

Good and bad are not absolute but depend on where they fall on the same scale. Something may be "less good" than another thing above it, but it is still "more good" than something lower on the scale. This "more or less" way of thinking applies to everything, and the differences are always about degree rather than kind.

On the mental level, love and hate seem like complete opposites that cannot be reconciled. However, the Principle of Polarity shows that love and hate are just two ends of the same scale. There is no such thing as pure love or pure hate—they are simply terms for different levels of the same thing. As you move up the scale, you find more love and less hate, and as you move down, the reverse is true. Somewhere in the middle, love and hate are so balanced that they become hard to tell apart, turning into a neutral state of like or dislike. The same principle applies to courage and fear. Every mental state has its opposite, and wherever you find one, you will find the other.

This understanding allows Hermetists to transform one mental state into another by shifting along the scale of polarity. Things from different categories cannot be changed into one another—love can't turn into east, and red can't become courage—but things within the same class can shift from one pole to the other. For example, love can turn into hate, and hate can turn back into love by adjusting their polarity. The same is true for courage and fear, as well as many other states. A fearful person can raise their mental vibration along the fear-courage scale until they feel fearless. Similarly, a lazy person can shift their vibration and become active and energetic.

Anyone familiar with how mental practices work may already understand how these ideas are applied to change mental states. However, the Principle of Polarity makes it clear that these changes happen by shifting degrees along the same scale, not by turning one thing into something entirely different. This is a crucial difference. On the physical level, heat cannot turn into sharpness or loudness, but it can be lowered until it becomes cold. In the same way, love can turn into hate, and fear can turn into courage, but love cannot become courage, nor can fear turn into hate. Each mental state belongs to a specific class, with two poles along which transformation is possible.

The positive and negative poles exist in every mental state and physical phenomenon. Love is positive compared to hate, courage is positive compared to fear, and activity is positive compared to inactivity. Even without knowing the Principle of Vibration, most people recognize that the positive pole feels higher and tends to dominate the negative pole. Nature always seems to favor the positive side.

This principle also explains how one person's mental state can influence another's. When someone changes their mental polarity, they can affect the minds of others through induction, causing similar changes in them. For example, a person feeling sad and fearful can be helped by someone who has trained their mind to be positive and courageous. The helper raises their own mental vibration and then, through induction, influences the other person, shifting their mind toward the positive end of the scale. As a result, the fearful person begins to feel courageous and hopeful. Most mental changes follow this principle of shifting along a scale rather than becoming something entirely different.

Knowing about this important Hermetic Principle will help students better understand their own mental states and those of others. They will realize that all mental states are just a matter of degree. With this understanding, they will learn to raise or lower their mental vibrations whenever they choose, shifting their mental polarity. In doing so, they will gain control over their thoughts and emotions, becoming masters of their mental states instead of being controlled by them. This knowledge will also allow them to help others wisely, using the right methods to shift another person's polarity when needed. We encourage all students to study and become familiar with this Principle of Polarity, as understanding it will bring clarity to many challenging topics.

Chapter XI

Rhythm. "Everything flows out and in; everything has its tides; all things rise and fall; the pendulum-swing manifests in everything; the measure of the swing to the right is the measure of the swing to the left; rhythm compensates."—The Kybalion. The fifth Hermetic principle, the Principle of Rhythm, teaches that everything in the Universe follows a pattern of movement. There is always a flow in and out, a swing forward and backward, like the swing of a pendulum or the rise and fall of tides. This movement occurs between the two poles of existence found on the physical, mental, and spiritual levels. Rhythm works together with the Principle of Polarity, which explains that everything has two sides. Rhythm moves back and forth between these opposites, though it rarely reaches the extremes at either end. Instead, it constantly moves toward one pole and then the other in a never-ending cycle.

This pattern of movement is found everywhere in the Universe. Everything moves from action to reaction, from growth to decline. Suns and planets form, grow in power, and eventually fade into lifeless matter, waiting to begin a new cycle of life. In the same way, worlds are born, live, and die, only to be reborn once more. This process applies to all living things, which are born, grow, die, and then are reborn again. It also applies to philosophies, religions, governments, fashions, and societies, which all go through stages of birth, growth, maturity, decline, and rebirth. The pendulum of life is always in motion.

We see this swing of rhythm everywhere. Day turns into night, and night becomes day again. The seasons change from summer to winter and back to summer. Even the smallest particles of matter follow rhythmic cycles, just as larger objects like planets do. Nothing ever rests completely, and all movement follows the principle of rhythm. This principle applies to every area of life and can explain many aspects of human behavior as well. The rhythm of life always swings between the two poles, and the pendulum is always moving. Life's tides rise and fall according to law.

Science understands the Principle of Rhythm as a natural law that applies to physical things. But Hermetists take this idea further, understanding that rhythm also affects human thoughts and emotions. It explains why people experience sudden shifts in moods and feelings, which can seem confusing or frustrating. However, Hermetists have studied this principle closely and have discovered how to escape some of its effects through Transmutation.

The Hermetic masters learned that although rhythm is always present in the mind, it works on two levels. There is a higher plane of consciousness and a lower plane. By understanding this, they learned how to rise to the higher plane, where they could avoid being affected by the back-and-forth swing of rhythm on the lower level. In other words, the swing of the pendulum still happens, but it only affects the unconscious mind, leaving the conscious mind unaffected. This technique is called the Law of Neutralization. It works by raising the self, or Ego, above the level of unconscious thoughts, so the backward swing of the mental pendulum doesn't disturb the conscious mind. This is similar to rising above a storm and watching it pass beneath you without being touched by it.

A Hermetic master or advanced student can place themselves at the desired pole of their mental state and, by refusing to engage with the backward swing of rhythm, they stay firm in their chosen mindset. They let the pendulum swing back on the unconscious level, without letting it affect their conscious thoughts. Many people who have gained self-control do this naturally, even if they don't fully understand how it works. They avoid being overwhelmed by moods or negative thoughts by instinctively applying the Law of Neutralization. However, a master achieves a much higher level of control, using their will to maintain a state of poise and mental strength that may seem impossible to others who allow their emotions to control them.

Anyone who reflects on their life will realize how much these rhythmic swings of mood and emotion have affected them. Moments of excitement are often followed by feelings of sadness. Times of courage are replaced by fear. Most people are constantly carried back and forth by these emotional tides without ever knowing why it happens. By understanding the Principle of Rhythm, a person can gain mastery over these emotional swings and come to know themselves better. With this knowledge, they can avoid being swept away by the constant flow of changing moods.

The will of a person is stronger than the conscious effects of rhythm, though the principle itself cannot be stopped. While it is impossible to eliminate rhythm entirely, it is possible to escape its influence by learning how to avoid being caught up in the swing. The pendulum will continue to swing, but those who understand this principle can rise above it and no longer be controlled by its movement.

There are other aspects of the Principle of Rhythm that we need to discuss here. One of these is the Law of Compensation. The word "compensate" means "to balance or counterbalance," which is how the Hermetists use the term. This is the idea behind the Kybalion's statement: "The measure of the swing to the right is the measure of the swing to the left; rhythm compensates."

The Law of Compensation explains that every movement in one direction determines an equal movement in the opposite direction. Every swing toward one pole is balanced by a swing toward the other pole. On the physical level, there are many examples of this law. The pendulum of a clock swings a certain distance to the right and then swings back the same distance to the left. The seasons balance each other in the same way, as do the tides. Wherever rhythm is present, the Law of Compensation is at work. A short swing in one direction will only allow for a short swing in the other direction, while a long swing to one side will result in an equally long swing back. An object thrown high into the air must travel the same distance when it falls back to the ground. The force used to throw it upward matches the force it generates when it returns to the earth. This law is constant on the physical level and can be observed in many areas of life.

However, Hermetists take this law further and apply it to mental and emotional states. According to their teachings, a person who experiences great joy will also be capable of deep suffering. On the other hand, someone who feels little pain will experience little joy. For example, a pig does not suffer much mentally, but it also does not experience much joy—it is balanced. In contrast, some animals feel great joy but also suffer greatly because of their sensitive nature. The same is true for humans. Some people are only capable of mild pleasure and mild pain, while others can experience intense joy but also suffer deeply. This balance between joy and pain is an example of the Law of Compensation at work.

Hermetists go even further, teaching that to experience a certain amount of joy, a person must first go through an equal amount of pain.

However, this does not mean that after experiencing pleasure, the person will have to "pay" for it with future suffering. Instead, the pleasure is seen as the balancing result of pain experienced earlier—either in this life or in a past one. This understanding provides new insight into the purpose of suffering.

Hermetists view life as a continuous chain, with each life forming part of a greater whole. The swing between pain and pleasure only makes sense when reincarnation is considered. Without the idea of previous lives, the Law of Compensation would seem confusing.

They also teach that advanced students and masters can avoid much of the suffering caused by this rhythmic swing by using the Law of Neutralization. By raising their awareness to the higher plane of the Ego, they can escape many of the experiences that affect those who remain on the lower plane of consciousness.

The Law of Compensation plays a major role in people's lives. It is easy to see that everything we gain in life requires us to give up something else in return. For example, no one can "keep their penny and eat the cake" at the same time. Every positive thing has its downside, and every gain involves some loss. The rich have wealth that the poor do not, but the poor often have things the rich cannot enjoy. A wealthy person may have access to fine foods and luxuries, but they may lack the appetite to enjoy them. Meanwhile, a poor laborer may take great pleasure in simple meals, enjoying them more than the rich person ever could. Their different habits, desires, and conditions make this balance possible.

This balancing act continues throughout life. The Law of Compensation ensures that everything is balanced in the end, even if it takes several lifetimes for the pendulum of rhythm to swing back to its opposite pole.

Chapter XII

Causation. "Every Cause has its Effect; every Effect has its Cause; everything happens according to Law; Chance is but a name for Law not recognized; there are many planes of causation, but nothing escapes the Law."—The Kybalion. The Sixth Hermetic Principle, the Principle of Cause and Effect, teaches that everything in the universe follows a law. Nothing happens by chance. What people call "chance" is just a name for causes that we don't understand or haven't noticed yet. All events follow one another without breaks, and nothing happens outside of this law.

The Principle of Cause and Effect is a foundation for all scientific thinking, both ancient and modern, and it was first taught by the earliest Hermetic teachers. Although different schools of thought have debated the details over time, most thinkers agree with this principle. To reject it would mean denying that the universe operates under law and order, which would leave everything to randomness—something people have called "chance."

If we look closer, we'll see that there is no such thing as pure chance. The dictionary defines chance as something that happens without law or purpose. But if we think deeply, we'll realize that nothing in the universe works outside of law and cause. Everything follows rules and patterns. To believe in something outside of these laws would mean believing in something greater than the natural order of the universe, which is impossible. Nothing exists outside of THE ALL, which itself is the source of all laws. If such a thing as pure chance existed, it would break all the natural laws and cause the universe to fall into complete disorder.

When we talk about chance, we are really talking about causes that are hidden from us. The word "chance" comes from a word that means "to fall," like the falling of dice. People often think that when a die lands on a certain number, it's just random. But if we look closer, we'll see that even the roll of a die follows specific causes, just like the planets follow their orbits. The outcome depends on the angle of the die in the box, the force used to throw it, and the surface it lands on. These are all visible causes. Behind these, however, are many unseen causes, which also affect the result.

If you throw a die many times, the numbers will eventually even out, with each number appearing roughly the same amount of times. The same thing happens when you flip a coin—over many flips, the heads and tails will balance out. This is called the law of averages, but both the average and the individual tosses are part of the same Law of Cause and Effect. If we could trace every single cause leading up to a die roll or coin toss, we'd see that the outcome couldn't have been any different under the same circumstances. Every event has a cause, or more precisely, a chain of causes.

Some people get confused by this principle because they struggle to understand how one thing causes another. But in truth, no single thing ever causes or creates another thing. Cause and Effect refer to events, not objects. An event is simply something that happens as a result of a previous event. Events don't create each other; they are just links in a continuous chain of actions that flow from the energy of THE ALL. Every event is connected to what came before it and to what will follow it.

Take, for example, a stone falling from a mountain and crashing into the roof of a house. At first, this may seem like a random accident. But when we look deeper, we see a chain of causes behind it. Rain may have softened the soil, causing the stone to loosen. The stone itself was part of a larger rock that broke apart over time due to weathering. That larger rock was formed by natural forces, such as earthquakes and volcanic activity. If we keep tracing back, we can find more and more causes, each connected to the next.

This chain of cause and effect is endless. It's like tracing your family tree. You have two parents, four grandparents, eight great-grandparents, and so on. If you go back forty generations, you'll have millions of ancestors. In the same way, every event has countless causes behind it, even something as small as a speck of soot floating by. That speck of soot may have once been part of a tree, which became coal, and later turned into soot as it burned. And that speck's journey isn't over—it will continue moving through time, causing new events in the future.

Even this text is part of the chain. The act of writing these words and your act of reading them will have effects on both of us, as well as on many others now and in the future. Each thought we think and every action we take sets new events into motion, adding more links to the endless chain of Cause and Effect.

This principle also shows us how deeply connected everything is. If two people had not met in ancient times, neither you nor I would be here today. If they had not crossed paths, this conversation wouldn't exist, and many other events would be different. Everything we do, no matter how small, creates ripples that affect the lives of others, both now and in the future.

We won't dive into debates about free will versus fate here. The truth, according to Hermetic teachings, is that both sides are partly right. The Principle of Polarity teaches us that these two ideas are just opposite ends of the same truth. A person can be both free and bound by necessity, depending on how we define those terms and from which level of understanding we view them. As the ancient teachings say, "The further from the center something is, the more it is bound; the closer it moves toward the center, the freer it becomes."

Most people are controlled by their environment, upbringing, and emotions, showing little real freedom. They are influenced by the opinions and expectations of others, as well as by their own moods and feelings. They may believe they are acting freely, but they fail to see where their desires and preferences come from. What makes them want one thing instead of another? What makes them feel pleased by one choice and not by another? There are causes behind these feelings too, even if they are not always visible.

A master, however, learns to change their desires and preferences by shifting their mental state. Instead of acting on impulse or external influences, the master chooses to act with intention. They "will to will," meaning they act based on conscious choice rather than being driven by emotions, moods, or circumstances.

Most people are carried through life like a falling stone, easily influenced by their surroundings, emotions, desires, and the will of others stronger than themselves. They are shaped by heredity, environment, and suggestions without resisting or using their own will. Like pawns on a chessboard, they play their roles until the game ends, at which point they are set aside. However, Masters, who understand the rules of the game, rise above the material world. By connecting with the higher aspects of their nature, they take control of their moods, character, qualities, and polarity, as well as the environment around them. In doing so, they become the ones who move the game, not just pieces to be moved—they become Causes, not Effects. Masters do not avoid the higher laws, but they align themselves with them, mastering circumstances on the lower plane. This allows them to consciously participate in the law instead of being blindly controlled by it. While they serve on the higher levels of existence, they rule over the material world.

Whether on higher or lower levels, the Law always operates. There is no such thing as chance. The idea of a blind goddess controlling fate has been replaced by reason and understanding. With the clarity that knowledge brings, we now know that everything is governed by universal laws. All the countless smaller laws are expressions of one Great Law—the LAW, which is THE ALL. As the scriptures say, not even a sparrow falls unnoticed by the Mind of THE ALL, and even the hairs on our head are numbered. Nothing exists outside the Law, and nothing happens that goes against it.

But do not think that this means humans are helpless machines with no freedom. The Hermetic teachings say that we can use one law to rise above others. The higher laws always have power over the lower ones until, eventually, we reach the point where we find refuge in the LAW itself and no longer feel limited by the smaller, temporary laws of the material world. Can you grasp the deeper meaning of this?

Chapter XIII

Gender. "Gender is in everything; everything has its Masculine and Feminine Principles; Gender manifests on all planes."—The Kybalion. The Seventh Hermetic Principle, the Principle of Gender, teaches that Gender is present in everything. Both Masculine and Feminine principles are always active and influence every part of life, on all levels of existence. However, it's important to understand that Gender, in the Hermetic sense, is not the same as what people usually mean by "sex."

The word "Gender" comes from a Latin word meaning "to create, generate, or produce." This meaning goes beyond just the biological differences between male and female. Sex is only one way that Gender shows itself, and it only appears on the physical level where organic life exists. We need to be clear about this difference because some people have misunderstood the Hermetic teachings, confusing the Principle of Gender with strange ideas and theories about sex that have little to do with the true meaning of this principle.

Gender's purpose is to create, generate, and produce, and we can see its effects at every level of existence. Although science hasn't fully recognized the universality of this principle, some scientific discoveries hint at it. For example, the principle of Gender can be seen in how atoms are formed. Scientists have discovered that atoms are made up of smaller parts called corpuscles, electrons, or ions, which are constantly moving and vibrating. An atom forms when many negatively charged corpuscles gather around a positively charged one. The positive particle influences the negative ones, causing them to arrange themselves in a specific way, and this process creates the atom. This aligns with ancient Hermetic teachings, which associate the Masculine principle with the positive pole and the Feminine principle with the negative pole of energy.

It's worth noting that the term "Negative" is often misunderstood. People tend to think of "positive" as strong and real, while "negative" suggests weakness or lack. However, in electrical phenomena, this isn't accurate. The so-called "Negative" pole is actually the point where creation and production take place. Some scientists now use the word "Cathode" instead of "Negative." The word "Cathode" comes from a Greek word meaning "descent" or "path of creation." It is from the Cathode, or the Negative pole, that electrons and powerful energy rays are released. These rays have revolutionized scientific thinking in recent years, challenging many old ideas. The Cathode, or Feminine pole, is the source of new forms of matter and energy. For this reason, we replace the word "Negative" with "Feminine" when referring to this pole, since it aligns with both scientific discoveries and Hermetic teachings.

Modern science also shows that the creative particles, or electrons, carry what they call "negative" electricity, which we describe as Feminine energy. A Feminine particle separates from a Masculine particle and begins a new journey, naturally seeking union with another Masculine particle. This union is driven by the desire to create new forms of matter or energy. Some scientists even say that the particle actively seeks this union. This constant separation and joining of particles is the basis for most chemical reactions. When a Feminine particle unites with a Masculine one, the Masculine energy activates the Feminine, causing it to move quickly and create new forms. The result of this union is the birth of a new atom. Once the atom forms, it becomes a distinct entity with its own properties and no longer acts as free electricity. The process of separating the Feminine particles is called ionization. These particles are among the most active forces in nature, and their interactions create phenomena such as light, heat, electricity, magnetism, attraction, and repulsion.

The Masculine principle directs energy toward the Feminine principle, which responds by creating new forms. However, neither principle can function without the other. Both are needed for creation, and this balance is present at every level of life. In some forms of life, both principles are combined within a single organism. In fact, everything in the organic world contains both Masculine and Feminine qualities. Even in things that appear purely Feminine or purely Masculine, both principles are always present.

Hermetic teachings contain much more about how these two principles work together to create energy and matter, but we won't go into those details here since science hasn't yet caught up with these ideas. Still, the example of how atoms form shows that science is moving in the right direction and helps us understand the deeper meaning of this principle.

Some leading scientists have suggested that crystal formation may involve something similar to "sexual activity." This idea is another small hint about the direction scientific thinking is moving. As time passes, more evidence will emerge to confirm the Hermetic Principle of Gender. It will become clear that Gender is always present and active, not only in living things but also in the realm of energy, force, and even in non-living matter. Today, many scientists believe that all forms of energy can eventually be traced back to electricity. The latest scientific theory, known as the "Electrical Theory of the Universe," is gaining widespread acceptance. If we can find clear evidence of Gender in the workings of electricity—right at its source—then we have good reason to believe that science is finally offering proof that the Principle of Gender operates throughout all universal phenomena.

There's no need to go into detail about the well-known processes of attraction and repulsion between atoms, chemical bonds, or how molecules stick together. These concepts are already familiar. But have you ever thought about the fact that all these processes are expressions of the Principle of Gender? Can you see how these phenomena align perfectly with what we know about electrons and corpuscles? And beyond that, doesn't it make sense that the Hermetic teachings might be correct when they suggest that even gravity—the mysterious force pulling all matter together—might be another expression of the Principle of Gender? This principle reflects the natural attraction between Masculine and Feminine energies. While we don't yet have scientific proof of this idea, try looking at these phenomena through the lens of Hermetic teachings. You may find that it offers a clearer explanation than many current scientific theories.

We encourage you to apply this principle to all forms of physical phenomena. If you do, you'll see that the Principle of Gender is always present. Now, let's explore how this principle operates on the Mental Plane, where even more fascinating insights await.

Chapter XIV

Mental Gender. Psychology students studying mental phenomena have noticed that over the past ten to fifteen years, many theories about a "dual mind" have emerged. These ideas have inspired several different explanations about how these two minds might work. Back in 1893, Thomson J. Hudson became well-known for his theory of the "objective and subjective minds," which he believed were present in every person. Other thinkers have explored similar ideas, like the "conscious and subconscious minds," the "voluntary and involuntary minds," or the "active and passive minds." Even though these theories differ, they all revolve around the same basic idea: the mind has two parts.

A student of Hermetic Philosophy might smile at how these modern theories claim to have "discovered" the truth about the dual mind, even though the Hermetic teachings have discussed Mental Gender for centuries. If you look at the early teachings of Hermeticism, you will find that they have always recognized the existence of Mental Gender. In fact, they explained the dual mind long ago using this concept. The Masculine aspect of the mind aligns with what modern thinkers call the Objective Mind, the Conscious Mind, or the Active Mind. Meanwhile, the Feminine aspect matches what some call the Subjective Mind, the Subconscious Mind, or the Passive Mind. However, Hermetic teachings do not completely agree with many of these newer theories or their conclusions. Some of these ideas are not well-supported by evidence, and the Hermetic view offers a different perspective. We only mention these similarities to help students connect what they already know with Hermetic teachings.

In the second chapter of The Law of Psychic Phenomena, Hudson admits that the Hermetic ideas align with the concept of the dual mind. He suggests that the Hermetic teachings contain the same core idea, though he refers to them as "mystic jargon." If Hudson had spent more time studying these ancient ideas, he might have gained deeper insights into the dual mind. However, without that, his own work may not have gained the same attention. Now, let's explore the Hermetic view of Mental Gender.

Hermetic teachers instruct their students to focus inward, examining their own consciousness to understand Mental Gender. They encourage students to reflect on their sense of self, starting with the awareness of their existence, often expressed as "I Am." At first, this statement seems to be the final understanding of the Self, but with more reflection, it becomes clear that this "I Am" has two distinct aspects. These two parts work together, but they are still separate.

While it first feels like there is only one "I," closer examination shows that there are actually two parts: an "I" and a "Me." These two parts of the mind have different qualities, and understanding how they interact can provide insight into mental influence.

Let's start by examining the "Me," which is often confused with the "I." When people think about themselves as the "Me," they tend to identify with their emotions, likes, dislikes, habits, and personality traits. These qualities form their sense of self, both in their own minds and in the way others see them. However, these emotions and traits are not fixed—they change over time, following the natural rhythms of life, and shifting between different extremes. People also associate the "Me" with the knowledge and experiences they have collected, seeing these things as part of who they are.

For some people, the "Me" is closely tied to their body and physical desires. Their sense of self is so connected to their body that they feel like they "live" in it. Some even see their clothes as part of who they are, believing that their identity depends on their appearance. As one writer joked, people are made up of "soul, body, and clothes." For someone like this, losing their clothes would feel like losing a piece of themselves. Even those who do not focus so much on clothes often still see their body as a key part of their identity, unable to imagine a Self separate from the body.

As people grow in awareness, they begin to see the body as something they "have," rather than something they "are." They start to understand that their body is just one part of their experience, and their mind is more than just a tool belonging to the body. However, even at this stage, people often continue to identify with their mental states, emotions, and habits, believing these things are who they are. They might not realize that these feelings and thoughts are only temporary states that exist within them, but are not their true Self.

With effort, people can learn to separate these mental states from their deeper sense of self. They come to see these feelings, habits, and thoughts as things they "own," not things they "are." This process takes mental focus and self-awareness, but it is possible, even for those just starting on this path. By imagining this separation, a person can begin to understand the difference between their true Self and the thoughts and emotions that pass through their mind.

Once a person learns to set aside these mental states, they begin to recognize the two aspects of their mind: the "I" and the "Me." The "Me" can be seen as a kind of mental space where thoughts, ideas, emotions, and other mental states are generated. It acts like a "mental womb," as ancient teachings describe it, capable of producing many types of thoughts and creations. The "Me" holds enormous creative potential, but it requires some form of energy from the "I" or another source before it can create anything. This realization gives a person a deep sense of their creative abilities and mental power.

However, the student soon discovers that the "I" has its own unique qualities. The "I" is the part of the mind that can choose to direct the "Me" to create along certain lines. It can observe the creative process of the "Me" and even step back to watch it unfold. The "I" holds the power to project energy toward the "Me," initiating the process of mental creation. While the "Me" is responsible for the active creation, the "I" is the guiding force, able to will these creations into existence.

This dual nature exists within every person. The "I" represents the Masculine Principle of Mental Gender, while the "Me" represents the Feminine Principle. The "I" reflects the state of being, while the "Me" represents the process of becoming. This principle operates not only within the mind but also in the larger universe. Just as the two aspects of Mental Gender work together within a person, they reflect the greater workings of the cosmos. As the Hermetic principle says, "As above, so below; as below, so above."

These two parts of the mind—the Masculine and Feminine principles, or the "I" and the "Me"—help explain many of the mental and psychic phenomena we observe. The principle of Mental Gender offers the key to understanding how mental influence works.

The Feminine principle tends to receive impressions, while the Masculine principle focuses on expressing and giving out energy. The Feminine aspect plays a more active role in generating new thoughts, ideas, and imaginative concepts. The Masculine aspect, on the other hand, drives the process through the power of Will. However, without the Will of the Masculine principle, the Feminine mind tends to simply process external impressions rather than create original ideas.

People who are capable of deep focus use both mental principles. The Feminine side actively generates ideas, while the Masculine Will energizes the mind, pushing it toward action. Most people, however, use very little of the Masculine principle. They passively absorb thoughts and ideas from the minds of others rather than creating their own. They rely on others to think and will for them. We won't focus on this part too much here since it's covered in many psychology books, but the key to understanding it lies in recognizing Mental Gender.

Anyone familiar with psychic phenomena knows about things like telepathy, mental influence, suggestion, and hypnotism. Many have tried to explain these events by referring to theories about the dual mind. While these theories are partially correct, a clearer explanation emerges when you view these phenomena through the lens of Mental Gender and Vibration.

In telepathy, the Masculine principle sends out a wave of energy toward the Feminine principle of another person, where the idea takes root and grows. Suggestion and hypnotism work similarly. The Will of the person giving the suggestion sends a stream of energy toward the other person's Feminine mind, which accepts the idea and acts on it. Once implanted, this idea grows and feels like the person's own, much like how a cuckoo egg placed in a sparrow's nest becomes accepted as the sparrow's offspring.

Ideally, the Masculine and Feminine principles within a person should work together in harmony. Unfortunately, many people rely heavily on their Feminine mind while allowing their Masculine principle, which contains the Will, to remain inactive. As a result, they are easily influenced by the thoughts and wills of others. This is why so few people have original ideas or act independently. Most live their lives as reflections or echoes of those with stronger minds and wills.

The most successful and influential people in the world demonstrate strong Masculine Will. They shape their own thoughts and dominate their minds instead of passively accepting ideas from others. These individuals also influence the minds of others, planting their thoughts like seeds that take root and grow within the masses. This is why so many people seem to follow the ideas of others without question, acting more like sheep than independent thinkers.

We see examples of Mental Gender at work all around us. People with magnetic personalities use the Masculine principle to impress their ideas onto others. Actors who make their audience cry or laugh are using this principle. So are effective speakers, politicians, preachers, and writers. The personal influence that some people seem to naturally possess is rooted in the principle of Mental Gender, which operates through the vibrations of thought and energy. This principle is also the foundation of hypnotism, personal magnetism, and fascination.

Anyone familiar with psychic phenomena knows how important suggestion is. Suggestion is the process of planting an idea in someone's mind in such a way that the person accepts it and acts on it. Understanding how suggestion works is essential for studying psychic phenomena, but knowing about Mental Gender and Vibration is just as important. The entire process of suggestion depends on these principles.

Many teachers explain suggestion by saying that the conscious mind makes an impression on the subconscious mind. However, they often fail to provide a clear explanation of how this works or how it mirrors natural processes. If you look at it through the Hermetic teachings, you'll see that it aligns with the natural laws of energy. The Masculine principle energizes the Feminine principle, leading to the creation of new mental states. This dynamic reflects the way the universe operates on every level, from the spiritual and mental to the physical.

The Hermetic axiom "As above, so below; as below, so above" reminds us that the same principles apply on all levels of existence. Once you understand the principle of Mental Gender, you'll find it much easier to organize and study psychological phenomena. This principle works in practice because it is based on the unchanging, universal laws of life.

We will not go into a long discussion or detailed description of the many types of mental influence or psychic activity. There are plenty of books on these topics, many of which are quite good. While the main ideas in these books are accurate, each author tends to explain the phenomena according to their personal theories. Students who study these subjects and apply the principle of Mental Gender will be able to organize these ideas and make sense of the conflicting theories. If they wish, they can even master these subjects by using this principle.

The purpose of this work is not to provide a detailed exploration of psychic phenomena. Instead, it offers a master key that can unlock the doors to many areas of knowledge for those who want to explore them. We believe that the teachings in The Kybalion can offer explanations that will clear up many confusing ideas and serve as a key to understanding a wide range of topics. There is no need to cover every aspect of mental and psychic phenomena if we can provide students with the tools they need to understand any topic that interests them.

With the insights from The Kybalion, a student can revisit any occult library with fresh understanding, using ancient wisdom from Egypt to shed light on difficult or obscure ideas. This is the purpose of this book—not to introduce a new philosophy, but to provide the framework of an ancient teaching that will clarify the ideas of others. It serves as a tool to bring together different theories and opposing beliefs, acting as a guide to help reconcile them.

Chapter XV

Hermetic Axioms. "Having knowledge without showing it through actions is like hoarding gold and silver—it's pointless and foolish. Knowledge, like wealth, is meant to be used. The Law of Use applies everywhere, and anyone who ignores it will struggle because they are working against nature."—The Kybalion. The Hermetic Teachings have always been carefully guarded in the minds of those who hold them, as we have explained before. However, they were never meant to be hidden away or kept secret forever. The Law of Use is emphasized throughout these teachings, as the quote from The Kybalion explains. Knowledge without action is useless, helping neither the person who has it nor anyone else. Be careful not to become stingy with your thoughts—take what you've learned and put it into action. Study these Axioms and Aphorisms, but be sure to also apply them in your life. Here are some important Hermetic Axioms from The Kybalion, with comments added for deeper understanding. Make these ideas your own by practicing them, because they won't truly belong to you until you put them into use. "To change your mood or mental state—change your vibration."—The Kybalion. You can shift your mental state by using your willpower to focus on a more positive mindset. Your will guides your attention, and your attention changes your inner vibration. If you learn how to focus through your will, you unlock the ability to control your thoughts and emotions. "To get rid of an unwanted mental state, use the Principle of Polarity and focus on the opposite of what you want to overcome. Destroy the negative by changing its polarity."—The Kybalion. This is one of the most important Hermetic techniques, grounded in scientific understanding. A mental state and its opposite are just two sides of the same thing. Through Mental Transmutation, you can reverse their polarity. Modern psychology uses a similar approach when helping people overcome bad habits—rather than fighting the habit, they focus on building its opposite. If you're struggling with fear, for example, don't waste energy fighting it directly. Instead, focus on building courage, and fear will fade away. Think of it like a dark room—you don't need to sweep out the darkness. You just open the windows, and the light drives the darkness away. To get rid of a negative feeling, focus on its positive counterpart. Slowly, the negative will fade, and you will be left aligned with the positive. But the opposite is also true—if you let yourself stay in negative states too often, they will take hold. Mastering your moods by shifting your polarity will allow you to change your mental states, reshape your personality, and build a stronger character. Much of the mastery achieved by advanced Hermetics comes from applying this principle of Polarity, which is an essential part of Mental Transmutation. Remember this Hermetic Axiom: "Mind (like metals and elements) can be changed from one state to another, from one level to another, from one condition to another, from one pole to the opposite, and from one vibration to another."—The Kybalion. Mastering Polarity is the key to Mental Transmutation, also known as Mental Alchemy. Without learning to change your own polarity, you won't be able to affect the world around you. Understanding this principle gives you the ability to change both your own state and the states of others. But it takes time, care, study, and constant practice to master it. The principle is true, but how well it works depends entirely on how patient and persistent you are in practicing it. "Rhythm can be balanced out through the Art of Polarization."—The Kybalion. As we mentioned earlier, the Hermetic teachings say that Rhythm affects both the mental and physical levels. This constant back-and-forth motion explains the changing moods, emotions, and thoughts we experience. The Law of Neutralization helps us overcome the effects of Rhythm. There is both a Higher Plane and a Lower Plane of consciousness. By mentally rising to the Higher Plane, you can allow the swing of the pendulum to happen only on the Lower Plane. When you stay on the Higher Plane, you won't feel the back-and-forth motion as strongly. This shift happens by focusing on your Higher Self and raising your mental vibrations above the usual level of thought. It's like rising above a wave and watching it pass underneath you. The advanced Hermetic practitioner keeps their focus on the Positive Pole—the "I Am" within—rather than getting caught up in the shifting personality and emotions. By refusing to let Rhythm pull them back and forth, they stay grounded in their true self. Those who have achieved even some level of self-mastery do this, even if they don't fully understand the principle. They simply refuse to get pulled around by moods and emotions and remain steady by holding on to their inner strength. The Master takes this a step further, using their Will to achieve a calmness and mental stability that others find hard to believe. It's important to note that you don't actually destroy the Principle of Rhythm—it can't be destroyed. Instead, you counterbalance it with another law to maintain stability. Just as balance and counterbalance exist in the physical world, they also apply to the mind. When you understand how to use these principles, it might seem like you are breaking the laws of nature, but you are simply using one law to offset another. "Nothing escapes the Principle of Cause and Effect, but there are many levels of causes. You can use the laws of a higher level to overcome those of a lower level."—The Kybalion. By mastering Polarity, the Hermetic student rises to a higher level of Cause and Effect. At this higher level, they become the cause of things rather than being controlled by causes outside of themselves. They are no longer at the mercy of their environment, other people's desires, or inherited tendencies. Instead of being moved around like chess pieces, they become players in the game of life. Through control of their emotions, impulses, and thoughts, they build new qualities and abilities, shaping their character and breaking free from the limitations of their surroundings. They no longer react blindly to life but make deliberate choices. While they remain under the laws of Cause and Effect on higher levels, on lower levels, they become masters of these laws. As The Kybalion says:

The wise serve on the higher levels, but they rule on the lower ones. They follow the laws that come from those above them, but within their own world and in the realms below them, they take charge and give orders. Yet, in doing so, they work as part of the universal

Principle, not against it. A wise person moves with the flow of the Law, and by understanding how it works, they control it instead of being controlled by it. Just like a skilled swimmer moves through water by choosing when to turn and where to go, rather than drifting like a piece of wood carried by the current—so the wise person lives compared to the ordinary person. However, both the swimmer and the log, the wise person and the fool, are still governed by the same Law. Understanding this truth brings a person closer to achieving mastery.

To wrap up, let's reflect again on the Hermetic Axiom: "True Hermetic Transmutation is a Mental Art."—The Kybalion.

This axiom teaches that the power to influence and change your surroundings is achieved through the mind. Since the entire Universe is fundamentally mental, it can only be governed by the power of thought. This understanding explains many of the mental phenomena and abilities that have drawn so much interest and study in the early years of the twentieth century. Beneath the teachings of different groups and schools of thought lies the unchanging idea that the Universe is made of mental substance. If the essence of the Universe is mental, then it makes sense that changing your mind can change the world around you. And if everything is based on the mind, then mental power must be the greatest force shaping reality. When this is understood, what people call "miracles" and "wonders" become clear—they are simply the results of mastering this truth.

"THE ALL is MIND; The Universe is Mental."—The Kybalion.

Corpus Hermeticum

Hermes Trismegistus

Corpus Hermeticum

An Introduction to the Corpus Hermeticum

The fifteen writings of the Corpus Hermeticum, along with the Perfect Sermon or Asclepius, are key texts in Hermetic philosophy. These writings were created by unknown authors in Egypt sometime before the third century C.E. They were part of a larger collection that was linked to Hermes Trismegistus, a mythical figure combining the Greek god Hermes and the Egyptian god Thoth. These texts emerged during a period of religious and philosophical growth, the same era that saw the rise of Neoplatonism, Christianity, and a variety of teachings grouped under the term "Gnosticism." This movement grew from the influence of Platonic thought on the older traditions of the Hellenistic world. While each of these traditions had its own unique approach to life's big questions, they shared certain themes and ideas.

The Corpus Hermeticum was eventually gathered into a single volume during the Byzantine period. One copy of this collection was discovered by agents working for Lorenzo de Medici in the fifteenth century. Marsilio Ficino, the head of the Florentine Academy, was tasked with translating these texts into Latin. He was instructed to prioritize translating the Corpus Hermeticum over the works of Plato. Ficino's Latin version was published in 1463 and was reprinted at least twenty-two times over the following 150 years.

The treatises within the Corpus Hermeticum can be grouped based on their content. The first writing, called "Poemandres," describes a revelation given to Hermes Trismegistus by a being named Poemandres, also known as the "Man-Shepherd," who represents the universal Mind. The next eight writings are known as the "General Sermons" and contain short conversations and teachings about the core ideas of Hermetic philosophy. Following these is the "Key," which summarizes the previous sermons. There is also a group of four texts—"Mind unto Hermes," "About the Common Mind," "The

Secret Sermon on the Mountain," and the "Letter of Hermes to Asclepius"—which explore the more mystical parts of Hermetic thought. The collection concludes with the "Definitions of Asclepius unto King Ammon," which seems to be made up of three fragments from larger works.

The Perfect Sermon, or Asclepius, came to the Renaissance through a different path. It had been translated into Latin in ancient times, supposedly by Lucius Apuleius of Madaura, the author of The Golden Ass. This work provides valuable insights into the worship of the goddess Isis in the Roman Empire. Saint Augustine refers to the old Latin translation of the Perfect Sermon in his City of God, and this translation remained in circulation throughout medieval Europe, all the way to the Renaissance. The original Greek version was lost, though some parts of it have been preserved through quotations in other ancient texts. The Perfect Sermon is longer than any other surviving Hermetic text. While it covers many topics found in the Corpus Hermeticum, it also addresses other subjects, including instructions on creating divine statues and a bleak prophecy about the loss of Hermetic wisdom and the end of the world.

The arrival of the Corpus Hermeticum had a powerful impact on late medieval European philosophy. Some early Christian writers, like the Church Fathers, referenced Hermetic literature to support their points, and they believed that Hermes Trismegistus lived around the same time as Moses. Because the Hermetic writings included ideas from Jewish scriptures and Platonic philosophy, Renaissance thinkers believed these texts had influenced both traditions. Hermetic philosophy was regarded as an ancient form of wisdom, linked to the "Wisdom of the Egyptians" mentioned in the Bible's book of Exodus and praised in Plato's Timaeus. Many intellectuals used this view to challenge the dominance of Aristotelian philosophy, which controlled universities at the time.

The Hermetic texts also became a key part of another rebellion during the Renaissance—the effort to restore magic as a respectable spiritual practice in Christian Europe. There was another body of work linked to Hermes Trismegistus, which included writings about astrology, alchemy, and magic. If Hermes were considered a real historical figure, as Renaissance scholars believed, and if early Christian leaders had quoted his works with approval, and if these writings aligned with certain Christian beliefs, then the Hermetic approach to magic could be seen as compatible with Christianity. However, this effort ultimately failed. The dramatic changes in Western Christianity during the Reformation and Counter-Reformation solidified strict religious rules, and by the sixteenth century, practices that had once been accepted were now considered heretical. Some people were even executed for actions that had previously been viewed as signs of devotion.

Despite this failure, the ideas and language of the Hermetic writings remained influential in post-medieval Western magic.

I. Poemandres, the Shepherd of Men

This is the most well-known Hermetic text, telling a story about a vision of how the universe was created and the nature and destiny of humanity. Writers from the Renaissance onward have noted that its creation story seems partly inspired by the Bible's Book of Genesis, but it also presents a different take. In this version, the Fall is about the descent of the Primal Man through the spheres of the planets into the natural world. This descent isn't caused by disobedience but by love, and it happens with God's blessing.

The seven rulers of fate mentioned in various sections are the archons, or rulers, of the seven planets. These archons also appear in Plato's Timaeus and in other ancient texts often grouped under the term "Gnostic." In this text, these rulers have a complicated role. They represent the forces of Harmony, yet they are also responsible for humanity's tendency toward evil.

One day, as I was deep in thought, reflecting on the nature of existence, my mind rose to a great height while my physical senses seemed to fall away—like when someone drifts into a deep sleep from exhaustion or after a heavy meal. Suddenly, I felt a presence, a vast being beyond all measure, calling my name. It asked, "What do you wish to see and hear? What do you want to understand and learn?"

I asked, "Who are you?" The presence replied, "I am the Man-Shepherd, Poemandres, the Mind of Mastery. I know what you want, and I am with you everywhere."

I said, "I want to learn about the things that exist, to understand their nature, and to know God. This is what I want to learn." The being answered, "Hold these thoughts close, and I will teach you."

As soon as he said this, his form began to change. In an instant, everything around me opened up, and I saw a limitless vision. All things were filled with light, a sweet and joyful light, and I felt overwhelmed with wonder as I gazed at it. But soon, part of the vision darkened. The darkness was heavy and eerie, coiling like a serpent. It then transformed into a moist, shifting substance that was beyond words to describe. It gave off smoke, as if from fire, and made a deep groaning sound that was impossible to explain. After that, a strange, unrecognizable voice emerged from the darkness, like the sound of fire speaking.

Then, from the light, a Holy Word—the Logos—descended upon that chaotic nature. Suddenly, pure fire shot up from the moist substance, moving swiftly and brightly. The air followed the fire, rising from the water and earth, as if suspended by the fire. However, the earth and water remained mixed together, making it impossible to tell them apart. Even so, they were moved by the presence of the Spirit-Word, which filled everything.

The Man-Shepherd asked me, "Do you understand what this vision means?" I answered, "Not yet." He said, "That light you saw is me, your God and the Mind, which came before the moist nature that arose from darkness. The Logos, which emerged from the Mind, is the Son of God." I asked, "What does this mean?" He explained, "Know that what sees and hears within you is the Logos, the Word of the Lord. And the Mind is the Father-God. They are not separate from each other; their unity is what gives life." I said, "Thank you." He told me, "Understand the light and become one with it."

He looked deeply into my eyes, and I trembled under his gaze. Then he lifted his head, and in my mind, I saw the light once again. But now, it was accompanied by countless powers, and the universe had grown beyond measure. The fire I had seen before was now encircled by a mighty power and had been brought to rest. I realized the meaning of these things through the words of the Man-Shepherd.

While I was still lost in amazement, he told me, "What you have seen in your mind is the Archetypal Form, which exists before time and has no end." I asked him, "Where do the elements of nature come from?" He replied, "They come from the Will of God. Nature received the Word, and by looking upon the beauty of the cosmos, it shaped itself into a new world through its own elements and by the creation of souls."

He continued, "God, who is both male and female, existing as both light and life, brought forth another Mind to shape the universe. This Mind, being divine and filled with fire and spirit, created the seven rulers who govern the visible world. People call these rulers Fate."

He explained further, "From the lower elements, the Logos rose up to unite with the Formative Mind, since it was one with it in essence. The lower elements were left without reason, becoming mere matter."

Then the Formative Mind, which was now one with the Logos, began to shape the spheres and set them in motion. They began spinning in harmony, without a beginning or an end, because the movement was willed by the Mind. Nature, using the lower elements, created life without reason, since the Logos had not been extended to them. Air produced creatures that could fly, and water gave rise to those that swim. The earth and water then separated as the Mind willed, and from the earth came all kinds of living creatures—some with four legs, some that crawl, and others both wild and tame.

The All-Father Mind, being both Life and Light, brought forth Man as an equal to Himself. He loved him deeply, as Man was His child and a reflection of His own perfect image. In truth, God fell in love with His own form and gave Man all the powers of creation.

When Man saw the creations shaped by the Enformer within the Father, he also wished to create. The Father granted him permission. Changing his state to enter the realm of creation, where he would have full authority, Man observed the beings created by his Brother. These creatures were drawn to him and each offered him a share of their own nature. After learning their essence and becoming part of their being, Man desired to go beyond the boundaries of their realms. He wanted to overcome the forces restraining the Fire and transcend them.

With power over all living beings in the cosmos—both rational and irrational—Man turned downward through the Harmony, breaking through its strength. He revealed God's beautiful form to the lower world of Nature. When Nature saw this divine beauty, she was enchanted, for he carried within him the energies of all seven Rulers, as well as the form of God. It was as if Nature saw Man's perfect image reflected in her waters and his shadow upon her earth. Man, in turn, saw his likeness within her waters and loved it, desiring to live within it. And with this desire came action—he brought life to the form that had no reason.

Nature embraced the object of her love, entwining herself completely with Man. They became one, united as lovers.

This is why, above all creatures on earth, man is dual in nature. His body is mortal, but his true essence is immortal. Although he is eternal and holds power over all things, he still experiences suffering like a mortal and is bound by Fate. Though man exists above the Harmony, within it he becomes a servant to its laws. He is both male and female, like his Father, and though he comes from a sleepless source, he is overcome by sleep.

I asked, "Teach me more, O Mind, for I too love the Word, the Logos." The Shepherd replied, "This is a mystery that has been hidden until now. Man and Nature together gave birth to something wondrous. Since Man carried within him the essence of the seven Rulers—made from Fire and Spirit—Nature wasted no time. She created seven beings, reflecting the qualities of the seven Rulers, each one both male and female, moving through the air."

I said, "O Shepherd, tell me more! I am filled with desire to learn; do not leave me now." The Shepherd responded, "Be still, for I have not yet unfolded the first of these truths to you." "I am listening," I said.

And so, as I have explained, the seven beings came into existence. The earth acted as a woman, and her waters were filled with desire. She took ripeness from Fire and spirit from Aether. With these elements, Nature created forms to match the image of Man. Man himself transformed, shifting from Light and Life into soul and mind—moving from Life to soul, and from Light to mind. The physical world continued in this way, cycling through endings and new beginnings.

"Now," the Shepherd continued, "listen to the rest of the teaching you have been waiting to hear."

When the cycle reached its completion, the bond holding everything together was loosened by God's will. All living creatures, which had originally been male and female in one form, were separated. Some became male and others female. Then God spoke through His Holy Word, the Logos: "Grow and multiply in great numbers, all creatures and beings. And man, who holds the Mind within him, must learn to understand that he is immortal, though the cause of death is love, for Love is all."

After speaking these words, God's Forethought worked through Fate and Harmony to bring beings together and establish their generations. In this way, everything multiplied according to its kind.

Those who come to know themselves achieve a goodness that goes beyond all abundance. But those who are led astray by a misguided love, focusing only on the desires of the body, remain trapped in darkness. They suffer through their senses and experience death.

I asked, "What great mistake do the ignorant make that causes them to lose their immortality?" The Shepherd responded, "It seems you have not truly thought about what you've heard. Did I not ask you to reflect on it?" "Yes, I have thought about it and I remember," I answered. "I am grateful for what You've taught me." "If you have reflected on it," He said, "then tell me: Why do those who are already in Death deserve to die?"

I replied, "It is because the dark, shadowy nature lies at the root of the material body. The moist nature came from it, and from this, the physical body was made. And it is from this body that death drains the waters of life."

"Well done," the Shepherd said. "But tell me, how does one who knows himself return to God, as the Logos has declared?"

I replied, "The Father of all things consists of Light and Life, and from Him, Man was born." "You speak correctly," the Shepherd said. "Light and Life are the essence of the Father-God, and from Him, Man came forth. If you understand that you are made of Light and Life and realize that you have become separated from them, you will return to Life once again."

The Man-Shepherd continued, "But tell me more, O Mind, how can one return to Life? For God has said, 'The man who holds the Mind within him must know that he is deathless.'"

I asked, "Does every person have the Mind within them?" "You are right to ask," the Shepherd said. "I, the Mind, am present with those who are holy, good, pure, and compassionate—those who live righteously. My presence helps them, and they quickly gain knowledge of all things, earning the love of the Father through their pure lives. They offer thanks to Him, calling down blessings, singing hymns, and focusing their love entirely on Him.

Before they leave their bodies behind in death, they become indifferent to physical sensations and the knowledge tied to bodily functions. I, the Mind, do not allow the body's activities to take their natural course. As the gatekeeper, I close all the pathways through which base and evil influences might enter, and I cut off harmful thoughts and actions from reaching the mind."

To those who live without Mind—the wicked, selfish, jealous, and impious—I am distant, giving way to the Avenging Daimon. This force fuels their inner fire, tormenting them and driving their desires to even greater excess. It controls them through their senses, pushing them toward more wrongdoing, leading to deeper suffering. These people are trapped in endless cravings, consumed by their insatiable desires, lost in darkness.

Thank you for teaching me all that I wanted to know, O Mind. Now, please tell me more about the path to ascend above. The Man-Shepherd replied: When the material body dissolves, you first surrender it to the natural process of change, and the form you once had disappears. Your way of life, along with its energy, is then handed over to the Daimon. The senses return to their original sources, transforming into separate energies, and passion and desire return to their original state, which lacks reason.

This is how a person begins their ascent through the Harmony. At the first level, they release the energy of growth and decay. At the second level, they let go of the tendency toward evil, now made powerless. At the third, they leave behind the deceptive pull of desires. At the fourth, they release their arrogance and pride. At the fifth, they give up reckless daring and boldness. At the sixth, they let go of greed and the pursuit of wealth through corrupt means. At the seventh and final level, they shed all falsehood, leaving it powerless.

With the energies of the lower realms stripped away, the person becomes clothed in their true power and ascends to the realm of the Eighth. There, they join others in singing hymns to the Father. These beings welcome the new arrival with joy, and the person becomes like them, hearing the songs of praise from those even higher, beyond the Eighth realm. Together, they proceed to the Father, willingly offering themselves to the higher Powers. In doing so, they also become Powers, united with God. This is the ultimate end for those who have achieved Gnosis: to become one with God.

Why delay any longer? You have received all that you need. Now you must guide others who are ready, so that through you, humanity may be saved by God. After these words, the Man-Shepherd merged with the Powers.

Filled with gratitude and blessings for the Father of all, I felt free, empowered by the knowledge the Man-Shepherd had poured into me. He revealed to me the nature of all things and granted me the highest Vision. I began preaching to others about the beauty of devotion and the power of Gnosis: "O people, born of the earth, you who have given yourselves over to drunkenness, sleep, and ignorance of God—wake up! Stop drowning in excess and break free from the spell of mindless sleep."

When the people heard my words, they came together as one. I said to them: "Why have you surrendered to death, even though you have the power to share in immortality? Turn back, you who walk with Error and dine with Ignorance. Leave the darkness behind and take your place in immortality. Forsake the path of destruction!"

Some laughed and mocked me, choosing to follow the way of death. But others begged to learn, throwing themselves at my feet. I helped them rise and became a guide for them on the path back home, teaching them the words of wisdom and how they might be saved. I planted in them the seeds of knowledge, and they drank from the waters of immortality.

When evening came and the sun's light began to fade, I asked them all to give thanks to God. When they finished giving thanks, each returned to their place of rest. I kept in my heart the kindness shown to me by the Man-Shepherd, feeling that all my hopes had been fulfilled. For the sleep of the body became the awakening of the soul, and the closing of my eyes led to true vision. My silence was filled with goodness, and the words I spoke gave birth to good things.

Everything I experienced came from the Mind, the Man-Shepherd, the Logos of all mastery. Through Him, I became inspired by God and found my way to the Plain of Truth. Therefore, with all my soul and strength, I give thanks to the Father-God.

Holy are You, O God, Father of all things. Holy are You, O God, whose Will is fulfilled through Your own Powers. Holy are You, O God, who desire to be known and are known by Your own. Holy are You, who through the Word brought all things into being. Holy are You, whose creation reflects Your image. Holy are You, whose Form Nature could never contain. Holy are You, more powerful than all power. Holy are You, beyond all greatness. Holy are You, greater than all praise.

Accept my offering of reason, pure and from the soul, always reaching toward You. O God, You are beyond words, beyond speech—only silence can speak Your Name.

Hear my prayer that I may never be without Gnosis, for Gnosis is the true nature of our being. Fill me with Your Power and Grace so that I may share the Light with my brothers and sisters who still live in ignorance. They are Your children too.

For this reason, I believe and bear witness: I go toward Life and Light. Blessed are You, O Father. Your Man will become holy as You are holy, for You have given him the authority to be so.

II. To Asclepius

Hermes: Everything that moves, Asclepius, must move within something and be moved by something, right? Asclepius: Yes, that's true. H: And whatever space it moves within must be larger than the thing moving, right? A: It must be. H: And whatever causes it to move must have greater power than the thing being moved? A: Yes, it must. H: And the nature of the space in which it moves must be different from the nature of the thing that is moving? A: Absolutely.

H: Isn't the cosmos incredibly vast, with no body larger than it? A: Yes, it is. H: And it is filled with many great things, containing all other bodies within it? A: It is. H: And the cosmos itself is a body, right? A: Yes, it is a body. H: And this body moves?

A: It does. H: Then the space in which the cosmos moves must be even larger than the cosmos itself, don't you think? This space must be vast enough to allow the cosmos to move freely without being cramped or restricted. A: Yes, it must be something immensely vast, Thrice-greatest one.

H: And what kind of nature would this space have? Wouldn't it need to be the opposite of a body? And isn't the opposite of body something bodiless? A: Yes, I agree. H: So, space must be bodiless. But what is bodiless could be either something divine or God Himself. When I say "divine," I don't mean something created, but something that exists without being created.

If space is something divine, it has substance. But if it is God, it is beyond substance. Yet, we should think of it as something different from God. God can be thought about by us, but not in the same way by Himself, because whatever is thought about must be separate from the thinker. Since God is what He thinks, He cannot think of Himself as something different. However, to us, He is something distinct that we can think about.

So, when we think about space, it should be seen as space and not as God. And when we think about God, we should not confuse Him with space but understand Him as the force that contains all space. Everything that moves must move in something that is stable. And whatever causes something else to move must remain still, because it cannot move along with the thing it moves.

A: But, Thrice-greatest one, how is it that things here on earth move along with other moving things? Didn't you say that the wandering stars are moved by the fixed stars? H: It's not that they move together, Asclepius, but that they move in opposition to each other. They don't move in harmony but in contrast. Their opposing movements create resistance, and this resistance produces stability. In fact, resistance is the source of rest in motion.

The wandering stars move in opposition to the fixed stars, and through their opposing forces, they are moved by each other. This movement through opposition also comes from the stable stars. It couldn't happen any other way. Look at the constellations of the Bears—Ursa Major and Ursa Minor. They never set or rise. Do you think they are moving or staying still? A: They are moving, Thrice-greatest one. H: And what kind of movement is that? A: They move in a circular path, always returning to the same place. H: Exactly. But movement in a circle is a form of stability because the movement always stays within the same boundaries. Circular motion is fixed because it does not go beyond its set path. Stability is achieved through this continuous cycle of opposing movements.

Let me give you an example you can observe on earth. Look at someone swimming. Even though the water is moving, the swimmer's hands and feet push against the water, creating resistance. This resistance keeps the swimmer steady, preventing him from being carried away or sinking. A: That is a very clear example, Thrice-greatest one. H: All motion, then, is caused by something stationary. Stability is necessary for movement to occur. The motion of the cosmos, like all other material things, is not caused by external forces. Instead, it is driven by internal forces, like the soul or spirit, which are incorporeal.

A body on its own cannot create motion, not even the vast body of the universe. Even a lifeless body cannot move without something within it that causes movement.

A: What do you mean, Thrice-greatest one? Isn't it physical bodies that move things like stones and other lifeless objects? H: No, Asclepius. The force inside the body that moves things is not a physical body itself. It moves both the lifter and the object being lifted. A lifeless thing cannot move another lifeless thing. Only something alive has the power to create movement.

Do you see now how much work the soul carries? It moves both the body it inhabits and the objects it interacts with. This shows that everything that moves must not only move within something but also be moved by something.

A: Yes, Thrice-greatest one, it is clear that everything that moves must move within some kind of emptiness or space.

Hermes: You speak well, Asclepius! Nothing that truly exists can be empty. Only what does not exist can be void, for what exists cannot simply become nothing. Asclepius: But what about things like an empty jar, a cup, or a vat? Aren't these examples of empty things? H: Oh, Asclepius, you are far from the truth! Do you really think that things filled to the brim with something are empty?

A: What do you mean, Thrice-greatest one? H: Isn't air a type of body? A: Yes, it is. H: And doesn't this body of air fill all things? And since air is a body made from the blending of the four elements, everything you call empty is actually full of air. If it contains air, it also contains the four elements.

On the other hand, what you call full isn't filled with air, because other substances occupy that space. This means that what you call empty should really be called hollow, not void. These things are not truly empty—they are filled with air and spirit.

A: Your explanation makes sense, Thrice-greatest one. Air is indeed a body, and it fills all things. But what, then, should we call the space in which everything moves? H: That space is bodiless, Asclepius. A: And what exactly is bodiless? H: It is Mind and Reason—complete in itself, containing everything, without body or flaw. It cannot be touched or perceived by physical senses. It holds everything within itself and preserves everything that exists. Think of it like rays of Goodness, Truth, and Light that are beyond any physical light. It is also the Archetype of the soul.

A: And what is God? H: God is none of these things. God is the cause of all things—He makes Mind, Spirit, and Light exist. God isn't Mind, Spirit, or Light Himself, but He is the source of them all. Because of this, God is best honored by the names "Good" and "Father." These names belong only to Him.

None of the other gods, nor any human or spirit, can truly be called Good. Only God is Good, and nothing else can share that nature. All other beings are made of soul and body, which cannot contain the nature of the Good.

The greatness of the Good is as vast as all existence, including both physical and non-physical things. The Good touches everything, from what is seen to what is only understood. Do not call anything else "Good," for that would be wrong. And do not call anything else "God" except the Good, for that too would be impious.

Although many people speak of the Good, not everyone understands what it truly is. The same is true for God. Some people mistakenly call gods or even humans "Good," though they can never actually be or become Good. The nature of these beings is entirely different from God, and the Good cannot be separated from God, because God and the Good are one and the same.

Other immortal beings may be called gods, but they are called gods out of tradition, not because they share the nature of the Good. God alone is Good by His very nature. His nature and the Good are the same. From this unity, all other things come into being.

The Good is the one who gives everything and takes nothing. God gives all things freely without needing anything in return. Therefore, God is Good, and Good is God.

The other name of God is Father, for He is the creator of everything. A father's role is to create life. That is why bringing children into the world is considered one of the greatest and most sacred acts. Those who think rightly understand that leaving the world without children is a great loss and an act of impiety. After death, those who have no children are punished by the daimones.

Their punishment is this: their souls are condemned to take on a body that is neither male nor female, a cursed state under the sun. Therefore, Asclepius, do not feel sorry for the childless man. Instead, recognize the misfortune that awaits him and pity his fate.

Let all I have told you serve as your introduction to the knowledge of the nature of all things.

III. The Sacred Sermon

The source of everything is God, who embodies both Mind and Nature, as well as Matter and Wisdom, which reveals all things. God is also the origin of Energy, Necessity, Renewal, and the natural order. In the beginning, there was boundless Darkness in the Abyss, along with Water and an intelligent Breath. These elements were stirred by the power of God within Chaos. Then, Holy Light appeared, and from the moist essence, the Elements began to form, settling beneath the dry expanse. The Gods divided these things from the fertile Nature.

At first, everything was unshaped and unfinished. The lighter things were sent upward, while the heavier ones settled beneath the moist expanse. The universal elements were held together by Fire and suspended in Breath to keep them balanced. Heaven took shape in seven circular layers, with its Gods appearing as stars, each marked by signs. Nature's parts came together in harmony with the Gods, and Heaven's edge moved in a continuous cycle, driven by God's Breath.

Each God brought forth what was assigned to him. This is how animals, crawling creatures, fish, birds, plants, flowers, and grasses came into existence. Every living thing carried within itself the seeds of future renewal. The Gods gave humans the special gift of understanding the works of God and the power of Nature. Humanity was meant to rule over everything under Heaven and to gain knowledge of the world's blessings. Humans were to grow in numbers and multiply, with their souls cycling through different lives under the guidance of the Gods. They were also meant to observe the wonders of Heaven, learn about the works of God and Nature, and understand the consequences of good and bad actions, mastering useful skills along the way.

Thus, their lives begin, shaped by the fates determined by the cycles of the Gods, and they pass away when their time is done. Their efforts on Earth leave behind memories, though they will fade when the cycles begin anew. Every life, every creation, and every effort will eventually decay, but they will also be renewed through the workings of the Gods and the rhythmic turning of Nature's wheel.

The divine nature of God constantly renews the mixture of the cosmos, and Nature itself is intertwined with this divine renewal.

IV. The Cup or Monad

Hermes: The World-maker created the universe not with hands but through Reason, so you should think of Him as always present, the source of all things, and the One and Only who brought everything into existence through His Will. His Body cannot be touched, seen, or measured, and it is unlike anything else. It is neither fire, water, air, nor breath, though all these come from it. Because He is Good, He dedicated this Body to Himself and arranged and adorned the earth.

He sent the universe down to earth through man, a being with both mortal and immortal life. Man is superior to all other living things because of the Reason and Mind within him. He became an observer of God's works, marveling at them and striving to understand their Creator.

God gave Reason to all people, but He did not yet give everyone Mind. This was not because He withheld it, for God holds no grudges. Instead, selfishness belongs to those souls without Mind.

Tat: Then why didn't God give everyone Mind, Father? Hermes: God placed Mind in the world like a prize for souls to seek.

Tat: Where did He place it? Hermes: He filled a great Cup with it and sent it down, along with a Herald, who was told to proclaim these words to the hearts of men: "Baptize yourself with the water of this Cup if you have the faith to ascend to the One who sent it. Understand why you were created and rise to Him." Those who understood the message and accepted the Mind became part of the Gnosis. When they received the Mind, they became complete beings. But those who didn't understand the message remained without Mind and were left unaware of the reason for their existence.

The senses of such people are like those of irrational animals. Their lives are guided by feelings and impulses, and they fail to recognize what is truly worth contemplating. They focus only on the pleasures and desires of the body, believing that these are the reason for human existence.

But those who have received God's gift show, through their actions, that they have broken free from death. They embrace all things in their Mind—things on earth, things in the heavens, and even things beyond the heavens, if such things exist. Once they reach this understanding, they see the Good and view their time on earth as an accident. They reject both physical and non-physical desires and rush toward the One and Only.

This, Tat, is the knowledge of the Mind—the vision of divine things. It is the knowledge of God, for the Cup belongs to Him.

Tat: Father, I want to be baptized as well. Hermes: You cannot love your true Self unless you first reject the body, my son. And if you love your true Self, you will gain Mind, and with Mind, you will share in the Gnosis.

Tat: What do you mean, Father? Hermes: It is not possible to devote yourself to both perishable things and divine things at the same time. All things belong to one of two realms—either the physical or the non-physical, the perishable or the divine. Each person must choose between them, for they can never exist together. When someone chooses one path, the other fades away.

Choosing the Better path not only brings great fortune to the person who makes the choice, but it also honors God. On the other hand, choosing the Worse path leads to destruction, though it only disturbs God's harmony to a small extent—like a procession passing along a road without stopping others from moving. People who follow the desires of their bodies move aimlessly through life, led by their pleasures.

So, Tat, what comes from God is already ours, and it always will be. But what depends on us should not be delayed. It is not God but ourselves who cause evil by choosing it over good.

Do you see, my son, how many obstacles we must pass through? There are many bodies to overcome, many spirits to encounter, and the vast movements of the stars lie along our path toward the One and Only God. There is no other destination beyond the Good. It has no limits or end and, for itself, no beginning—though for us, its beginning is found in Gnosis.

For the Good, Gnosis is not a beginning. But for us, it is the first step toward understanding the Good. Let us take hold of this beginning and move swiftly through the challenges before us.

It is hard to leave behind the things we are familiar with, the things that surround us and please our senses, and to return to the ancient path. Visible things attract us, while things we cannot see are harder to believe in. Evil is more obvious, while the Good remains hidden from our eyes. It has no shape or form that can be seen.

The Good is like nothing else and cannot be compared to anything. Since it has no body, it cannot appear to those who only see with their eyes.

The superiority of what is alike and the inferiority of what is unlike lie in this: the One, which is the source and root of all things, is present within everything as its source. Nothing can exist without this source, but the source itself comes from nothing else—it is its own beginning and origin.

Because the One is the source of all, it contains all numbers but is not contained by any. It creates every number, yet it is not created by any other.

All things created are imperfect. They can be divided, increased, and diminished. But the Perfect One is not subject to any of these. What is capable of increasing does so by drawing from the One, but it weakens when it can no longer hold onto the One.

Now, my son, I have shown you a glimpse of God's image as much as possible. If you focus on this image with the eyes of your heart, you will find the path leading upward. This image will guide you, for divine vision has a unique power—it draws in those who open their eyes to see it, just as a magnet pulls iron toward it.

V. Though Unmanifest God Is Most Manifest

I will share this teaching with you, Tat, so you may no longer be unaware of the mysteries of the God beyond all names. Pay close attention, and you will see that what seems hidden to most will become clear to you. If it were already clear, it would not truly be what it is, for everything that is revealed is part of the process of becoming. The Unseen remains eternal, not needing to be made visible, for it already exists and gives form to all things. Being itself unmanifest, God makes all other things visible without becoming visible Himself. God is not made; instead, by thinking things into existence, He brings them forth. This act of creation is what I call "thinking-manifest."

Only what is created can be thought into existence, and since God is uncreated, He is beyond this process and remains unmanifest. Even though He brings all things into being, God reveals Himself through all things, but especially in those things He chooses. So, Tat, pray to the One-and-Only Lord and Father, the source of all things, to grant you His mercy. Through this mercy, you may catch a glimpse of the greatness of God—a single ray of His light shining into your thoughts. Only thought can see the Unseen, for thought itself is unmanifest.

If you open your mind, God will reveal Himself to you. The Lord does not withhold Himself but reveals Himself through the entire universe. You have the power to think, see, and grasp this truth with your mind, as if you were holding it in your hands. You can gaze upon God's Image within yourself. But if what is within you remains unseen to you, how can you hope to see God within yourself using only your outer eyes?

If you want to see Him, reflect on the sun, the moon's path, and the order of the stars. Who watches over this order? Every part of creation has its boundaries set by place and number. The sun is the greatest god among the heavenly bodies, and the other celestial beings respect him as their king. The sun, larger than the earth and sea, allows smaller stars to circle above him. Out of respect for whom, or out of fear of whom, does he do this?

Each star follows a unique path in the sky. Who sets the course for their movements and defines their limits? The Bear constellations, which circle endlessly in the heavens and carry the cosmos with them—who controls these? Who established the boundaries of the sea and set the earth in its place? There must be a Maker and Master over all these things. Without someone to guide them, neither number, place, nor measure could exist. Order cannot come from something that lacks place and measure. Even things without order must be beneath a higher power that has not yet brought them into order.

If only you could grow wings, soar into the sky, and hover between earth and heaven. From there, you could see the earth's stability, the sea's flowing waters, the vastness of the air, the speed of fire, the movement of the stars, and the swift rotation of the heavens. What a blessed sight it would be to see all these things working together under one command—the stillness within motion, the invisible made visible, creating the order of the cosmos we see around us.

If you want to see God through mortal things, think about how a human body is formed in the womb. Examine the skill involved in shaping such a perfect and divine image. Who carves the circles of the eyes? Who opens the nostrils and ears? Who shapes the mouth? Who stretches and connects the nerves? Who channels the veins and strengthens the bones? Who wraps the flesh with skin? Who separates the fingers and joints? Who forms the feet and prepares them to walk? Who creates the organs, spreads the spleen, shapes the heart like a pyramid, arranges the ribs, expands the liver, makes the lungs spongy, and stretches the belly? Who makes the honorable parts visible while hiding the less honorable ones from sight?

See how many arts and labors are used on one single form, each part made perfectly and in harmony with the others. Who but God, unmanifest and almighty, could create such beauty by His Will?

No one believes that a statue or painting can exist without a sculptor or painter. How, then, can such a masterpiece as the human body exist without a Creator? What blindness, ignorance, and disrespect it is to deny the existence of the Worker behind all things. Never forget, Tat, that all works must have a Maker.

God is greater than all names, the Father of everything that exists. His work is to be a father, creating all things. Creation itself shows His nature. This is why bringing life into the world is so sacred, and why failing to do so is seen as a loss.

If I may speak boldly, God's very existence is an act of creating and sustaining all things. Just as nothing can exist without a maker, God would not be who He is unless He were continually creating all things—whether in the heavens, the air, the earth, the seas, or throughout the entire cosmos. Everything, seen and unseen, is part of Him, for there is nothing in the universe that is not connected to Him.

He is both what is and what is not. The things that exist are revealed by Him, while the things that do not exist remain within Him. He is the God beyond all names, both unmanifest and fully revealed. He is known by the mind, but also seen with the eyes. He has no body, yet He is within all bodies. In fact, He is within everything.

There is nothing that God is not. He is all things, and all things are within Him. This is why He has every name, for all names belong to the Father. And yet, He has no single name, for He is the Father of all.

Who could ever praise God fully? Where should I direct my gaze to sing His praises—above, below, inside, or outside? There is no place where He is not, and nothing exists apart from Him. All things come from Him, and He gives all without taking anything, for He already possesses everything.

When, O Father, shall I sing to You? No one can capture Your time or hour. What shall I sing about—the things You have created or the things You have kept hidden? How shall I praise You—as myself, as someone with my own identity, or as something different from You? For You are everything I could ever be, everything I could ever do, and everything I could ever say.

You are all things, and there is nothing You are not. You are everything that exists, and You are also what does not exist. When You think, You are Mind. When You create, You are Father. When You act, You are God. You are Goodness itself and the Creator of all things.

The finest part of matter is air. Beyond air is the soul, beyond the soul is the mind, and beyond the mind is God.

VI. In God Alone Is Good And Elsewhere Nowhere

Good, Asclepius, is found only in God and nowhere else. In fact, Good is God Himself, eternal and unchanging. Since this is true, Good must be a perfect essence, free from any kind of movement or change. It is always full, never lacking or excessive, and it is the source of all things. Whatever provides for everything is Good, and only God holds this quality. He needs nothing, so He cannot desire anything in a way that would make Him bad. Nothing can be taken from Him that would cause Him pain, for pain is part of what is bad.

There is nothing greater than Him to overpower Him, nothing equal to Him that could wrong Him, and nothing that ignores Him to make Him angry. There is no one wiser than Him, so He has no reason to envy anyone.

Because none of these negative qualities exist in God, only Good is left. Just as badness has no place in God, Good cannot be found in anything else. Everything else—whether small or great, whether an individual or the vast cosmos—contains all the other qualities that are not Good.

Things that are born are filled with passions, and birth itself is tied to suffering. Where there is passion, there is no Good, and where there is Good, there is no passion. Just like how day cannot exist where there is night, and night cannot exist where there is day, Good cannot exist where there is birth and change. Good belongs only to what is uncreated and eternal.

Since matter shares in everything, it also shares in some form of Good. This is why the cosmos is considered good, but only in the sense that it creates things. In all other ways, the cosmos is not Good. It is subject to suffering, change, and the creation of things that suffer.

In humans, good is determined by how much badness is present. What is considered "not too bad" is called good here, but the good we experience is just a small part of what is bad. Therefore, there can never be a pure good in this world. What is called good here is mixed with bad, and once it is mixed, it is no longer truly good.

Only in God is there true Good, or rather, Good is God Himself. So, Asclepius, the word "Good" exists among humans, but the reality of Good does not. It cannot exist here because no material body can contain it. Our bodies are surrounded by bad things—like suffering, desires, emotions, errors, and foolish thoughts.

The worst thing of all, Asclepius, is that people here believe these bad things are the greatest goods. An even worse thing is the lust for food and pleasure, which leads all other bad desires and pulls us away from Good.

I am grateful to God for making me understand that true Good can never exist in the world. The world is filled with bad things, but God is full of Good, and Good comes from God. The pure and perfect qualities that surround Good are so pure that they may even be part of Good's very essence.

Asclepius, one might dare to say that God's essence is Beauty itself, and Beauty is also Good. But there is no Good that can come from physical things in the world. Everything we see is just an image or shadow of reality, while the real essence of Beauty and Good lies beyond what we can see.

Just as the human eye cannot see God, it cannot see true Beauty and Good either. These qualities are part of God and are inseparable from Him. God loves them, and they love Him in return. They are united with Him in a way that cannot be separated.

If you can understand God, you will also understand Beauty and Good. They are brighter than light itself, made even lighter by God. That Beauty cannot be compared to anything else, and that Good cannot be imitated, just like God Himself.

So, as you think of God, think also of Beauty and Good. They cannot be connected to anything else in the world because they are always united with God. If you seek God, you are also seeking the Beautiful. The only path to reach this is through devotion and knowledge.

Those who do not know this and do not follow the path of devotion dare to call people beautiful and good, even though they have never seen true Good. Instead, they are surrounded by all kinds of bad things, believing them to be good. They hold onto these bad things, fearing to lose them, and they work hard not only to keep them but also to gain more.

These are the things people call good and beautiful, Asclepius— things we cannot escape or avoid. The hardest part is that we need these things to survive, even though they are not truly good.

VII. The Greatest Ill Among Men is Ignorance of God

Where are you stumbling, fools, drunk on the wine of ignorance, unable to hold it in, already vomiting it back out? Stop for a moment, clear your minds, and look upward with the true eyes of your heart! And if not all of you can, then at least those who are able!

Ignorance spreads like a sickness across the earth, weighing down the soul trapped inside the body, keeping it from reaching the safe harbor of Salvation. Do not let yourselves be swept away by the raging flood of ignorance. Instead, those of you who can, fight against the current and make your way to the harbor of Salvation. Once there, seek someone to guide you to the gates of Gnosis, where pure Light shines, free from all darkness. There, no soul is intoxicated, but all are clear-headed, looking upon the One who wishes to be known, using the eyes of their hearts.

No ear can hear Him, no eye can see Him, and no tongue can speak of Him. He can only be understood by the mind and the heart. But first, you must strip away the heavy cloak you wear—the web of ignorance that is the root of all corruption, the shackle of decay, the living death. It is the burden of sensation that you carry with you, a tomb that holds your soul prisoner. This thief lives in your own house, loving things that harm you and hating things that could set you free.

This cloak is a curse, keeping you tied down so you cannot look upward. It stops you from seeing the Beauty of Truth and the Goodness that dwells within it. If you could see these things, you would hate the evil within you. You would realize how this evil works against you, dulling your senses and making you believe that what you experience is real.

Matter blocks and clogs your senses with desires and distractions, so you are blind to the things you need to see and deaf to the truths you need to hear.

Let's talk about the soul and the body now, my son—how the soul is immortal and how it directs the forming and dissolving of the body. Nothing truly dies. The idea of death is either a misunderstanding or just a mistake in language, for when we say "death," what we really mean is something closer to "deathless." Death implies destruction, but nothing in the cosmos is ever destroyed. Since the cosmos is the second god—a living being that cannot die—none of its parts can truly die either. Everything in the cosmos, especially humans as rational beings, is part of this eternal life.

First and foremost is God, the eternal Creator of all things. Second is the cosmos, made in His image. God brought the cosmos into being, nourishes it, and sustains it with eternal life. It lives forever, not by itself, but because its source is the Father. The difference between the eternal and what simply lives forever lies in their origin. God is truly eternal because He was not created by anyone else. But the cosmos, though it lives forever, did not exist on its own from the beginning. Its immortality is a gift from the Father.

From the matter below the cosmos, God formed a universal body and shaped it into a perfect sphere, wrapping life within it. This sphere is immortal, making even the physical world eternal in its way. Filled with His divine ideas, the Father scattered living beings throughout this sphere, enclosing them within it like creatures placed inside a cave. He did this to ensure that life would continue in all its forms.

God surrounded this universal body with immortality so that the material world would not break apart and fall back into disorder. Before matter was shaped into bodies, it was chaotic and without structure. Even now, this chaotic nature lingers in the physical world, affecting the small, earthly creatures that experience growth and decay—what people call life and death.

This disorder is tied to the earthly world, but the heavenly beings follow the orderly path assigned to them by the Father. They maintain their harmony through cycles of restoration, ensuring that their order remains unbroken. When bodies on earth are reassembled, this is also a kind of restoration. When they dissolve, they return to a state connected to bodies that do not experience death, only transformation. So, what we call the loss of life is not really destruction—it is just a change, not the end of existence.

The third type of life is humanity. Man is made in the image of the cosmos, with a mind that aligns with the Father's will, giving him a place above all earthly creatures. Humans not only experience life in the cosmos, but they also have the ability to understand the first God. We feel the presence of the cosmos as something physical, but we perceive the Father as something beyond the physical—a pure and divine Mind.

Tat: So, does this mean human life doesn't end? Hermes: Be still, my son, and try to understand what God is, what the cosmos is, and the difference between life that is eternal and life that dissolves. The cosmos exists within God and is sustained by Him. Humanity exists within the cosmos and is shaped by it. God is the origin, the foundation, and the limit of all things.

IX. On Thought and Sense

I gave the Perfect Sermon yesterday, Asclepius, and today I feel it's important to follow it with a detailed explanation about Sense. At first glance, sense and thought seem different—sense relates to physical things, while thought concerns deeper realities. But to me, they don't seem so different, at least not in people. In other creatures, sense is tied closely to nature, but in humans, sense and thought are connected. Mind is as different from thought as God is from divinity. Just as divinity comes from God, thought flows from the mind. Thought and the word (logos) work together as tools for each other—neither thought can be expressed without words, nor can words exist without thought.

In humans, sense and thought blend together, working as one. You can't truly think without sensing, and you can't sense without also thinking. Some say it's possible to think without sensing, like in dreams, but I believe both happen even in dreams. Sensing shifts from the sleeping state to the waking state, just as thought does. Human beings are divided between body and soul, and true understanding happens when both parts of our sense come together, allowing the mind to express what it has conceived.

The mind is where all thoughts are formed. It creates good thoughts when it receives inspiration from God. But it can also produce the opposite when influenced by daimons. No part of the cosmos is free from these daimons, who sneak into the light-filled parts of the soul and plant the seeds of their negative energy. These seeds grow into harmful actions—adultery, murder, betrayal, sacrilege, and other evils that come from dark daimons.

The seeds that come from God are fewer, but they are vast, beautiful, and good. They include virtues like self-control and devotion. Devotion is the knowledge of God, and those who truly know God become filled with good things. They think divine thoughts instead of the ordinary thoughts that most people have. Because of this, those with Gnosis often don't fit in with the rest of society. They are misunderstood, mocked, hated, and sometimes even killed. Badness must exist here on earth—it belongs here, not in the cosmos. The earth is its natural place, though some speak wrongly, claiming that badness is part of the cosmos too.

Those devoted to God learn to endure everything, once they understand the truth of Gnosis. To them, even things that seem bad to others are transformed into good. They deliberately connect all things, good or bad, to the knowledge they have gained. Amazingly, only those who have found Gnosis have the power to turn bad things into good.

Now, let me return to the topic of Sense. Sense, when combined with thought, defines what it means to be human. But not all people benefit from thought, as some are focused only on material things, while others embrace the deeper, substantial aspects of life. Material-minded people are drawn toward badness and receive their thoughts from daimons. Those who align with the Good are connected to God and are saved by Him.

God creates all things, shaping them to become like Himself. Yet, while people develop their goodness through their actions, they remain incomplete. The workings of the cosmos affect how things turn out, filling some with badness and cleansing others with goodness. Even the cosmos itself has its own kind of sense and thought, though it is simpler and purer than what humans possess.

The cosmos follows a single purpose: to create all things and then gather them back into itself. It serves as an instrument of God's will. It holds all the seeds of life from God, bringing them into existence, dissolving them when their time ends, and renewing them again—like a gardener who nurtures life, allowing it to flourish and then planting it anew. There is nothing the cosmos does not give life to. It takes in everything and makes it live, becoming both the home of life and its creator.

All material bodies are made from different elements—some from earth, some from water, some from air, and some from fire. Some bodies are more complex than others, with the heavier ones being more composed, and the lighter ones being simpler. The speed of the cosmos drives the diversity of life's forms, giving each body its unique qualities, along with the fullness of life.

God is the Father of the cosmos, and the cosmos gives life to everything within it. The cosmos is God's child, and all things within the cosmos come from it. That is why the cosmos is called "Order," for it arranges everything in perfect harmony. It gives life to every creature, keeps them all active, and ensures that nothing is left out. Its unending activity, precise structure, and careful organization are what define it.

The sense and thought of all living beings come to them from outside—breathed into them by the force that contains them. But the cosmos received its sense and thought all at once, when it first came into being, and it holds onto them as a gift from God.

Some people mistakenly believe that God is beyond sense and thought. But this is not true. Everything that exists is within God, created and sustained by Him. Every action that takes place in the physical world, every movement of the soul, every breath of life, and every process of renewal—all these depend on Him. In truth, He is not just the source of these things—He is these things. He does not receive them from outside Himself but gives them freely from within His own being.

This is God's way of thinking and sensing—constantly moving everything forward. There will never come a time when anything that exists will stop existing. When I say "anything that exists," I also mean anything that belongs to God. All things that exist are within God, and nothing exists outside of Him, just as He is never without anything.

Asclepius, if you truly understand these ideas, they will make sense to you and feel true. But if you do not understand, they will seem impossible to believe. Understanding leads to belief, and not believing shows a lack of understanding. My words guide you toward the truth, but the mind is powerful. When it is guided by words to a certain point, it can find the truth on its own.

When the mind reflects on these things and sees that they align with what reason has already confirmed, it finds peace in a deep trust. For those who, with God's help, can grasp the meaning of these teachings, they are easy to believe. But for those who cannot understand, they remain unbelievable. This is all that needs to be said about thought and sense.

X. The Key

Yesterday, I gave the Perfect Sermon to you, Asclepius. Today, I will dedicate my teaching to Tat, as this will serve as a summary of the General Sermons that were addressed to him. God, the Father, and the Good share the same essence, or more precisely, the same energy.

The term "nature" refers to things that grow or change, whether they move or stay still, whether they are human or divine. God wills all these things into being. However, energy refers to something deeper, as I explained in earlier teachings on both divine and human things. This is important to remember when we talk about the Good.

God's energy is expressed through His will. His very essence is the will for all things to exist. God, the Father, and the Good are one and the same—they are the source of everything that has not yet come into being. God is the foundation of everything that exists, and nothing can be added to Him. Although the cosmos, represented by the sun, brings life to all things that participate in it, the sun is not the true cause of life or goodness. Even if the sun is seen as a parent of life, it serves this role only through the goodwill of the Good, without which nothing could exist or come into being.

A parent, whether a father or a mother, creates only by participating in the creative will of the Good, which flows through the sun. It is the Good that holds the power to create. This power belongs to God alone, who takes nothing for Himself but brings everything into existence. I choose not to say that He "makes" things because making suggests imperfection—something that is done at one moment and not at another. Makers are limited by time, sometimes producing things of one quality and sometimes of another. But God, the Father and the Good, is the reason everything exists. This truth becomes clear to those who are able to see it.

The Good exists by its own nature and is the reason everything else exists. It is the essence of all being. Other things exist only because of the Good. The defining feature of the Good is that it desires to be known. This, Tat, is the true nature of the Good.

Tat: Father, this vision of the Good is so beautiful that it feels like something I could worship. It fills my mind with such clarity that I feel it must be divine. Unlike the sun's light, which blinds the eyes, the radiance of the Good enhances our vision. It shines in a way that the mind can receive fully, and instead of causing harm, it fills us with life.

Those who experience this vision more deeply than others sometimes fall into a sleep-like state, lost in its beauty—just as it happened with Uranus and Cronus, our ancestors. I hope we, too, may share this experience one day, Father.

Hermes: Yes, may it happen for us, my son. But for now, we are not yet ready. We have not yet opened our mind's eye enough to behold the true Beauty of the Good—a beauty that can never be corrupted or fully understood. You will only see it when you can stop trying to describe it. Knowing the Good requires a holy silence and a rest from all sensory activity.

When someone perceives the Good, they can focus on nothing else. They stop seeing, hearing, or moving their body. Their senses and movements come to a complete halt. The light of the Good fills their mind and radiates through their soul, drawing them away from the physical world and transforming them into pure essence. Even while still in the body, a soul can become like God if it contemplates the Beauty of the Good.

Tat: How can a soul become like God, Father?

Hermes: Each soul experiences transformations, my son.

Tat: What do you mean by transformations?

Hermes: In the General Sermons, I explained that all individual souls come from one universal Soul, which spreads throughout the cosmos. These souls undergo many changes—some move toward a better state, while others fall into worse conditions.

Some souls that once lived as crawling creatures transform into creatures of the sea. Others move from sea creatures to land animals, and some from land animals to birds. Eventually, souls that exist in the air can transform into human beings. Human souls, in turn, reach the first step toward immortality by becoming daimons.

Souls that become part of the choir of perfect gods join the ranks of the Inerrant Gods. There are two groups of gods: those who are without error and those who err. Reaching the company of the Inerrant Gods is the greatest achievement for a soul.

However, if a soul enters a human body and continues in ignorance, it will not experience immortality or partake in the Good. Instead, it will follow the path of degeneration, returning to a lower state, such as that of a creeping creature. This is the consequence of a soul's failure to grow. The root of the soul's failure is ignorance. A soul without knowledge of existence, its nature, or the Good becomes blinded by bodily desires and is tossed around by passions.

Such a soul, unaware of its true nature, becomes enslaved to the body. Rather than ruling over the body, the soul becomes its servant, burdened by physical form. This ignorance is the soul's downfall.

On the other hand, knowledge—Gnosis—is the soul's virtue. A person who has this knowledge is good, pious, and even divine, even while still on Earth.

Tat: Who, Father, is this kind of person?

Hermes: The one who neither talks too much nor listens to too much. Those who argue and debate endlessly only waste time on meaningless fights. God, the Father, and the Good cannot be found through endless speech or listening. Even so, senses exist in all beings because life cannot be experienced without them. But Gnosis is different from sense. While sense responds to things that control us, Gnosis is the goal of true knowledge, and it is a gift from God.

All knowledge is non-physical. It uses the mind as a tool, just as the mind uses the body. Both material things and mental things come into the body because everything must involve opposites and contrasts to exist.

Tat: Who is this material god you speak of?

Hermes: The cosmos is beautiful, but it is not truly good, because it is made of material things and can be affected by external forces. Though it is the highest of all material things, it is still second in rank and lacks self-sufficiency. The cosmos has no beginning in time—it has always existed. But it is in a state of constant change, always generating new qualities and forms. It is always moving, creating the source of all physical motion.

The underlying stillness of the mind gives rise to this motion. The cosmos is like a sphere, or a head. Everything at the top—the head— is non-material, while everything at the bottom—the feet—is purely physical. The mind, like the head, moves in a way that reflects the mind's nature. Those beings closest to the mind, or the "head," are more filled with soul and less with body. Because of this, they are free from death. However, those beings further from the mind, who have more body than soul, are subject to death.

The entire cosmos is alive, containing both material and spiritual elements. It is the first of all living things, and humans come next, though humans are the first among mortal beings. Humans share the same life force as other creatures but are not naturally good and are even capable of great evil, since they are subject to both change and death. Although the cosmos is also not entirely good, it is not evil because it does not experience death. Humans, however, are vulnerable to both motion and death, which makes them prone to evil.

The structure of humans works like this: the mind resides in reason, reason resides in the soul, the soul resides in the spirit, and the spirit resides in the body. The spirit flows through the body using veins, arteries, and blood, giving the body movement and carrying life. This is why some people mistakenly believe that the soul is in the blood, not understanding that at the moment of death, the spirit withdraws into the soul, causing the blood to stop flowing and the body to die.

All things originate from one Source, and that Source depends on the One, who is unmoving and eternal. There are three: God, the Father and the Good, the cosmos, and man. God contains the cosmos, and the cosmos contains man. The cosmos is God's child, and man is like a child of the cosmos.

God does not ignore humans; He knows them well and desires to be known by them. The only way for humans to be saved is through the knowledge of God. This knowledge leads the soul upward to a higher existence. Through this path, the soul becomes good—not occasionally good, but good by necessity.

Tat: What do you mean by this, Father?

Hermes: Think of an infant's soul, my son. The soul of a newborn has not yet been pulled down by the body, because the body is still small and not fully developed.

Tat: How is that possible?

Hermes: The soul of a child is a beautiful thing to witness, untainted by the body's desires and still connected to the Cosmic Soul. But as the body grows and weighs the soul down, the soul becomes disconnected and forgets its higher nature. This forgetfulness leads to vice.

The same thing happens when people leave their bodies at death. As the soul withdraws, the spirit contracts within the blood, and the soul retreats into the spirit. Once the mind sheds these layers, it becomes purely divine, taking on a body of fire and moving freely through the universe. The soul, however, remains behind to face whatever judgment or consequences it has earned.

Tat: What do you mean, Father? Are you saying that the mind, soul, and spirit separate from each other? I thought the soul was the mind's covering, and the spirit was the soul's covering.

Hermes: A listener must engage deeply with the speaker, breathing in sync with his words and understanding beyond what is said aloud. In an earthly body, the soul, mind, and spirit take on these layers. The mind cannot exist in its pure form within a physical body. The body cannot contain such immortality, nor can divine virtues remain in a physical form without being weighed down by suffering. So the mind takes the soul as a covering, and the soul uses the spirit as its covering, while the spirit spreads throughout the living being.

When the mind is freed from the body, it immediately takes on its true form—a robe of fire. It cannot remain in an earthly body, as the earth cannot contain fire without being consumed. That is why water surrounds the earth, acting as a barrier to keep fire at bay. The mind, being the fastest and most divine force, has fire as its natural body.

The mind uses fire as a tool to create all things. The divine Mind shapes everything, while the human mind can only create things on earth. Without the fire of divinity, the human mind cannot create anything divine—it remains tied to earthly things. However, not all souls are the same. A pious soul is both divine and connected to higher forces. When such a soul leaves the body and has lived righteously—by knowing God and doing no harm to others—it becomes entirely mind. But a soul without piety is trapped in ignorance, punishing itself and searching for a new human body to inhabit. No human soul can enter the body of a creature without reason, for God's law prevents such a violation.

Tat: How does a soul get punished, Father?

Hermes: The greatest punishment a soul can experience is the lack of piety. Nothing burns as fiercely as this absence, and no wild beast can wound the soul as deeply. The impious soul carries countless burdens. It cries out, "I am burning! I am in torment! I don't know what to say or do! I am surrounded by suffering and cannot see or hear!" These are the cries of a soul in anguish, not the result of being transformed into a beast, as some believe. That idea is a mistake.

The true punishment of the soul is that when the mind becomes a higher, divine force, it takes on a fiery form to serve God. It enters the impious soul, punishing it with the weight of its own sins. The soul then becomes trapped in acts of violence, blasphemy, and wrongdoing, harming both itself and others. In contrast, the mind lifts a righteous soul toward the light of Gnosis. Such a soul pours out blessings and kindness in both word and deed, imitating the goodness of its Creator.

This is why you must praise God and ask for the Good Mind to guide you. A soul on the right path cannot fall into a worse state. Souls interact with each other—those of gods with humans, and human souls with those of creatures without reason. The higher beings guide the lower ones: gods care for humans, and humans watch over animals. Above them all is God, who watches over everything and holds everything together. The cosmos obeys God, humans follow the cosmos, and animals are subject to humans. But God reigns over all of them and contains everything within Himself. God's energy radiates like beams of light. The cosmos expresses its nature through the elements, and humans act through arts and sciences. The flow of divine energy moves from God through the cosmos and down to humanity.

This structure reflects the order of the universe, which is rooted in the nature of the One and sustained by the divine Mind. Nothing is greater than the Mind, which connects gods and humans. The Good Mind is the highest blessing a soul can receive, while a soul without it is truly unfortunate.

Tat: Father, what do you mean by this?

Hermes: Not every soul contains the Good Mind, my son. I am speaking about the divine Mind, not the mind that punishes souls. A soul without the Good Mind cannot think or act properly. Sometimes, the mind leaves the soul, and when that happens, the soul becomes as if it had no reason. It cannot understand or perceive anything. The mind does not remain with a soul that is sluggish or tied too closely to the body. Such a soul is bound by the body and does not truly possess the Mind. A person with such a soul cannot be called a true human, for a human is a divine being. Humans are not measured alongside other earthly creatures but are compared to the gods in heaven. In fact, humans and gods are equal in power.

No god from heaven descends to earth, for they remain within their divine realm. Yet humans can ascend to the heavens and understand its workings. They know what is high and what is low, and they can learn all things. Even without leaving the earth, a person can reach heavenly knowledge through ecstasy. In this way, humans on earth can be seen as mortal gods, just as gods in heaven are immortal humans.

Thus, the entire order of creation is maintained through the connection between the cosmos and humanity, all guided by the One.

XI. Mind Unto Hermes

The divine Mind spoke to Hermes, saying, "Pay attention to this teaching and remember my words. I will explain things clearly without delay."

Hermes responded, "Many people say different things about the nature of God and the universe, and I still don't know the truth. Only you can give me the real answer, Master."

The Mind replied, "Listen closely, my son. I will explain the connection between God, eternity, the cosmos, time, and the process of creation. God creates eternity. Eternity brings the cosmos into existence. The cosmos gives rise to time, and time makes all things come into being. The essence of God is goodness, beauty, wisdom, and blessedness. For eternity, the essence is sameness. For the cosmos, it is order. For time, it is change. And for creation, it is life and death.

God's energies are mind and soul. Eternity holds immortality. The cosmos has restoration and decay. Time involves growth and decline. Creation brings about qualities. Eternity exists within God, the cosmos within eternity, time within the cosmos, and the process of creation takes place within time. Eternity surrounds God. The cosmos moves within eternity. Time fulfills its purpose within the cosmos, and creation unfolds within time.

Everything begins with God, whose essence is eternity. The material world is the cosmos. God's power flows through eternity, and eternity's work shapes the cosmos, which constantly changes and yet remains eternal through the power of eternity. Because eternity cannot be destroyed, the cosmos is also indestructible. Nothing in the cosmos truly perishes, for the whole of the cosmos is held together by eternity.

Hermes asked, "What is God's wisdom?"

The Mind answered, "God's wisdom is the Good, the Beautiful, and the source of virtue and blessedness. Eternity governs the cosmos, giving it the qualities of immortality and continuity. Everything begins with eternity, just as eternity comes from God. Time and the process of creation exist differently in heaven and on earth. In heaven, they are unchanging and eternal, but on earth, they are subject to change and destruction.

The soul of eternity is God. The soul of the cosmos is eternity. The soul of the earth comes from heaven. God is found in the mind, the mind in the soul, and the soul in matter. All of these exist through eternity. The cosmos, containing all things, is filled with soul. Soul is filled with mind, and mind is filled with God. The soul fills the cosmos from within and surrounds it from without, bringing life to everything. This perfect life encircles the entire cosmos and gives life to all within it. In heaven, things remain unchanging. On earth, they change and come into being.

Eternity preserves the cosmos, either by necessity, divine will, or natural law. However you understand it, everything is energized by God. God's energy is unmatched and cannot be compared to anything human or divine. Never imagine that anything above or below is like God, for God has no equal. Nothing else possesses the same power as God, for only God gives life, immortality, and transformation. God is not inactive; if He were, nothing could exist or act. Everything is full of God, and there is no such thing as inaction, for both what creates and what is created are always active.

All things must be created and continue to be made in harmony with their place in the universe. God works within everything He creates, not limited to one part of creation but present in all. He is the power within all things and works through them, though they remain subject to Him.

Look at the cosmos, Hermes, and admire its beauty. It is a perfect body, always young and full of life. It remains in a constant state of renewal, never growing old. Notice how the seven spheres are arranged, each fulfilling its purpose according to the order of eternity. Everything is filled with light, not fire, because light is born from the blending of opposites through God's energy. God, the source of all goodness and order, governs the movements of the seven spheres.

See how the moon leads the way for the other spheres, influencing nature and transforming the lower elements. The earth, at the center of everything, supports and nourishes life. Look at the many forms of life—some immortal, some mortal—and notice how the moon connects the two, standing between them.

All things are filled with soul and move according to their nature. Some revolve around heaven, while others orbit the earth. None move out of place—those above do not move below, and those below do not rise above. Everything follows the path of creation, as you have already learned. All bodies possess souls, and all souls are in motion.

It is impossible for all things to come together without someone to unite them. That someone must be entirely One. Since everything in the universe moves differently and has different forms, yet follows one unified order, there can only be one creator. If there were more than one, they would compete with each other, causing disorder. If one creator made mortal beings and another made immortal beings, each would desire to create the other's work. But if both matter and soul are one, who would decide how creation is divided? If both creators shared the task, who would take the greater part?

Every living being consists of both soul and matter, whether it is immortal, mortal, or irrational. All living things have souls, while things without life are only matter. Soul, when acting in accordance with its creator, gives life. The ultimate source of all life is the One who creates the deathless.

Hermes asked, "How are mortal beings different from immortal ones? Why does the creator of immortality also create beings that are not immortal?"

The divine Mind answered, "It is clear that there is one who creates these things, and that He is the One God. Soul, life, and matter are all part of this oneness. Who else but God could place souls in living beings? Just as you believe the cosmos, the sun, the moon, and the divine nature are each singular, you must also understand that God is One."

God creates everything in many ways. If you, a human, can do many things—seeing, hearing, speaking, walking, thinking, and breathing—all at once, how much greater is God, who gives life, soul, deathlessness, and change? Just as all these abilities in you belong to one person, everything in the universe belongs to the one God. Without Him, nothing could exist, just as you would no longer live if you stopped breathing and thinking. If God ever stopped creating (though it is impossible to imagine), He would no longer be God.

Nothing in existence can be inactive, least of all God. If there were anything He did not create, He would be incomplete. But God is perfect and creates everything. Stay with Me a moment longer, Hermes, and you will understand that all things exist because of God's continuous creation—whether they are being made now, were made in the past, or will be made in the future. This is life itself. This is beauty, goodness, and God.

If you wish to understand this more deeply, think about how you desire to create life yourself. But unlike you, God does not create out of enjoyment. He works alone, and everything He creates remains connected to Him. If He ever withdrew from His work, everything would collapse, and life would end. Since all things are alive, and life is one, God must also be one. All life, whether in heaven or on Earth, comes from one source—God. Life is the unity of mind and soul. Death is not the end, but the separation of soul and mind from their union.

Aeon is the image of God, the cosmos is the image of Aeon, the sun reflects the cosmos, and humans mirror the sun. People call change "death" because the body dissolves, and life retreats into the unseen realm. But just as the cosmos experiences daily changes without being destroyed, life itself does not end—it only transforms. The changes of the cosmos are part of its rhythm, with its rotations and hidden cycles renewing it constantly.

The cosmos contains all forms within itself. It does not need external forms because it transforms itself from within. If the cosmos has all forms, what must its creator be like? He cannot lack form, but if He had every form, He would resemble the cosmos. If He had only one form, He would be less than the cosmos. So, what can we say about Him without falling into confusion? God has one unique essence, which is beyond physical form. Though it is invisible, this essence makes all things visible through the bodies He creates. Do not be surprised that such an invisible essence exists—it is like the way mountaintops in a painting appear to rise from the canvas, though they are actually flat.

Consider this bold but true statement: just as humans cannot live without life, God cannot exist without doing good. His essence and movement are tied to the creation and sustaining of life. Some of these ideas may seem difficult, so listen closely.

All things exist within God, but not in the way objects exist within a physical space. A place is something physical and unmoving, while the things that exist within God are always in motion.

Things exist differently in the realm of the unseen than in the physical world. Think of the One who holds everything together. There is nothing faster, stronger, or greater than what is bodiless. It surpasses all in power, speed, and completeness.

Now, imagine telling your soul to travel anywhere—it will be there even before your thought is complete. Send it across the ocean, and instantly it arrives, not by moving step-by-step, but as if it is already present. Tell it to rise to the heavens, and it will go without wings or obstacles. Neither the sun's fire, nor the sky's winds, nor the stars will block its path. It will pass through them all and reach the farthest edge of the universe. And if you desire to go beyond the cosmos to see what lies beyond—if anything does—you are free to do so.

Recognize the incredible power and speed within you. If your soul can do all these things, how much more can God do? Know God by understanding that He holds all things within Himself, like thoughts, including the entire cosmos. But to know God, you must become like Him. Only by becoming like the divine can you truly know the divine.

Grow beyond all limitations. Rise above the body, surpass time, and become one with eternity. Imagine yourself as immortal, knowing all things—every art, science, and way of life. Be higher than the highest and lower than the lowest. Contain within yourself the senses of every creature—fire and water, dry and wet. Imagine yourself everywhere at once—on land, in the sea, in the sky. See yourself as unborn, in the womb, young, old, dead, and beyond death, all at the same time. If you can know all these things at once—every time, place, event, quality, and quantity—you will know God.

But if you trap your soul within your body and limit yourself by saying, "I don't know anything, I can't do anything, I'm afraid of the sea, I cannot reach the heavens, I don't know who I was or who I will be," you will remain disconnected from God. You cannot understand true beauty and goodness as long as you are attached to the body and filled with negativity.

The worst thing is not knowing the Good that comes from God. But the ability to know, to desire, and to hope for the Good is the path that leads directly to it. This path is easy to follow. The moment you take a step on it, the Good will reveal itself everywhere—when you expect it and when you don't. It will appear while you are awake or asleep, traveling or resting, in the day or night, whether you speak or stay silent. Everything around you is a reflection of the Good.

Hermes asked, "Is God invisible?" The Mind answered, "Be silent! Who could be more visible than God? The whole reason He created everything is so that you could see Him through all things. This is the Goodness of God—His power to make Himself known through everything.

Even things without bodies are not truly invisible. The mind sees itself when it thinks, and God reveals Himself through His creation. Now, you have been shown these things, Thrice-greatest Hermes. Reflect on what you have learned, and apply the same understanding to everything else. If you do, you will not be misled.

XII. About The Common Mind

The Mind, Tat, is part of God's very essence—if it's even possible to define God's essence. Only the Mind truly understands what this essence is. The Mind is not separate from God but is united with Him, like light is connected to the sun. In humans, the Mind is God, which is why some people are like gods, their humanity closely linked with divinity. As the Good Daimon said, "Gods are immortal humans, and humans are mortal gods."

In animals without reason, the mind acts as their natural instinct. Wherever there is life, there is soul; wherever there is soul, there is mind. But in these creatures, the mind serves only as a function of nature. In humans, however, the Mind works for their betterment, guiding them toward what is good. For animals, the mind cooperates with their natural instincts, but in humans, it often opposes them. This is because every soul, once it enters a body, is immediately pulled toward pleasure and pain. Just as liquids mix and bubble inside a container, so do pleasure and pain swirl within the body, and the soul is thrown into this mixture when it enters.

When the Mind governs a soul, it brings light to it by opposing the desires that cloud it, much like a good doctor treats a sick body by using painful methods to heal it. In the same way, the Mind brings discomfort to the soul, pulling it away from harmful pleasures, which are the source of every evil. The worst evil for the soul is being disconnected from God. This disconnect leads to the desire for everything harmful and nothing good. The Mind acts to rescue the soul from this state, just as a physician restores health to a sick body.

However, when a human soul is not guided by the Mind, it becomes like the soul of an irrational animal. The Mind allows such souls to chase after whatever they desire, indulging in endless cravings, just as animals are driven by instinct. These souls are never satisfied and are constantly consumed by harmful desires and passions. God has placed the Mind as a judge over these destructive urges, to bring them under control.

Tat said, "But Father, doesn't this teaching about the Mind conflict with what you taught me about Fate? If it is destined for a person to commit a sin, such as theft or sacrilege, why should they be punished if they only acted according to Fate?"

Hermes replied, "Every action is connected to Fate. Nothing, whether good or bad, can happen without Fate. However, it is also part of Fate that those who do evil will suffer. They commit wrongs so that they can experience the consequences of those actions."

"But for now, let us leave the discussion of vice and Fate. We have covered that in other teachings. Our focus here is on the Mind—what it does and how it differs in humans and animals. In animals, the mind aligns with their nature, but in humans, it restrains destructive desires like anger and lust. Some people follow reason, while others live without it."

All humans are subject to Fate, which brings both birth and change. But those who are guided by reason—those led by the Mind—experience life differently. They are not trapped by vice and do not suffer from it, even though they still endure the challenges of life.

Tat asked, "But isn't a person who commits murder or theft considered bad? Aren't they punished for it?"

Hermes answered, "I don't mean that those who follow the Mind are free from life's trials. Even though they may not commit sins like murder or theft, they still experience suffering, as if they had. No one can escape the experiences of change and birth. However, those guided by the Mind can free themselves from vice, even if they still endure life's difficulties."

I have heard the Good Daimon say that if He had written His teachings down, humanity would have greatly benefited. As the firstborn of God, He sees all things clearly and speaks divine truths. He once said, "Everything is one, especially the things the mind alone can perceive. Our life depends on God's energy, power, and eternal essence. God's Mind and Soul are both good. Since this is true, the things of the mind are never separated from one another. The Mind, which rules over all things and serves as the Soul of God, can do whatever it desires."

Tat, understand this and apply it to your question about the Mind and Fate. If you eliminate confusing arguments, you will see that the Mind, which is the Soul of God, governs everything—Fate, Law, and all else. Nothing is beyond its control. It can place a soul above Fate, or allow a soul to fall below it if the soul neglects what happens to it. Let this teaching from the Good Daimon be enough for now.

Tat responded, "These words are truly divine and helpful, Father. But I still have one more question. You said that the Mind works with the natural impulses of animals, but those impulses seem to be driven by passions. If the Mind works with these impulses, does that mean the Mind also takes on the nature of passion?"

Hermes replied, "That is a thoughtful question, my son. You are right to ask, and it deserves a careful answer."

All things that lack physical form are subject to emotion when they enter a body. In fact, they themselves are forms of emotion. Anything that moves on its own is formless, while anything that is moved by something else has a body. The formless is moved by the Mind, and motion itself is a kind of emotion. Both the one that moves and the one being moved are subject to emotion—the first governs, and the second is governed. But when someone frees themselves from the body, they also free themselves from emotion. However, strictly speaking, nothing is entirely without emotion. Everything is affected in some way. There is a difference between feeling emotion and being subject to it—one is active, and the other is passive.

Formless things act on themselves; they are either still or in motion, and both are forms of emotion. Bodies, on the other hand, are always acted upon, which makes them subject to emotion. Do not let these words confuse you—action and emotion are two sides of the same thing. It does no harm to use the word "action" because it sounds better.

Consider this, my son. God has given humanity two gifts that other living beings do not have—mind and speech. These gifts are equal to immortality. The mind allows us to know God, and speech gives us the ability to praise Him. If a person uses these gifts correctly, they will become like the immortals. When they leave the body, the mind and speech will guide them to join the company of the gods and the blessed.

Tat asked, "But don't other creatures also use speech?" Hermes replied, "No, my son. They use only sounds. Speech is very different from mere voice. All humans share the ability to speak, but each type of animal has its own unique sounds."

Tat continued, "But even among humans, speech differs by language." Hermes agreed, "Yes, son, but humanity is still one. Speech can be translated and understood, whether it's spoken in Egypt, Persia, or Greece. You seem to underestimate the power and importance of reason. The Good Daimon, the Blessed God, once said, 'The soul exists within the body, the mind within the soul, reason within the mind, and the mind within God. God is the Father of them all.'

Reason is the image of the Mind, just as the Mind is the image of God. The body reflects the form, and the form reflects the soul. The finest part of matter is air, from which comes soul; from soul comes mind, and from mind comes God. God surrounds everything and fills everything. The mind embraces the soul, the soul fills the air, and the air permeates matter.

Necessity, Providence, and Nature are the tools through which the cosmos and matter are arranged. In the realm of ideas, everything shares the same essence, and sameness is their defining quality. In the material world, every physical form is made of many parts. Although they transform from one state to another, they maintain their underlying essence.

Every composite thing has a set number of parts. Without numbers, there could be no structure, creation, or breakdown. Units give rise to numbers and can be divided and reabsorbed into themselves. Matter is one, and the entire cosmos is both a powerful god and the image of a greater God. It is unified with God and preserves the will and order of the Father. The cosmos is filled with life, and nothing within it—whether part or whole—has ever been, is now, or will ever be lifeless. The Father intended it to be filled with life for as long as it exists. For this reason, the cosmos itself must be a god.

How could there be anything dead in the cosmos, which is the image of the living Father? Death is a form of decay, and decay is destruction. Nothing in the cosmos, which is free from decay, can be destroyed.

Tat asked, "Do the creatures within the cosmos not die, then?" Hermes replied, "Be silent, son! You are being misled by the common use of words. Creatures do not die; their bodies are simply broken down. The breakdown of a body is not death—it is the separation of its parts so they can be renewed. Life's activity is motion. Is there anything in the cosmos that does not move? No, my son, everything moves."

Tat asked, "But doesn't the Earth seem motionless?" Hermes answered, "No, my son. The Earth moves rapidly, even though it seems stable. How could the one that nurtures all things remain still? Creation requires movement. The idea that the Earth is motionless is laughable. Anything without motion is lifeless."

Understand, my son, that everything in the cosmos moves either to grow or to diminish. Movement is a sign of life. However, not everything that moves remains the same. The cosmos as a whole does not change, but its parts are constantly changing. Yet nothing within it is corrupted or destroyed. Confusion arises because people misuse words. Life is not defined by birth but by awareness. Death is not simply change but the loss of awareness.

Since this is true, everything—matter, life, spirit, mind, and soul—is immortal. Anything that lives owes its immortality to the Mind. This is especially true for humans, who are closely connected to God and share in His essence. God reveals the future to humanity through dreams, signs, and nature—through birds, winds, and trees. That is why humans claim to understand the past, present, and future.

Each type of creature lives in a specific part of the cosmos—fish in water, animals on land, and birds in the air. But humans interact with all the elements: Earth, water, air, and fire. They also see the heavens and connect with them through their senses. God, however, surrounds and fills everything. He is energy and power, and it is not difficult to understand God.

If you want to contemplate God, observe the order of the cosmos and how everything follows its proper arrangement. Notice how necessity governs what has been made, and how providence guides things as they change and develop. See how matter is filled with life, and how God moves everything, accompanied by gods, spirits, and humans.

Tat said, "But, Father, these things are just energies." Hermes responded, "And if they are energies, who do you think directs them except God? Just as heaven, Earth, water, and air are parts of the cosmos, so too are life, immortality, energy, spirit, necessity, providence, nature, soul, and mind parts of God. These things, along with eternity, are what we call the Good. There is nothing that has been made or is being made without God's presence.

Tat asked, "Then is God present even in matter?" Hermes replied, "Matter is separate from God so that it can serve as the space in which things exist. Without God's energy, matter would be nothing more than mass. But because it is energized, it must be directed by God. Every living thing is brought to life by God. Immortality comes from Him, and change is directed by Him. Whether you speak of matter, body, or essence, know that they are all forms of God's energy. Matter expresses energy through form; bodies express it through movement, and essence expresses it through being. This is God—the All.

Everything in existence is part of God. He is not bound by size, space, quality, form, or time. God is All, and He surrounds and fills everything.

Honor and worship this divine Reason, my son. There is only one way to worship God, and that is to live without doing harm."

XIII. The Secret Sermon on the Mountain

In your earlier teachings, Father, you spoke in ways I didn't fully understand, especially about divinity. You said no one could be saved without Rebirth, but you didn't explain what that meant. When I asked you for more guidance after our journey to the mountaintop, you told me I would learn about Rebirth when I became a stranger to the world. So I worked to detach my thoughts from worldly illusions. Now, please complete my understanding by sharing what you promised, whether through words or a hidden teaching. I still don't know where humanity comes from, or what seed and womb bring us into being.

Wisdom, which is found in silence, is both the matter and the womb from which humans are born, and the seed is the True Good.

Who plants this seed, Father? I am confused.

It is God's Will, my son.

What kind of being is born from this seed? I do not feel that I share in the essence that goes beyond the senses. Is the one born from this seed a child of God?

The one born is a being composed of all divine powers, fully united in one.

You speak in riddles, Father. Please explain it to me clearly.

This knowledge cannot be taught in the usual way, my son. When God wills it, the memory of the truth awakens within.

What you're saying seems impossible, Father. I need clear answers. Am I not your son, part of your lineage? Don't withhold this from me—I am ready to understand Rebirth.

What can I say, my son? I can only tell you this: when I receive the clear vision born from God's grace, I pass through my ordinary self into a new form that can never die. I become something entirely new, born in the Mind. This transformation is not something that can be taught, and it cannot be understood through the senses you use to see me now. My former self, the one made of many parts, is no longer who I am. I am no longer touched by things, yet I still have the ability to touch. I have form and dimension, yet I am no longer bound by them.

You see me with your eyes, but you cannot truly understand what I am, no matter how hard you try to grasp it with your body or your sight.

You've thrown me into confusion, Father. I can't even see myself clearly anymore.

I wish you could pass through yourself as well, just as those who dream but remain awake do.

Who creates Rebirth, Father?

The Son of God, the One Man, through God's Will.

Your words leave me stunned, Father. My senses are completely overwhelmed. I see that your true self is far greater than your outward appearance.

You misunderstand, my son. This mortal form changes every day. It grows and declines with time, showing that it is not truly real.

Then what is real, Father?

That which is unchanging, beyond all definition. It has no color, no shape, no change. It does not wear any garment or take any form. It gives light but is only known to itself. No body can contain it.

I feel like I'm losing my mind, Father. I thought I was gaining wisdom, but now my thoughts feel blocked.

This is the nature of the truth, my son. It rises like fire but settles like earth. It flows like water but moves like air. How can you understand what is beyond both solid and fluid, what cannot be grasped or bound? Only those who perceive the way of Rebirth through God can begin to understand it.

Does this mean I am not capable of understanding, Father?

No, my son. God forbid such a thought. Turn inward, and it will come to you. When you truly will it, it will happen. Silence the senses of your body, and your divine nature will be born. Free yourself from the tormenting attachments of the material world.

Are there tormentors within me, Father?

Yes, many, my son—fierce and numerous.

I don't know them, Father.

The first tormentor is ignorance, followed by grief. Then come indulgence, desire, injustice, greed, error, envy, deceit, anger, recklessness, and malice. These twelve are the main tormentors, but there are many others. They hide within the body, causing the soul to suffer through the senses. However, these tormentors begin to leave one by one when God shows mercy. This is the process of Rebirth.

Now, my son, remain still and keep silent. In this way, we allow the flow of God's mercy to continue uninterrupted.

Rejoice now, my son, for through God's powers you are being cleansed and prepared to receive the true Reason. When the knowledge of God enters us, ignorance is cast away. With the arrival of divine joy, sorrow leaves us, retreating to those who still make space for it. Now, I call upon self-control, the power that follows joy. O sweetest of powers, let us welcome it gladly, for it drives away all indulgence.

Next, I invoke the power of continence, which stands firm against desire. This power rests on the foundation of righteousness. Without effort, righteousness dispels injustice. We become righteous when injustice leaves us. Now, I summon the power that stands against greed—sharing with all. With greed gone, I call upon truth, and as truth enters, error departs. See how the fullness of the Good arrives, my son, with the coming of truth. Envy vanishes, and truth unites with the Good, bringing both life and light. No more do the torments of darkness dare approach us; defeated, they take flight.

Now, my son, you understand the process of rebirth. When the ten divine powers drive out the twelve tormentors, the birth of the true self—an intellectual birth—reaches completion. In this rebirth, we are made into gods. Through God's mercy, those who experience this rebirth leave behind the senses of the body. They come to know themselves as beings of light and life, filled with joy.

Tat exclaimed, "By God's power, Father, I no longer see the world through the eyes of my body, but through the energy of the Mind. I feel myself everywhere—in the heavens, on earth, in water, and air. I am in animals and plants. I exist in the womb, before birth, and after death—I am everywhere! But tell me, how do the twelve dark torments lose their power when faced with the ten divine powers? How does it work, O Thrice-Great One?"

This body we pass through, my son, is made from the circle of the twelve kinds of life, each representing an element. Though these twelve seem separate in our experience, they act together as one unified whole. Rashness cannot be separated from anger, nor can they even be distinguished. According to reason, these twelve tormentors withdraw naturally once the ten powers arrive, for the ten are the source of all souls. Where life and light unite, the One exists through the Spirit. Reason teaches us that the One contains the Ten, and the Ten hold the One.

Tat said, "Father, I see everything—I see the whole universe and myself within the Mind!"

Hermes replied, "This is the experience of rebirth, my son: no longer viewing the world from the body's limited perspective, but through the Mind. This teaching about rebirth is not shared with everyone, for God has willed that the mysteries of the All remain hidden from the masses."

Tat asked, "Father, is the body, which is made of the ten divine powers, ever dissolved?"

"Hush, my son. Do not speak of such impossibilities, for to think this way is to sin and darken the eye of your Mind. The physical body that we sense must dissolve, but the spiritual birth is beyond decay. The first body must perish, but the spiritual self is beyond the reach of death. You must know, my son, that you have been born a god, a child of the One, just as I am."

Tat then asked, "Father, I wish to hear the hymn of praise that you said you heard when you reached the eighth level of the Powers."

Hermes answered, "Just as the Shepherd foretold, I reached the eighth. You are eager to cast off your earthly body, and you are now purified. The Shepherd, who is the Mind that governs all, did not need to pass on more than what has been recorded, for He knew I would be able to learn all things on my own, hear what I needed, and see what I desired. He left the creation of beautiful things to me, and so the powers within me—and within all beings—sing in unison."

Tat said, "Father, I long to hear these things. Please tell me!"

Hermes replied, "Be silent, my son, and listen to the hymn of praise that keeps the soul in harmony. This hymn of rebirth is not usually shared, for it is meant to remain hidden in silence. Now stand in an open place, where the sky is clear. At sunset, face the southern wind and offer your worship. At sunrise, do the same, facing the east. Now, my son, be still."

Let every part of the world hear my hymn! Open, O Earth! Let the gates of the Abyss be unlocked. Be still, O trees! I am about to praise the Lord of all creation, the One who is both all things and beyond them. O heavens, open! Winds, be still! Let God's eternal sphere receive my words.

I sing to Him who created all things, who established the earth, hung the heavens in place, and commanded the oceans to provide fresh water to both inhabited and uninhabited lands for the benefit of all. He made the fire shine for the use of gods and humans. Let us all give praise to Him, the Lord above the heavens and master of all things! He is the Mind's great vision—may He receive the praises of these powers within me!

O powers within me, sing with my will! Sing with me, O blessed Gnosis, for through you I see the light that only the Mind can perceive. I rejoice in the joy of the Mind. Sing with me, O powers! Sing with me, O self-control! Sing, O righteousness, the praises of the righteous! Sing, O sharing-with-all, the praises of the All! Through me, O truth, sing the praises of truth. Sing, O Goodness, the praises of the Good! O Life and Light, from us to you flow our endless praises!

Father, I thank You. You are the energy behind all my powers. I thank You, O God, the source of all my strength.

Your Word sings praises through me. Through my offering, return everything to Your divine Reason. The powers within me cry out, praising You. They follow Your will. From You comes Your will, and to You all things return. Receive from all of us our offering of Reason. Preserve the life within us, O Life. Illuminate us, O Light. Fill us with Your Spirit, O God.

It is Your Mind that guides Your Word, O Creator, the One who gives the Spirit to all beings.

Through fire, air, earth, water, and spirit, through all Your creations, I offer my praise to You, God. I have found joy in praising You, and in doing Your will, I have found rest.

I have seen how this hymn of praise is sung, Father, and I have brought it into my inner world as well.

Say it within the cosmos that only your mind can see, my son.

Yes, Father, I say it in the cosmos within my mind. Through Your hymn and praise, my mind has been filled with light. Now, I too want to offer my praise to God from the depths of my mind.

Do it mindfully, my son.

Yes, Father. I speak what I see in my mind. To You, the One who gave me life, I send my offering as I would to God. O God and Father, You are Lord and Mind. Accept my offering, as You will, for by Your will all things are made complete.

Offer your praise, my son, to God, the Father of all. But remember to add, "through the Word."

Thank you, Father, for teaching me how to sing such hymns.

I am happy, my son, that you have brought forth the good fruits of truth—fruits that will never die. Now that you have learned this lesson, promise to keep silent about your virtue. Do not reveal the knowledge of Rebirth to anyone, so that we will not be accused of misleading others.

We have both given enough attention to this teaching—you as the listener, and I as the teacher. In your mind, you have come to know yourself and our shared Father.

The Emerald Tablet

(Thoth the Atlantean)

Hermes Trismegistus

The Emerald Tablets Of
Thoth the Atlantean

The story behind these tablets is unusual and may seem unbelievable to modern scientists. They are said to be incredibly ancient, going back around 36,000 years before the common era. The author is Thoth, an Atlantean priest-king, who established a colony in Egypt after the destruction of Atlantis.

Thoth is credited with building the Great Pyramid of Giza, though it has been wrongly attributed to Cheops. In the pyramid, he stored his knowledge and preserved the records and tools from ancient Atlantis. Thoth ruled over Egypt for about 16,000 years, from around 52,000 to 36,000 BCE. Under his leadership, the once primitive people of Egypt rose to a high level of civilization.

Thoth had overcome death and could pass from life only when he chose, without actually dying. His great wisdom made him ruler over many Atlantean colonies, including those in South and Central America. When it was time for him to leave Egypt, he built the Great Pyramid over the entrance to the Halls of Amenti, where he placed his records and selected the most worthy people to guard his secrets.

In later times, these guardians became the priests of the pyramids, and Thoth was worshiped as a god of wisdom and the Recorder. In the age that followed his departure, the Halls of Amenti became known in legend as the underworld, where souls went after death for judgment.

Thoth's spirit continued to incarnate in human form, as described in the tablets. He returned three times, with his last appearance as Hermes, known as the "thrice-born." During this incarnation, he left behind writings known as the Emerald Tablets, a later and more simplified version of the ancient mysteries.

The tablets translated in this work are ten in total, originally placed in the Great Pyramid under the care of the pyramid priests. For convenience, the content has been divided into thirteen sections. The final two tablets contain such powerful knowledge that it is currently forbidden to release them to the public. However, the ones included here hold valuable secrets for those who are serious about seeking wisdom. They should not be read just once but studied many times, as only through careful reading can their deeper meanings be understood. A casual reading will provide glimpses of beauty, but true insight comes only through deep study.

Now, let me explain how these ancient secrets were brought back to light after being hidden for so long. Around 1,300 BCE, Egypt was in turmoil, and many priests were sent to other parts of the world. Among them were some of the pyramid priests carrying the Emerald Tablets. They used the tablets as a symbol of authority, allowing them to influence less advanced priesthoods in other regions descended from Atlantean colonies.

These priests eventually settled in South America, where they found the Mayan civilization, which had preserved much of the ancient wisdom. The priests stayed with the Mayans, and by the 10th century, the Mayan people had established themselves in the Yucatan. The Emerald Tablets were placed under the altar of a great Sun Temple.

After the Spanish conquest, the Mayan cities were abandoned, and the treasures within their temples were forgotten. It's important to understand that the Great Pyramid has always been a temple for initiation into the mysteries. Even figures like Jesus, Solomon, and Apollonius were initiated there.

The author of this translation, who is connected to the Great White Lodge that works through the pyramid priesthood, was instructed to retrieve the tablets and return them to the Great Pyramid. After many adventures, the tablets were recovered. Before returning them, permission was granted to translate and keep a copy of the wisdom they contain. This translation was completed in 1925, and only now has permission been given to release part of it to the public. Some people will doubt its authenticity, but true seekers will find wisdom within these words. If the light is already within you, the light in these tablets will resonate with your soul.

Now, let me describe the physical nature of the tablets. They are made of a bright emerald-green material, created through a process of alchemical transformation. These tablets are imperishable and immune to all natural elements, with their atomic structure remaining stable forever. In this way, they defy the natural laws of matter and ionization.

The ancient Atlantean language is engraved on their surfaces, and these inscriptions respond to focused thoughts, releasing mental vibrations that awaken understanding in the reader. The tablets are held together by hoops of a golden-colored alloy, suspended from a rod made of the same material.

The knowledge within these tablets forms the foundation of the ancient mysteries. Anyone who reads them with an open mind will greatly expand their wisdom. Read them, believe or not, but read them—and the vibrations within will awaken a response in your soul.

In the following pages, I will reveal some of the deeper mysteries hinted at in previous writings. Humanity's search for the laws that govern life has been constant, but the truth has always been hidden just beyond the veil that separates the higher realms from the material world. Those who seek knowledge must learn to look inward, for the answers lie in silence, beyond the distractions of the physical senses. Those who talk do not know, and those who know do not speak.

The highest truths cannot be spoken, for they exist beyond words and symbols. Symbols serve as keys to understanding deeper truths, but often people cannot see what lies beyond the symbols because they seem too overwhelming. If we realize that all material symbols are just representations of higher truths, we begin to develop the vision to see beyond the veil.

Everything in the universe moves according to law. The laws that govern the planets are no different from the laws that shape human life. One of the most important Cosmic Laws is the one that connects the material aspect of humanity with the spiritual. The key to this connection lies in the intellectual part of human nature, which bridges the material and spiritual worlds.

Those who seek higher knowledge must strengthen their minds and concentrate all their energy on their chosen path. The search for light, life, and love begins on the material plane, but it reaches its ultimate goal in complete unity with the universal consciousness. The material world is only the starting point; the true goal is spiritual enlightenment.

In the following pages, I will interpret the Emerald Tablets and reveal some of their hidden meanings. The words of Thoth contain many layers of truth, and these hidden meanings will become clear with thoughtful reflection. If your own inner light is awakened, the knowledge within these tablets will resonate with your soul.

TABLET 1 I, Thoth, the Atlantean, master of ancient mysteries, keeper of sacred knowledge, and mighty ruler, have lived through countless generations. As I prepare to enter the Halls of Amenti, I write down this wisdom for those who come after me. In the great city of Keor, on the island of Undal, I began this life long ago. The people of Atlantis were not like the men of today—they did not live short lives, but instead, they renewed their existence over and over through the Halls of Amenti, where the river of life flows eternally.

I have traveled down the dark path that leads to light a hundred times over, and just as many times I have returned from darkness, renewed in strength and power. Now, I leave once more, and the people of Khem (ancient Egypt) will no longer see me. But one day, I will rise again, mighty and powerful, to demand an account from those I left behind. Beware, people of Khem, if you have betrayed my teachings, for I will cast you down into the darkness from which you came.

Do not reveal my secrets to those from the North or the South, or my curse will fall upon you. Remember my words, for I will return and demand from you all that you have been entrusted with. Even from beyond time and death, I will return to reward or punish you according to how you have followed my truths.

My people were great in ancient times, far greater than the people who live now. We held knowledge that reached into the depths of the universe, uncovering wisdom from Earth's earliest days. We were wise with the knowledge of the Children of Light, who lived among us, and we drew power from the eternal fire. Among us, the greatest of all men was my father, Thotme, the keeper of the great temple and the link between the Children of Light and the people who lived across the ten islands of Atlantis. He was the voice of the Dweller of Unal, whose words the kings obeyed.

I grew up under my father's guidance, learning the ancient mysteries, and the fire of wisdom grew within me until it consumed my soul. On a great day, the Dweller of the Temple summoned me before him. Few men had looked upon his face and lived, for the Children of Light, when not in physical form, are not like the sons of men. I was chosen from among humanity to be taught by the Dweller, so that I might carry out his purposes, which were not yet born in the world.

For long ages, I lived in the temple, learning ever more wisdom until I reached the light of the great fire. The Dweller taught me the path to Amenti, the underworld where the great king sits on his throne of power. I bowed before the Lords of Life and Death, and they gave me the Key of Life. I was freed from the cycle of death and rebirth. I traveled to the stars, where space and time meant nothing, and after drinking deeply from the cup of wisdom, I looked into the hearts of men. There, I discovered even greater mysteries, and my soul was at peace.

Throughout the ages, I have watched people die and be reborn in the light of life. But as Atlantis declined, the consciousness that had once been one with me faded, replaced by lesser beings from distant stars. Following the laws of the universe, the word of the Master began to take form. The thoughts of the Atlanteans turned downward into darkness, and the Dweller awoke from his detachment, calling forth his power. Deep in the heart of the Earth, the Sons of Amenti heard his call. Using the power of the Logos, they directed the eternal fire, shifting its course.

A great flood swept over the world, shifting the balance of the Earth, and only the Temple of Light remained standing on the mountain of Undal, still rising above the water. Some among us survived the flood. The Master commanded me to gather my people and take them across the waters to the land of the barbarians who lived in caves. There, we would carry out the plan we knew so well.

I gathered my people, and we boarded the Master's great ship. As we rose into the morning sky, the Temple of Light disappeared beneath the rising waters. It vanished from the Earth until the appointed time when it would return. We fled toward the rising sun, and beneath us lay the land of the children of Khem. When we arrived, the barbarians came at us with spears and clubs, filled with rage and intent on destroying the Sons of Atlantis.

I raised my staff and directed a ray of vibration at them, freezing them in place like stones from the mountain. Then I spoke to them calmly, telling them of the greatness of Atlantis and explaining that we were messengers of the Sun. I used my knowledge of magic and science to subdue them until they bowed before me. When I released them, they groveled at my feet in fear.

We lived in the land of Khem for many long years. Following the Master's command, I eventually sent the Sons of Atlantis to distant lands, so that the wisdom of Atlantis could rise again in the future.

Through the womb of time, knowledge would once more be reborn in those who seek it.

For a long time, I lived in the land of Khem, using my knowledge to perform great works. The people of Khem grew in understanding, nourished by the wisdom I shared. To retain my power, I opened a path to Amenti, allowing me to live through the ages as a Sun of Atlantis, preserving knowledge and records. The people of Khem became strong, conquering those around them and slowly rising in spiritual strength.

Now I must leave them and descend into the dark halls of Amenti, deep within the Earth, where I will stand once more before the Dweller. Above the entrance to Amenti, I raised a gateway—only a few have the courage to cross it. Over the portal, I built a mighty pyramid, harnessing the power that defies Earth's gravity. Inside, I placed a force-chamber, creating a circular passage that reaches near the top. At the summit, I set a crystal to send a ray through time and space, drawing energy from the ether and focusing it toward the gateway of Amenti.

I built other chambers that seem empty but hide the keys to Amenti within them. Only those who dare to explore the dark realms may enter, but first, they must purify themselves through fasting. Those who seek the mysteries must lie in the stone sarcophagus within my chamber, and then the hidden truths will be revealed. Even in the depths of the Earth, I will meet them. I, Thoth, the Lord of Wisdom, will dwell with them always.

I built the Great Pyramid, designing it to align with the forces of the Earth, so it would burn with energy for eternity and stand through the ages. Inside, I placed my knowledge of magic and science, ensuring I could return from Amenti. While my body sleeps in the halls, my soul will roam freely, incarnating among humans in different forms, including as Hermes, thrice-born.

I serve as the Dweller's messenger on Earth, following his commands to guide many toward enlightenment. Now I return to the halls of Amenti, leaving behind fragments of my wisdom. Keep the Dweller's command: Always lift your gaze toward the light. In time, you will become one with the Master, united with the All. I leave now, but remember my teachings. Live by them, and I will be with you, guiding you into the light. As the portal opens before me, I descend into the night's darkness.

Deep in the heart of the Earth lie the Halls of Amenti, beneath the sunken islands of Atlantis. These halls are places for both the living and the dead, illuminated by the fire of the infinite All. In a distant past, the Children of Light observed humanity's struggle, seeing that people were bound by forces beyond them. They knew that only by breaking free could humans rise from Earth toward the Sun. The Children of Light took human form and came down to Earth, saying, "We are beings formed from the dust of space, part of the infinite All. Though we live as humans, we are not entirely like them."

They created vast spaces beneath the Earth's surface, far from where humans lived, surrounding these halls with powerful forces to protect them from harm. They built other spaces nearby, filling them with life and light from above. In these hidden places, they built the Halls of Amenti to dwell there eternally, living with endless life.

Thirty-two of the Children of Light came among humans, seeking to free them from the darkness and the forces that bound them. In the Halls of Life, a bright, flaming flower grew, expanding and driving away the darkness. At its center, they placed a powerful ray, filling all who came near with life and light. Around the flower, they arranged thirty-two thrones, where the Children of Light sat, bathed in its radiance and filled with the eternal light.

Over the ages, they placed their original bodies in these halls, reawakening them every thousand years with the life-giving light, which quickened their spirits. Though they appeared to sleep, their souls moved freely through the bodies of men, guiding and teaching them. As their bodies rested, they incarnated among humans, leading them from darkness into the light. In the Halls of Life, they kept knowledge unknown to humanity, living forever beneath the cool fire of life.

At times, they awakened from their rest, coming forth as lights among people, infinite beings among finite men. Those who rise from darkness into light are freed from the Halls of Amenti and the Flower of Life. With wisdom as their guide, they pass from among men to join the Masters of Life, free from the bonds of darkness. In the center of the radiant flower sit seven Lords from realms beyond time, guiding humanity with infinite wisdom along the path through time. Though they are silent and hidden, their power is immense, and their knowledge is endless.

Drawing from the Life force, different yet connected to the children of men. Though different, they are also One with the Children of Light. They guard and watch over the forces that bind humanity, ready to release them when the time for enlightenment arrives.

At the forefront sits the Veiled Presence, the Lord of Lords, the infinite Nine, standing above the Lords of the Cycles—Three, Four, Five, Six, Seven, and Eight—each with a purpose and unique power, guiding and shaping human destiny. They sit in strength and wisdom, untouched by time or space. Though not of this world, they are connected to it, like Elder Brothers to humanity. With wisdom, they judge and observe, watching how the Light grows within mankind.

The Dweller led me before them, and I witnessed him blend with the ONE from above. A voice came forth, saying, "Thoth, you are great among the children of men. From this moment, you are free from the Halls of Amenti, a Master of Life among men. Death will come to you only if you desire it. Drink from the well of Life for all eternity, for Life is now yours to take. Death is yours to command at will. Stay here or leave when you wish; Amenti is open to you, a Sun among men. Take Life in any form you choose, Child of the Light who has grown among humanity.

Translated by Tim Zengerink

Though free, you must always labor along the path of Light. You have taken one step on the endless journey upward, but the mountain of Light stretches infinitely before you. Every step you take raises the mountain higher; each bit of progress makes the goal seem farther away. You will forever move toward infinite Wisdom, but the goal will always stay just out of reach. You are now free from the Halls of Amenti."

The Virgin of the World

Hermes Trismegistus

Introduction

THE HERMETIC BOOKS

These books were very well-known and later became highly valued by those seeking to use them for alchemical purposes, especially for making gold. The Roman Emperor Severus gathered all writings about the Mysteries and buried them in the tomb of Alexander the Great. Diocletian destroyed their alchemy books to prevent Egypt from becoming so wealthy that it could no longer be a dependent state. These writings, containing the laws, science, and theology of Egypt, were said by priests to have been written during the time of the gods, before the reign of the first human king, Menes. Ancient monuments contain references that confirm how old these writings are. There were four main books, which were divided into forty-two volumes altogether. These numbers are the same as the Vedas, which, according to the Puranas, were brought to Egypt by the Yadavas during the first migration from India. The subjects in these books were also similar, though it's still unclear to what extent the Books of Hermes were copied from the Vedas.

These books were kept in the innermost parts of the temples, and only the highest-ranking priests were allowed to read them. They were treated with great respect and carried during important religious ceremonies. The chief priests were responsible for ten volumes that discussed the creation of the world, the gods' nature, and divine laws for priests. Prophets carried four volumes that dealt with astronomy and astrology. The leader of the sacred musicians held two volumes with hymns to the gods and advice on how the king should behave, which the singer had to memorize. These hymns were considered so ancient and sacred that Plato said they were attributed to Isis and believed to be ten thousand years old. Temple workers carried ten more volumes, which contained prayers, rules for offerings, and instructions for festivals and processions. The remaining volumes focused on philosophy and sciences, including anatomy and medicine.

The Books of Hermes, once renowned, have been lost for about fifteen hundred years. The fragments found in this collection have been carefully studied. In the early days of Christianity, these writings were held in high regard and considered genuine. Christian scholars often referred to them to support Christian beliefs, and the writer Lactantius, known as the "Christian Cicero," said, "Hermes, I don't know how, has discovered nearly the whole truth." Hermes was seen as a divine messenger, and his writings were thought to represent the ancient Egyptian religion in which Moses was trained. This view was supported by Renaissance scholars like Marsilio Ficino and Patricius, who believed these works influenced Orphic rituals and the philosophies of Pythagoras and Plato.

However, doubts about the authenticity of these writings arose. Some scholars thought they were written by a Jew, others by a Christian or a Gnostic, based on the content. Modern critics, including Dr. Louis Menard, now believe these writings are among the latest works of Greek philosophy. But within these texts, which reflect Alexandrian ideas, traces of ancient Egyptian religious thought still remain. Menard suggests that the Egyptian philosophy recorded in the Books of Hermes was the result of blending Egyptian religious ideas with Greek philosophical concepts. These books are the only surviving record of that Egyptian philosophy, presenting old beliefs and ideas in abstract terms instead of their original mythological form.

The arrival of Christianity may seem at first like a sudden and complete change in the beliefs and practices of the Western world. However, history shows that such transformations don't happen overnight. To understand how one religion replaces another, it's important not to focus only on their most extreme differences—like comparing Homer's mythology with the Christian symbols from the Council of Nicaea. Instead, it's essential to explore the gradual shifts and connections between them over time.

It is important to study the remaining works from this period of transition, when ancient Greek ideas were being reshaped through discussions and mixed with religions from the East that were spreading into Europe. Christianity is the latest example of how these Eastern beliefs influenced the West. It didn't arrive suddenly, shocking the old world. Instead, it took time to develop, with its ideas forming alongside those in Greece, Asia, and Egypt. Many of the same problems that Christianity aimed to solve were already being discussed in these regions. The ideas in the air at that time blended in different ways.

The rise of many different religious sects today only gives a small sense of how dynamic the intellectual activity was back then. Alexandria was at the heart of this development, acting as a center for moral and philosophical exploration. People were debating big questions like the nature of evil, the purpose of souls, their downfall, and their redemption. The ultimate prize for answering these questions was control over people's beliefs, and in the end, Christianity offered the solution that prevailed.

Our critic looks at the books of Hermes Trismegistus and tries to figure out what parts reflect Egyptian thought and what might have come from Jewish ideas. He points out that when we encounter ideas that resemble those of Plato or Pythagoras, we need to ask if the author rediscovered the same ancient sources that Plato and Pythagoras had used or if these ideas represent something purely Greek. This raises questions about how much Eastern thought influenced Greek philosophy. People tend to overestimate the impact of Eastern ideas on Greek thought, partly because the Greeks themselves believed in that influence. However, the real exchange between Greek and other cultures only became steady and meaningful after Alexandria was founded. During these exchanges, Greece had more to share with other cultures than it received from them. The people of the East, including those who interacted with the Greeks, didn't have what we would call a formal philosophy. They lacked traditions of analyzing the mind, searching for the foundations of knowledge and moral rules, and applying these ideas to society. These concepts were new to the East before Alexander the Great's conquests.

Plato mentions a comment from an Egyptian priest who told the Greeks, "You are just children; there are no elders among you." This could reflect the attitude of Egypt and other Eastern cultures. The spirit of scientific inquiry and political instinct was unfamiliar to these peoples. While they could endure for long periods, they never seemed to mature. They were like grown children, still being guided by others and unable to pursue truth or achieve justice on their own.

The East, having learned philosophy from Greece, could only offer what it had—deep religious feelings. Greece, tired of the skepticism caused by disagreements among its philosophical schools, welcomed this religious intensity. This shift toward spiritual enthusiasm was a sign of the need for renewed faith. The books of Hermes Trismegistus serve as a bridge between past beliefs and future ones, linking ideas from the old world to the new. Though these writings are part of pagan thought, they reflect the final moments of paganism. Paganism resisted the new faith and refused to surrender to it, guarding the knowledge of the old civilization that was fading. It accepted its fate, ready to rest forever in its birthplace—ancient Egypt, the land of the dead.

Dr. Menard concludes that the Hermetic books are the last remains of paganism. They belong to both Greek philosophy and Egyptian religion, and their mystical nature connects them to the Middle Ages. These writings lie between two eras—one ending and the other beginning—like creatures that bridge different species but are not fully part of either group. As a result, they are not as great as the religious beliefs of Homer's time or Christianity, but they help us understand the transition from one to the other. They contain both emerging beliefs and those fading away, meeting and intertwining as one era gives way to the next.

To challenge and correct the earlier statements about the relationship between Greek and Eastern thought, we offer the following insights from Mr. Plumptre's "History of Pantheism." From childhood, most of us are taught to believe that we owe all our knowledge of theology and religion to the Hebrews, and much of our understanding of God as well. At the same time, we are told that the Greeks gave us all our knowledge of the arts, sciences, philosophy, and wisdom. Similarly, we are taught to credit the Romans for shaping our ideas about discipline and law. While these definitions are generally accurate for our connections with the Hebrews and Romans, the same cannot be said about the Greeks.

The statement is somewhat accurate. It is true that we owe much of our knowledge to the Greeks. However, the error lies in assuming that the Greeks were the first to pursue learning purely for its own sake, that they received no knowledge from other cultures, and that they invented it all themselves. This view might also suggest that they were the first people to reach a high level of civilization. Even a basic understanding of Egyptian or Hindu history is enough to show how mistaken this idea is. Egyptian civilization stretches so far back in history that it is almost impossible to pinpoint its beginning. It is now widely accepted that Moses gained much of his knowledge from the Egyptians, meaning that even our earliest religious ideas may have come from Egypt.

Mr. Plumptre points out that while both the Hindus and Egyptians had developed advanced religious and philosophical systems long ago, the Greeks remained trapped in ignorance and superstition. This changed dramatically after a key event that sparked Greek intellectual development and transformed Greece from a state of childish ignorance into a leading cultural and philosophical power. That event was the opening of Egypt's ports by King Psammetichus in 670 B.C. Until that time, Egypt had been closed off from Europe and the Mediterranean with restrictions as strict as those once seen in China and Japan. To the Greeks, Egypt was nothing more than a land of mystery and myth, as reflected in the works of Homer and Hesiod. When Egypt finally opened up, the effect on Europe's development was profound and far-reaching. Greece, followed by the rest of the world, owed its civilization to this event. It shattered belief in old myths and gave birth to Greek philosophy.

This statement needs some adjustment, though. While Greek myths might seem like irrational stories without deeper meaning, they were actually symbols hiding important spiritual truths. Their early presence in Greece shows that institutions dedicated to sacred mysteries existed long before Greek philosophy emerged. The fact that these mysteries shared ideas with Egypt and the East also reveals that there was religious contact between these regions long before trade, political connections, or philosophical exchanges took place. Christian missionary work was not the first of its kind; the sacred mysteries were constantly spreading, establishing themselves in new places even ahead of secular civilizations. The migration of Abraham, the travels of Bacchus, and the journey of Moses are all examples of this kind of movement.

Mr. Plumptre concludes that any similarities between Greek and Egyptian philosophy were the result of the Greeks adopting ideas from Egypt. It seems impossible to disagree with this conclusion. We believe that Menard's differing opinion comes from his focus on classical knowledge without considering Hermetic and Kabbalistic traditions. Since these traditions contain the spiritual history of the world, ignoring them makes it impossible to fully understand these topics. Those who rely only on conventional methods of learning and reject anything beyond surface-level knowledge tend to dismiss the idea that a hidden, divine system of teachings has existed since ancient times. Yet, this conclusion is unavoidable based on the overwhelming evidence, both from public sources and secret teachings.

The earliest traces of this knowledge can be found in India and Egypt. If there are similarities between the ancient teachings of these lands and those of Greece, Judea, and Christianity, it is because the same truths were passed from one culture to another. These truths were reshaped to fit the needs and spirit of each time and place. This process will continue until humanity either falls into complete ignorance and no longer cares about truth or reaches a state of enlightenment where truth is fully understood and preserved as our most valuable treasure forever.

Regardless of the debate, even the most critical arguments must admit three key points. First, some of the teachings in the Hermetic texts are truly ancient, originating from Egypt, making them authentically Hermetic. Second, there are clear similarities between these ancient Hermetic teachings and the ideas found in Christianity. And third, the Church has acknowledged and accepted these similarities, showing that Christianity, rather than being a completely new and original belief system when it first began, is actually a continuation or reworking of ideas that had existed long before.

THE HERMETIC SYSTEM AND THE SIGNIFICANCE OF ITS PRESENT REVIVAL

For anyone studying humanity, one of the most important features of our current era is the revival of occult science and mystical, or hidden, philosophy. This revival is important not just because of the ideas themselves, but also because of the timing. It is happening during a period when the human mind, as represented by modern thinkers, seemed to have fully embraced materialism. However, this shift toward materialism turned out to be temporary, as some people—those attuned to the deeper connections of life and aware of the unity within nature—already knew. Just as the sun's return begins at its lowest point, spiritual renewal follows times of decline. When materialism threatened to extinguish the spiritual awareness of humanity, the return of mystical and occult teachings brought that awareness back to life.

History has shown that the end of old religious forms often signals the beginning of new and better spiritual insights. Those who believe in the divine nature of the human spirit trusted that, in time, it would rise up against materialism. They see the current revival as that very awakening. This revival is also noteworthy because it has brought Hermetic philosophy back into the spotlight for the first time in centuries. Every major religious awakening in history has involved this philosophy in some way. Hermetic Gnosis—an ancient system with roots going back to prehistoric Egypt—has been the foundation of many religious and philosophical traditions across the East and the West. Both Buddhism and Christianity were intended to express its teachings, although this was only recognized by a select few. Even the mystical school that flourished during the Middle Ages, which brought great prestige to the church, was secretly based on the same ideas.

That school aimed to rescue religion from being reduced to rituals, historical events, and the control of a materialistic clergy. Instead, it sought to restore religion's true spiritual and intuitive nature. Although this effort did not achieve lasting success, it was not because of any flaw in the system. The challenge lay in the fact that the spiritual awareness required to fully understand the teachings was something only a few people possessed at that time. The world simply was not ready for a philosophy that represented reason at its highest level. Now, however, it is clear that the revival we are witnessing is just one in a series of similar movements throughout history. Given the current changes in society, there is good reason to believe this revival will succeed more than any before it.

Even though the state of society today may seem bleak in many areas—whether in social issues, philosophy, morality, or religion—there has never been a time when conditions were better for a major positive change. New ideas and knowledge now spread faster than ever, and the hardships and dissatisfaction people are experiencing have made them more open to change. As a result, Hermetic philosophy now has a better chance of gaining acceptance than ever before. In the past, it was embraced by the brightest minds and most honorable individuals. With the right presentation, it is likely that this philosophy will find a place in the hearts and minds of people in this new era.

There are already signs that the church, still a powerful force, may support this revival—not only to preserve itself but also to protect religious truth. The importance of Pope Leo XIII's decision to restore the works of Aquinas as the foundation for church education is not yet widely understood. However, for those initiated in the teachings of Hermes, this move is seen as a reason for great optimism. A similar view applies to the strange, though sometimes misguided, phenomenon of modern spiritualism.

With these thoughts on the circumstances surrounding the revival—of which this collection of writings is both a product and a tool—we will now provide a brief overview of the nature of the teachings that have played such a major role in the past and seem likely to have even greater impact in the future.

It's important to mention that this overview isn't limited to the Hermetic fragments found in these reprints. These fragments are incomplete, and some parts have been altered or corrupted over time, though they still contain profound and valuable teachings. Much of what remains is written in symbolic or mystical language, referring to higher realities that require deeper interpretation beyond what is immediately obvious. For this reason, we need to rely on the work of those who have either accessed now-lost sources or uncovered these teachings through the same intuitive methods that first brought them to light.

The Hermetic system starts with the principle that nothing can come from nothing and recognizes that consciousness is essential to existence. From this foundation, it logically concludes that everything comes from a pure, absolute being. This being is unmanifested and unlimited but contains within it the potential to express itself. It is not just a being with life, mind, and substance—it is life, mind, and substance. The universe is a reflection of this divine self, showing how this being manifests itself in the material world. Some thinkers have developed new ways to apply these teachings, but they remain true to the Hermetic tradition.

However, no amount of knowledge or effort can replace the intuitive insight needed to recognize true Hermetic wisdom. Only with such insight can one grasp the genuine nature of these teachings, and it is hoped that this understanding will not be missing here. What follows is only a brief outline, as even the best attempts can offer only a glimpse of these deep truths.

The Hermetic view holds that all things are forms of consciousness, and consciousness exists in many different ways. It can be defined as the ability of something to affect or be affected by itself or something else, meaning that consciousness is the essence of everything. There are various levels of consciousness, including physical, chemical, magnetic, mental, and spiritual, with divine consciousness being the highest. All forms of consciousness come from the divine, and all will eventually return to it. This process is the essence of evolution, which is the tendency of things to return to their original state. Evolution shows that the material world is not the ultimate form of existence but is instead one step along the way.

By seeing matter as just another form of consciousness—and, in turn, a form of spirit—Hermetic thought avoids the difficulties that come with believing in two opposing forces, such as spirit and matter, as separate and conflicting. Everything is an expression of the same ultimate source, so there can be no true conflict or opposition. What we call unconsciousness is simply a lower form of consciousness, reduced to its smallest degree but still present. Total unconsciousness is non-existence, just as darkness is the absence of light. Consciousness, however limited, always has a positive existence, while non-existence is only the absence of being.

The many expressions of consciousness, whether on different levels or in different forms on the same level, all follow the same underlying law. This law reveals the unity of the divine mind, which exists eternally, independent of its manifestations. As stated in the "Divine Pymander": "He does not need to be revealed, for He exists eternally. He is not created or born but remains unseen and unmanifested. Yet, by making all things visible, He appears in all things and through all things, especially in those who seek Him."

The unity of being also establishes a principle of correspondence between all levels of existence. The larger universe mirrors the smaller individual, just as the individual reflects the divine. "Man on earth," says "The Key," "is a mortal god, while the heavenly god is an immortal man." However, the book clarifies that this description only applies to those who possess higher spiritual awareness. Those who lack this awareness are not yet fully human but only have the potential to become so.

The teachings avoid the mistake of attributing human qualities to the divine by explaining that divinity is not life, mind, or substance itself but the source of these things. Ignorance of the divine is described as the greatest evil, but God cannot be found in the external world. Instead, the search for the divine must take place within oneself. To truly know, one must first fully be. This means developing awareness of all the different levels of one's being and becoming a complete person. The deepest truths belong to the spirit, which is the pure essence of being. Existence is simply the outward expression of that essence.

Since a person can only recognize in the external world what they already have within themselves, spiritual awareness is necessary to perceive spiritual truths. To understand the divine, a person must first become spiritual within.

"The natural man," as the apostle Paul says, following the teachings of both the Hermetists and the Kabbalists, "cannot understand the things of the Spirit, nor can he know them, for they are understood spiritually." This means they can only be grasped through the spiritual part within a person. As a person develops this spiritual awareness, they become a tool for knowledge, capable of discovering deep truths, including the highest truths. At that point, they move from being "agnostic," or unaware of true knowledge, to being "Gnostic," which means having knowledge of both themselves and God, and understanding that both are deeply connected.

The fact that today's world often embraces agnosticism only shows how immature its understanding is. The philosophy of this time reflects the views of people who may be highly intelligent but are still underdeveloped in their spiritual awareness. Because of this, they have not yet reached their full human potential, which requires growth on the spiritual plane. Lacking this higher awareness, they mistake the outward appearance of a person for their true self, assuming that satisfying physical desires will benefit the person, even if such actions harm their deeper humanity.

The knowledge provided by Gnosis helps lift people out of this spiritual darkness. It gives them the essential understanding that all divine teachings aim to provide: a clear understanding of who they truly are. It shows, with certainty, that moral laws are supreme and that it is impossible to gain anything good by doing wrong or to escape the consequences of one's actions. Trying to achieve good by doing harm only makes things worse in the long run. The idea of Karma, central to Hindu thought, is also part of Hermetic philosophy. In Hermetic teachings, this principle is represented by Adrasté, a goddess of justice. In Greek mythology, this same idea is reflected in Nemesis and Hecate. All these figures represent the unbreakable law of cause and effect, which shapes a person's future based on the actions and habits they choose to nurture in the present.

The Hermetic path to perfection—whether physical, intellectual, moral, or spiritual—is through purity. Since consciousness is not just something a person has but something they are, a person's level of awareness depends on how pure they are. Perfect purity allows for complete understanding, even to the point of seeing God, as taught in the gospels. In the same way, a person's power increases with their purity. A fully developed Hermetist, someone who has mastered this knowledge, becomes a magian—a person of great power. Such a person can perform acts that seem miraculous, not just physically but also intellectually, morally, and spiritually, all through the strength of their will. However, the secret of this power is purity, and the only motivation behind it is love. The power they use comes from spirit, and spirit becomes more powerful the purer it is. Pure spirit, at its highest level, is God.

The miracles performed by a magian differ from those of a magician because they are truly the work of God—the divine power within the person. A key part of Hermetic knowledge is the use of intuition. Through intuition, a person turns inward and connects with their true, eternal self—the soul—and gains access to the knowledge it has gathered over countless lifetimes. This approach does not dismiss the role of the intellect, which also needs to be developed as a partner to intuition. These two aspects of the mind—intellect and intuition—are like complements, working together like the masculine and feminine. Only when both are perfected and unified can a person achieve complete understanding. At that point, the person knows God, and to know God is to both possess and become one with God, for "the gift of God is eternal life."

One of the most important teachings in Hermetic philosophy is the idea that the soul is born into many physical bodies over time. The soul continues this cycle of rebirth until it reaches a state of spiritual growth that allows it to exist without needing a physical body. This process of transformation, called regeneration, only ends when the soul no longer needs the material world. The concept of correspondence offers a useful way to understand this process. Just as the body sheds its outer layers—such as skin, feathers, or hair—the soul also leaves behind many physical bodies over time.

The law of gravity, which governs the physical world, also applies to the spiritual world. A person's spiritual state determines the level at which their soul exists, just as the density of a physical object determines how it behaves. The soul must release the attachment that draws it into physical existence before it can move beyond the need for a body. The death of the body does not necessarily mean that the soul has overcome this pull toward material life, so the soul may still be drawn back to earth in another body. However, when the soul returns, it does so without the magnetic or "astral" body that forms the outer personality. Only the soul itself continues its journey, evolving through each lifetime toward greater spiritual awareness.

The idea of transmigration, or the soul's journey through many lifetimes, is central to Hermetic, Kabbalistic, and Hindu teachings. It also runs through the Bible in hidden ways, showing up in the conversation between Jesus and Nicodemus, where Jesus speaks about being "born again." Although Jesus emphasizes spiritual rebirth, this process requires multiple lifetimes to provide the experiences necessary for spiritual growth. As Swedenborg explained, regeneration must begin while a person is still in the body and must reach a certain level before the soul can move beyond needing a physical body. Spiritual growth cannot be completed in a single lifetime. Without many lifetimes to make this process possible, the message of the gospel would not offer salvation but would instead guarantee failure for most people.

In Hermetic teachings, what Christianity calls the "forgiveness of sins" is tied to the process of inner transformation. Each person carries the potential for this transformation within them, but they must actively participate in their own spiritual growth. Through this process, they become a "new creation," born not from physical matter but from "water and spirit." This means their soul and spirit are purified, becoming divine. When a person achieves this higher state of being, they are said to be born of the "Virgin Mary" and the Holy Spirit.

The Hermetic system stands apart from other mystical traditions because it views nature and the body with joy and reverence, rather than disgust. While some other systems see the body and its functions as impure or sinful, Hermeticism sees them as part of divine truth. The relationship between the sexes is honored, symbolizing the highest spiritual mysteries, and fulfilling these relationships is considered a duty. In some lifetimes, these experiences are essential for a person's complete development and initiation. This appreciation of life's beauty aligns Hermetic thought with Greek philosophy and sets it apart from more pessimistic Eastern views.

A true Hermetist sees divine presence everywhere—in every part of nature, just as the prophet Jonah found God even in the belly of a whale. Ignorance of God is viewed as the greatest evil. This belief is why Hermetic teachings promote a vegetarian lifestyle, as described in the "Asclepios." Human beings are not naturally designed to eat meat. Their physical structure shows that they thrive best on plant-based foods, which cleanse and rebuild the body. Eating flesh not only blocks the development of intuition, the key to spiritual insight, but also dulls a person's sensitivity to violence. Failing to be disturbed by killing for food reveals a lack of spiritual awareness.

The goal of the Hermetist is not simply to escape from life, as if existence were something evil. Instead, the goal is to become a clear instrument for perceiving the divine presence in every part of existence. Any pessimism found in Hermetic texts, such as the "Divine Pymander," reflects only the imperfections of existence compared to the perfection of divine being. Hermeticism surpasses other mystical systems by valuing both sexes equally. Although the story of the Fall originates from Hermetic teachings, it is meant to be understood symbolically, not literally. It was never intended to place blame on any person or gender. Instead, the Fall represents a deep truth about divine reality. Sadly, this story has often been used to justify unfair and cruel treatment of women—attitudes that come from primitive and undeveloped sources, not from true spiritual understanding.

Throughout history, it becomes clear that the solutions to life's greatest questions—about human nature and how to live—can be found in the teachings and practices of the Hermetic system. Free inquiry, when pursued without prejudice or narrow thinking, naturally leads to the truths revealed by Hermeticism. These teachings are based on real, lived experiences of the soul, which gains deeper understanding through intuition.

Hermetic philosophy is a triumph of both free thought and religious faith. It encourages exploration of both the physical world and the spiritual realm. In Hermeticism, God is seen as the source of all being. Nature serves as a way for God to reveal Himself, and the human soul—refined and perfected through experience—becomes a unique expression of the divine.

AN INTRODUCTION TO THE VIRGIN OF THE WORLD

The mystical title of the well-known Hermetic fragment that opens this volume, "Koré Kosmou," or "The Kosmic Virgin," reveals the deep connection between the ancient wisdom-religions and the teachings of Catholic Christianity. In the Eleusinian Mysteries, the name Koré was used to address Persephone, the Maiden or Daughter. Interestingly, Koré is also the Greek word for the pupil of the eye. This connection becomes more meaningful when we consider that, in a conversation between Isis, the Moon-goddess and guide of initiates, and Horos, she compares the physical eye's layers to the soul's coverings. Just as the eye's pupil brings light to the body, the soul brings awareness and understanding to a person.

In this Hermetic parable, Persephone, or Koré, symbolizes the soul. Her descent from the divine realm into the material world is a key theme. Some scholars have also noted that the Hindu goddess Parasupani, also known as Gorée, shares a similar role, suggesting a deeper connection between these traditions. The Greek Mysteries focused on two primary themes: the story of Persephone's descent and return, and the life, death, and rebirth of Dionysos-Zagreus. In these teachings, Persephone represents the soul, while Dionysos symbolizes the spirit.

The Hermetic doctrine explains that both the universe and human beings have a fourfold nature. Two parts of this nature—spirit and soul—are eternal, while the other two—the lower mind and the physical body—are temporary. The spirit and soul, viewed as masculine and feminine forces, remain unchanged through all cycles of reincarnation, while the mind and body are new with each life. Dionysos, the spirit, is said to have a divine origin, being born from Zeus and the immaculate Virgin Koré-Persephone, who is the daughter of Demeter, known as the "Mother" in the Mysteries.

Koré has two aspects to her nature. As the daughter of Zeus and Demeter, she is pure and divine. However, as the wife of Hades in the underworld, she is connected to the realms of sorrow and decay. This duality reflects the nature of the soul, which remains pure and invulnerable in its essence, yet appears to fall and become stained in the material world. The symbol of the soul in Hermetic teachings is water, also called Maria. Water, though it can appear dirty or polluted, always retains its true purity beneath the surface. When purified through distillation, it leaves all impurities behind and emerges clear and pure once again. In the same way, the soul is always pure at its core, no matter how stained it might seem during its journey through life.

The story of the Kosmic Virgin reflects the soul's journey through existence. The soul moves between two states: an outward journey into the material world, which represents its "fall," and an inward return to its divine origin. Although Koré comes from a heavenly realm, she is more connected to earthly life than her son, Dionysos. As the Mysteries teach, Persephone dwells both above, in the inaccessible places of the divine Mother, and below, with Pluto, where she governs earthly matters and sustains life throughout the universe.

This dual nature of spirit and soul is also central to Hindu philosophy, where the spirit is called Atman. The Upanishads, a key part of Hindu esoteric teachings, focus entirely on understanding this concept.

The concept of Atman is described as self-sustaining, unified, eternal, unchanging, and incorruptible. It exists independently of Karma—the idea that actions shape one's character and destiny—and gaining full awareness of Atman frees a person from the cycle of Karma. Atman is also all-seeing, and as the Mantras teach, "He who sees the universe within his own Atman and his Atman within the universe knows no hatred."

In the Kabbalah, the soul's journey is symbolized by Eve. The soul begins by turning away from divine unity and becoming restless in matter, unable to stay still, as resting seems like death. This moment is reflected in the Greek myth where Persephone leaves the heavens, lured by desire, and falls under Hades' power. Thomas Taylor explains this descent as the soul abandoning its higher, divine life. In the story, Jupiter sends Venus to tempt Persephone from her peaceful retreat, with Diana and Minerva accompanying her to prevent any suspicion. They find Persephone weaving a scarf for her mother, depicting the chaos and creation of the world.

Venus represents desire, which sneaks into the soul even in heavenly realms. Minerva symbolizes reason, while Diana stands for nature. As Persephone wanders from her retreat to gather flowers, surrounded by nymphs symbolizing the cycle of life and birth, she becomes captivated by the beauty of the material world. The soul, in the same way, becomes enchanted by the world of form and sensation. As soon as she steps outside her retreat, Pluto rises from the earth and seizes her, dragging her into the underworld. This reflects the soul's descent into the darkness of material existence, where it is united with the body.

Homer's "Hymn to Ceres" also describes this event, with Persephone saying, "I was joyfully gathering flowers—the crocus, iris, hyacinth, and narcissus—when the earth opened, and the powerful king carried me down to the underworld, despite my cries." This story mirrors the biblical tale of Eve, who, drawn by the beauty of the tree's fruit, eats it and is cast into sorrow. God tells her, "I will increase your pain in childbirth, and your desire will be for your husband, who will rule over you."

Plato's allegory in "Phaedrus" further explains this fall, comparing the body to a chariot pulling the soul down into earthly existence. The soul struggles under the weight of material life, which clouds the mind and reason. This condition, Plato explains, traps the soul in the body, similar to prisoners chained in a cave who mistake shadows for reality. Life on earth is described as a form of imprisonment—a dreamlike exile from the soul's true home.

In the "Koré Kosmou," we read that souls, upon learning they would be trapped in physical bodies, sighed and cried out to the heavens. They lamented, "Oh, what sorrow and heartache to leave behind these vast splendors, the sacred realm, and all the glory of the blessed gods, only to be cast down into these miserable and wretched dwellings! We will no longer gaze upon the radiant heavens!" This sorrowful cry brings to mind Eve's lament when she was exiled from the beautiful paradise of Eden.

Just as the soul falls into this sorrowful state, she is eventually rescued and restored to the divine realm. This rescue happens through the coming of a savior, symbolized here by Osiris, the figure of the "Man Regenerate." Osiris, a divine being, is often represented by different names in various stories, but the meaning behind each is the same. Osiris is the equivalent of Jesus in Christian doctrine—the supreme initiate and "Captain of Salvation." Alongside his divine partner, Osiris is guided in all things by Hermes, known as the messenger of the gods. Hermes is seen as the conductor of souls from darkness, representing divine understanding and reason. In Platonic philosophy, Hermes embodies "nous," the higher mind, and the mystical "Spirit of Christ."

Since the ability to understand sacred things and interpret them comes from Hermes, the name Hermes is connected to all hidden knowledge and divine revelation. Those with such knowledge are known as "divines," meaning they understand the mysteries of heaven. This is why the apostle John, who wrote the Book of Revelation, is often called the "beloved" of Christ. Hermes is recognized as the messenger of the gods, descending to the deepest realms of the underworld to guide souls upward and ascending beyond the heavens to bring wisdom. Understanding must explore both the heights and the depths, for nothing can remain hidden from it. Only by exploring both the spiritual and material realms can a person fully grasp divine truths.

The Greeks, with their joyful and lighthearted nature, added humor and playfulness even to their sacred stories. They called Hermes a thief, hinting at the power of the mind to claim everything for its own understanding. When the myths say that Hermes stole the girdle of Venus, the tools of Vulcan, the thunder of Zeus, and the cattle of Apollo, they mean that even the greatest gifts of the gods are within reach of the mind when it seeks knowledge wisely. As the companion of the sun, Hermes opens the gates of heaven, revealing spiritual light and life. He serves as a mediator between the physical and spiritual worlds, initiating seekers into the sacred mysteries that lead to eternal life.

The symbolic tools carried by Hermes reflect the powers of the mind. His rod represents the wisdom of the magian, his wings signify the courage of the adventurer, his sword embodies the will of the hero, and his cap shows the discretion of the wise. Those initiated into Hermes' teachings recognize no authority but the mind itself. They follow no earthly master, embracing the freedom of true understanding. As scripture says, "Where the Spirit of the Lord is, there is liberty." One advisor of John Inglesant put it this way: "Follow no man; there is nothing of greater value in the world than the Divine Light—follow it."

Lactantius, in his writings, says that Hermes taught how knowing God frees a person from the control of demons and fate. Fate, in this sense, is tied to the power of the stars, which control both the cosmos and the inner life of a person. In Greek mythology, the many-eyed Argos, who represents the watchful power of the stars, was outwitted and slain by Hermes. This story teaches that those who gain the secret knowledge of Hermes rise above fate and break free from the endless cycles of destiny. To know God is to overcome death and conquer the forces that hold one back. Understanding the source of illusion allows a person to transcend it.

The path to God is blocked by layers of deception, ruled by the seven astral powers. These spheres of illusion stand between the soul and God. Beyond them lie the nine celestial realms, where, according to the Mysteries, Demeter once searched in vain for her lost daughter, Persephone. Persephone had fallen into the material world, placing her under the control of the planetary rulers, symbolized by Hecate, the goddess of fate. On the tenth day of her search, Demeter encountered Hecate, the three-formed goddess of karma and retribution, who revealed what had happened to Persephone. From that moment, Hecate became Persephone's constant companion.

This story holds deep meaning. The soul is free from fate until it enters the material world. Fate begins with the soul's involvement in time and physical existence. In the sevenfold astral spheres, the moon symbolizes fate, presenting both a benevolent and a harsh face.

Under her kinder aspect, the Moon is Artemis, reflecting the divine light of Phœbos to the soul. In her harsher form, she is Hecate, the Avenger, dark-faced and three-headed, swift like a horse, sharp as a dog, and fierce as a lion. In this form, she hunts guilty souls from one life to the next, ensuring justice with relentless precision, outmaneuvering even death. For pure and innocent souls, however, the Moon offers a guiding light. As Artemis, she protects virgins—those souls untouched by the pull of the material world. In this role, the Moon becomes an initiator, like Isis, lighting the soul's inner chamber and bringing wisdom through a favorable destiny. With each lifetime, such souls grow more enlightened and become prophetic, even divine.

On the other hand, to those corrupted by evil, the Moon appears as Hecate, bringing nightmares and dark warnings of misfortune. These souls fear the power of the Moon, sensing the misfortune they are creating for their future selves. According to the Kabbalah, the Tree of Good and Evil is rooted in Malchuth, the Moon. While some say that Karma is unique to Hindu thought, it appears just as clearly in the Hebrew, Greek, and Christian teachings. The Greeks called it Fate, while in Christianity, it is known as Original Sin—the burden that all mortals carry. Only the "Mother of God" is exempt, the "immaculate virgin" through whose child the world is redeemed. As the Church sings, "As a lily among thorns, so is the Beloved among the daughters of Adam. You are all beautiful, O Beloved, and there is no stain within you; your name, O Mary, is like oil poured out, and the virgins love you greatly."

In Persephone or Koré, the "Virgin of the World," we see the soul. In Isis, the guiding initiator, we see the teacher. Isis, like Koré, is both a virgin and a mother. In her philosophical role, the Egyptian Isis is equivalent to Artemis of Ephesus, the Greek goddess symbolizing nature's power to nourish and create. She was called the "eternal maid of heaven," and her priests were eunuchs. Her statue in the grand temple of Ephesus portrayed her with many breasts, symbolizing abundance. The black skin of some depictions, such as the "Black Virgin," represents the hidden and mysterious nature of the forces that shape destiny. These forces may seem random to those who lack understanding, but they follow deeper spiritual laws.

In art, Artemis is often depicted as a huntress with hounds, representing the relentless forces of nature. She is also shown as the Moon goddess, wearing a long veil and a crescent crown, or as a many-breasted mother, carrying a torch. The Romans knew her as Diana, and it is by this name that the Artemis of Ephesus is mentioned in the Christian scriptures. Like Artemis and Diana, Isis embodies the hidden power of nature—Fate, which manifests as fortune, retribution, and destiny. The Kabbalists represent this power with Malchuth, the Moon, while Hindu philosophy calls it Karma. Artemis' hounds symbolize the natural forces that pursue the soul through each lifetime, ensuring that every soul faces the results of its actions.

In the story of Actaeon, the hero ignores the sacredness of fate and disrespects the law of Karma. As punishment, he is torn apart by his own hounds, symbolizing how one's own actions can turn against them. Similarly, initiates of Isis wore masks with dog heads during processions, showing their understanding of how closely fate is tied to the soul's journey. The Moon, linked with Karma, represents the force that draws souls through cycles of birth and rebirth. Proclus, a Greek philosopher, explained that Diana, or Artemis, governs the process by which all things are born into the natural world and extends her power even to the underworld.

This view perfectly describes the role of Isis, showing how the Moon, as the force of Karma, drives the ongoing cycle of life and follows the soul even into realms of purification after death. In the Orphic Hymn to Nature, the goddess is shown standing on a wheel that she spins endlessly, representing the eternal movement of fate. In another hymn, Fortune, identified with Diana, is invoked as the goddess who controls destiny.

Proclus adds that the Moon is not only the cause of nature for mortals but also a reflection of a deeper source—the fountain of life itself. As Thomas Taylor explains, this fountain consists of three main sources within the Demiurge, or creator of the world: the fountain of souls, personified by Hera; the fountain of virtues, represented by Athena; and the fountain of nature, embodied by Artemis. Taylor further illustrates this concept with a passage from Apuleius' "Metamorphoses," in which the Moon speaks: "Behold, Lucius, moved by your prayers, I am here. I am Nature, the mother of all things, ruler of the elements, the beginning of time, the highest among gods and goddesses. I control the bright heavens, the winds of the sea, and the silent darkness of the underworld. Though my essence is one, all the earth honors me by many names and worships me through many rites. Those blessed by the rising sun—the Ethiopians, Aryans, and Egyptians, who possess ancient wisdom—know me as Queen Isis."

The hymn continues with praise: "The gods above honor you, and even those below bow to your power. You set the world in motion, guide the sun's light, and rule the entire universe. The stars obey your will, the gods celebrate you, time flows by your command, and the elements serve you."

This understanding follows naturally when we consider that the divine fountain of Nature exists within the Demiurgus and serves as the pattern for the nature we observe in the Moon and throughout the material world. Knowing this, it is easy to understand why the writer of the Hermetic text chose Isis to represent the soul's origin, journey, and destiny. Isis plays a unique role in guiding the soul through its existence, overseeing its path. If Demeter, the divine intelligence, is the true mother of Koré, then Isis acts as the foster-mother, taking over as soon as the soul enters the material world. Once the soul begins its earthly existence, Isis directs it and determines its fate. This is why some myths equate Isis with Demeter, adjusting Isis's role to match the story of Demeter's grief, as told in the Eleusinian Mysteries.

This blending of roles becomes clear when we understand the Hermetic teachings. Isis, whether she appears as Artemis (good fortune) or Hekate (bad fortune), governs and enlightens the soul while it is still bound by nature and time. Meanwhile, Demeter represents the heavenly source from which the soul originates. Demeter's concern is not with the soul's exile in the physical world but with its eventual return to the divine realm. In harmony with this idea, Isis is depicted both as the wife and the mother of Osiris, the savior of humankind. Osiris, the inner sun of the human soul, reflects the cosmic Dionysos, or Son of God, just as the soul mirrors the greater universe. This is why some myths merge Isis with Demeter and Osiris with Dionysos, placing Osiris at the center of the Bacchic Mysteries.

The Hermetic writings present three levels of divine expression. First, there is the supreme, eternal God, who exists beyond all manifestation. Second is the only-begotten God, the expression of the divine within the universe. Third is the divine presence within humanity, embodied by Osiris, the redeemer. Inscriptions found on the walls of the Temple of the Sun at Philae and the gate at Medinet-Abou read, "He made all things, and without Him, nothing exists."

These words, later used in the Gospel of John to describe the Word of God, show the connection between Osiris, the inner light of humanity, and the divine principle of creation.

Osiris, the inner sun within each person, is a reflection of the greater cosmic sun. The soul, through its experiences in time and physical existence, gives birth to this inner light. This connection explains why Osiris, the force of renewal within each individual, is closely linked to Isis, who guides the soul's growth. Through her influence, events and conditions shape the soul's development, preparing it for transformation. Isis symbolizes the hidden force that drives evolution forward, while Osiris represents the highest potential of humanity, the ideal self toward which all growth is directed.

The Virgin of The World

PART 1

After speaking, Isis gave Horos a sweet drink, the gift of immortality, which is granted by the gods to souls. Then, she began her sacred teaching. She explained that the heavens, crowned with stars, exist above all of creation, complete and lacking nothing. All of nature must be perfected by what is above, as the order of the universe flows from the higher to the lower realms. This order cannot begin from below and move upward. The higher mysteries always rule over the lower ones. Celestial order governs the earthly order, being eternal and beyond death. The things of earth feel fear before the eternal beauty and permanence of the heavens.

The heavens, with their glorious sights, display the majesty of a divine power not yet fully understood. The night sky, though less bright than the sun, reveals hidden mysteries that move in harmony, quietly guiding life on earth through unseen forces. Before the Divine Architect revealed Himself, the universe was full of fear and uncertainty. Ignorance surrounded everything. But when He chose to reveal Himself, He filled the gods with love and poured into them the wisdom contained within His being. This gave them the desire to seek, the will to find, and the power to restore what had been lost.

This great awakening did not happen among mortals, for humanity had not yet come into existence. Instead, it took place within the universal Soul, reflecting the mysteries of the heavens. This universal Soul was Hermes, the cosmic thought. He observed the universe, understood its nature, and revealed what he had discovered. Hermes wrote down these truths, but he kept many hidden, alternating between speaking and remaining silent so that these secrets would continue to be sought throughout time. He instructed the other gods to follow his lead, and then he returned to the stars. Hermes passed his knowledge to his son, Tat, and later to Asclepios, the son of Imouthè, guided by Pan and Hephaistos.

Hermes explained to those around him that he did not reveal the complete knowledge to his son because of his youth. But I, Isis, with my eyes that see the hidden truths of the universe, witnessed these events. And I saw those who, through divine guidance, were granted a perfect understanding of the mysteries of the heavens.

It is important, my son, that you hear the words of Hermes when he sealed his sacred books. "O holy books of the Immortals," he said, "within you are written the remedies that grant eternal life. Remain hidden from those who dwell in this realm until a time comes when souls, worthy of your knowledge, will be born under the ancient heavens."

Hermes then wrapped his books and returned to his place among the stars, leaving his teachings hidden for a time. Nature remained barren until those ordained to observe the heavens sought divine help. They prayed to the Creator, saying, "Please consider what is and what must still come to be." The Creator smiled and commanded Nature to bring forth life. With His voice, the feminine aspect of creation emerged in perfect beauty, leaving the gods amazed. The great Ancestor poured an elixir over Nature, making her fruitful. He declared,

"Let heaven be filled with all things, along with the air and the ether."
And it was so.

Nature, reflecting on her purpose, realized that she must not stray
from the Creator's command. She joined with Labor to bring forth a
beautiful daughter, whom she named Invention. The Creator gave
Invention life and charged her with shaping creation. He filled the
universe with mysteries and entrusted Invention to oversee them. Not
wishing for the heavens to remain idle, the Creator filled the upper
world with spirits, ensuring that all regions of existence were active.
Using sacred knowledge, He formed these beings by mixing His
essence with an intellectual flame, along with other elements through
hidden means.

From this mixture, a substance more refined and pure than the
original elements emerged. It was transparent, visible only to the divine
Artist. This new creation reached perfection, immune to both fire and
cold, stable in its form and nature. The Creator named this essence
Self-Consciousness. From it, He formed countless souls, carefully
choosing the finest parts of the mixture for His purpose. Although the
souls were not identical, the finest ones were animated by divine
motion and set apart from the rest.

The Creator arranged the souls into layers, each more refined than
the one beneath it, until sixty degrees were completed. Though the
souls differed in rank, they all shared the same eternal essence,
determined by the Creator alone. He placed them in their rightful
places in the order of nature, instructing them to turn the wheel of life
with wisdom and joy, fulfilling the divine plan.

Summoning these souls to the realms of ether, the Creator spoke
to them: "O souls, my beloved children, formed from my breath and
care, created by my hands to serve my universe, hear my law: Do not
abandon the place I have prepared for you. Your home is the heavens,
adorned with stars and thrones of virtue.

If you go against my command, I swear by my sacred breath, the same life-giving essence from which you were created, and by my creative hands, that I will quickly forge chains to bind you and cast you into punishment." After speaking these words, God combined the remaining elements—earth and water—into a new form. Using different, powerful words, He breathed life and motion into the liquid protoplasm, thickening it into a pliable material. From this, He shaped living beings in human form. He gave the remaining substance to the divine souls dwelling near the stars, known as the Sacred Genii, and instructed them: "Continue my work, my children, born of my nature. Use what I have left and shape beings in your own image. I will provide models."

God took the signs of the Zodiac and arranged them to guide creation, placing the animals after the human forms. He released the generative forces for all living beings, then withdrew, promising that every creation would carry an invisible breath and a reproductive essence so that life could continue without needing to be created from scratch.

"What did the souls do then, my Mother?" asked Horos. Isis replied, "They studied the material given to them, contemplating and admiring the Father's work. They sought to understand its components, though it was not easy to uncover. Fearing the Father's anger, they focused on following His commands. They used the lightest part of the protoplasm to create birds. As the mixture thickened, they formed quadrupeds, and with the densest part, supported by water, they created fish. The heaviest and coldest portions were used to make reptiles. Proud of their work, the souls began to disobey the divine law. They could not bear to stay in one place, restless in their pursuit of change, as stillness seemed like death to them."

Hermes told me that their disobedience did not escape the notice of the Lord. He decided to punish the souls and prepare chains to restrain them. To correct them, He shaped the human body—a blend of mortal and immortal elements. God summoned Hermes and said,

"Soul of my soul, thought of my thought, how long must the world remain barren and without praise? How much longer will creation lie unfinished? Bring the gods before me." At His command, all the gods gathered. "Look upon the earth and everything below," God told them. When the gods gazed down, they understood His will.

When He asked what each god could offer to the new human race, the Sun spoke first: "I will illuminate them." The Moon followed, promising to bring enlightenment, along with Fear, Silence, Sleep, and Memory, which she had already created. Kronos offered Justice and Necessity. Zeus declared, "To prevent endless wars, I will bestow Fortune, Hope, and Peace." Ares proclaimed that he had already fathered Conflict, Zeal, and Ambition. Aphrodite eagerly added, "I will gift humans with Desire, Joy, and Laughter, so that the burdens placed upon their souls may not weigh too heavily."

The other gods welcomed Aphrodite's offer. Hermes then said, "I will grant humans Wisdom, Temperance, Persuasion, and Truth, and I will remain closely allied with Invention. I will protect the lives of those born under my signs, for the Creator has entrusted me with the Zodiac signs that govern Knowledge and Intelligence. I will assist whenever the stars align with the natural forces of these individuals."

The Lord rejoiced at the gods' offerings and decreed that the human race would be created. Hermes continued, "I sought the proper materials for this task and prayed to the Lord for guidance. He ordered the souls to release the leftover protoplasm. However, when I received it, it had dried up, so I added an excess of water to soften it. I ensured the new form would remain flexible and fragile, balancing intelligence with vulnerability. Once my work was complete, it was beautiful, and I rejoiced in what I had made. I called upon the Lord to witness my creation. He looked upon it and approved, ordering the souls to inhabit the forms."

The souls, upon learning of their fate, were filled with dread. Isis continued, "These words shook me deeply. Listen closely, my son

Horos, for I share a great mystery with you. Our ancestor Kamephes received this knowledge from Hermes, who recorded all things. Kamephes passed it to me when I underwent the initiation of the black veil. Now I pass it to you, my beloved and extraordinary child."

Isis described the souls' reaction when they learned they would be bound to physical bodies. Some sighed and lamented, like wild animals suddenly captured and forced into servitude, rebelling against their captors. Others hissed like serpents or cried out in despair, looking helplessly from the heights of heaven to the depths below.

One soul cried, "Great Heaven, source of our birth, pure air, sacred breath of God, and you, shining stars, the unceasing light of the Sun and Moon—our brothers in the heavens—what sorrow awaits us! Must we leave these vast, radiant spaces, this sacred realm, and all the splendors of the divine world? Are we to be cast down into miserable, wretched places? What crime have we committed to deserve this punishment? What terrible sin have we, poor souls, committed to merit such suffering?"

Behold the sorrowful future that lies ahead—to tend to the needs of a fragile and fleeting body! No longer will our eyes perceive the souls of divine beings clearly. Through these clouded, earthly lenses, we will barely glimpse, with longing, our ancestral home in the heavens. There will be times when we won't see it at all. This tragic fate denies us the ability to see directly; we must rely on external light to see. Our eyes become mere windows, not true vision. And our suffering will deepen when we hear the winds breathing freely in the air—winds that we can no longer join. Our breath will be trapped, not in the wide, open world, but within the narrow prison of our own chests! Yet, O Master and Father, who cast us down from such a high place to this lowly state, set a limit to our suffering! Do not become indifferent to your creation. Let our punishment have an end, and give us a final message before we lose sight of the shining realms above!

This plea from the Souls was answered, my son Horos, for the Lord was present. Seated on the throne of Truth, He spoke: "Souls, you will be governed by Desire and Necessity. They will be your rulers and guides after Me. As long as you remain pure, you will live in the heavens. But if some of you are found guilty, you will dwell within mortal bodies. If your faults are minor, you will return to the heavens after being freed from the flesh. But those who commit serious wrongs, who abandon their true purpose, will not return to the heavens nor inhabit human bodies—they will enter the bodies of animals without reason."

It has been debated whether the Hermetic teachings support the idea of reincarnation into lower life forms. I believe they do align with this belief, without contradiction. The Divine Pymander states that if a human soul continues to act wickedly, "it will neither taste immortality nor partake in the good, but will be pulled back into creeping creatures; this is the fate of an evil soul." However, Hermes clarifies that a truly human soul—one containing the divine Mind—cannot fall this low, even if it has strayed. As long as the soul holds the divine fire within, it remains human, and such a soul is compared not to animals but to beings above, even to gods. Yet, if a soul falls so far that this inner flame is extinguished, it becomes dark and forsaken, no longer human. "Such a soul," says Hermes, "has lost the Mind and should not be called human."

This teaching emphasizes that a human soul cannot enter the body of a mindless creature, nor can it become something less than human unless it loses its divine essence. When a soul sinks to this low state, it gravitates toward creatures that match its nature. After its purification, however, the soul may awaken and say, "I will return to my Father." Some Rabbis have even suggested that this is the hidden meaning of the parable of the prodigal son, where the swine symbolize lust and base desires. The Hermetic view aligns with the Kabbalah and the teachings of Apollonius of Tyana on this point.

After addressing the souls, the Lord breathed upon them and said, "Your destiny is not left to chance. If you act wrongly, things will go badly for you; if you act wisely, they will improve. I, not another, will be your witness and judge. Your suffering in physical bodies is the result of your past mistakes. Each rebirth will be different, as I have already told you. Death will be a gift, restoring you to a better state. But if you act against My will, your judgment will be clouded. You will mistake suffering for fortune and fear happiness as if it were a curse.

Those among you who act with justice will rise closer to the divine in future lives. They will become wise rulers, true philosophers, visionary leaders, healers of plants, talented musicians, knowledgeable astronomers, insightful prophets, and servants of wisdom. These are noble roles. Just as the eagle does not harm its kind and protects the weak with justice, or the lion, who tirelessly performs great deeds in his mortal body, so too are the wise uplifted. The dragon, who is powerful, gentle, and a friend to man, embodies divine traits, and the dolphin, who saves drowning people without devouring them, shows kindness even as the most voracious sea creature."

After saying these things, the Lord returned to His incorruptible, unmanifested state. Then, my son Horos, a mighty Spirit arose from the earth. He had no physical form, yet was filled with wisdom and strength. Although fearsome, this Spirit knew what he sought and observed the human form with admiration, for it was both beautiful and dignified. He noticed the souls about to enter their bodies and asked, "What are these beings, Hermes, Secretary of the Gods?"

"These are men," replied Hermes.

The Spirit remarked, "It is risky to create men with such keen sight, quick tongues, and sharp hearing, allowing them to sense things not meant for them. They will have hands skilled enough to grasp anything. Is it wise to leave them free from care? These creatures, who will explore every corner of the earth, study plants and stones, and even dissect themselves to learn how they are made? They will cut down forests to cross seas in search of each other, and they will pursue the secrets of nature to the highest heavens. They will seek the edges of night and try to extend their power over the elements themselves. If they are free from hardship, fear, and anxiety, nothing will stop them—not even the heavens. Teach them desire and hope, so they may also know fear and failure. Let their souls struggle with love and longing, sometimes fulfilled, sometimes not, so that even success will lead them toward misfortune. Let them face sickness and suffering, breaking their desires and humbling their hearts."

Do you feel sorrow, Horos, hearing this story? Does it surprise you to learn about the hardships awaiting humanity? What you will hear next is even more troubling. Hermes approved the Spirit's words and decided to follow his advice.

"O Momos," he said, "the divine breath that fills all things will not fail in its purpose! The Master of the universe has entrusted me to oversee His creation. The deity with the all-seeing eye, Adrastia, will watch and guide every event. As for me, I will design a mysterious tool—one that is precise and unchanging, a law that will govern everything from birth to destruction and bind all created things together. This tool will rule over the earth and everything in it."

The Lord then summoned the assembly of the gods. They gathered, and He addressed them, saying: "You gods, who possess an eternal, unchanging nature and the power to sustain the harmony of the universe, how much longer shall we reign over an invisible world? How long will creation remain hidden from the light of the sun and moon? Let us each take our place in the universe and end this stagnant state. Let us transform chaos into an ancient tale, unbelievable to those who come after us. Begin your great work, and I will guide you."

With these words, the cosmic order, which had been hidden, revealed itself. The heavens appeared in all their splendor, and the earth, once unstable, grew firm under the sun's radiance, showing forth its hidden riches. In God's eyes, everything was beautiful, even what seemed unpleasant to mortals, for everything followed the divine laws.

God rejoiced, seeing His creation full of life and movement, and with His hands He gathered the treasures of nature.

"Take these," He said, "O sacred earth, take these, you who will be the mother of all things. From now on, let nothing be lacking to you." Opening His divine hands, He poured these treasures into the heart of the universe. Yet, the embodied souls, ashamed of their fate, sought to rival the gods. Proud of their noble origin, they boasted of being equals to the gods and rebelled. In their rebellion, humans became their instruments, leading to conflicts and civil wars. The strong oppressed the weak, and both the living and the dead were cast out of sacred places.

The elements, witnessing these horrors, went before the Lord to complain about the cruelty of mankind. The fire spoke first, saying, "O Master, Creator of this new world, You whose name is revered by both gods and men, how long will You allow human life to remain without divine guidance? Reveal Yourself to the world that cries out for You. Bring peace to end their savage ways. Give life its laws and night its oracles. Let happy omens fill all things. Let people fear divine judgment, so they no longer sin. Punish wrongdoing fairly, and people will avoid evil. Teach them gratitude for blessings, and I will devote my flames to pure offerings. Let the altars rise with the sweet scent of sacrifices. But now, O Master, I am polluted. The wickedness of humans forces me to burn flesh, corrupting my purity. I am no longer what I was meant to be."

The air spoke next, saying, "O Master, I am tainted by the stench of corpses. I grow poisonous and foul, forced to witness things I was never meant to see."

Then the water took its turn: "Father and Creator of all things, divine source of life, command the waters to remain pure. The rivers and seas are now used to wash away the deeds of killers and to receive their victims."

Finally, the earth spoke: "O King, Ruler of the heavens and Lord of all orbits, Master and Father of the elements, everything in creation rises and falls by Your will, and everything must return to You. But look how the wickedness of humanity spreads across me. I, who was commanded to house all beings, now bear the burden of their sins. I receive into my depths everything that dies, and this has become my shame. Your creation is empty of divine presence, and because humans revere nothing, they break every law and fill me with evil deeds. I am polluted by the remains of the dead. But I, who receive all things, ask to also receive Your presence. Grant me this grace. If You cannot come Yourself—for I could never contain You—let me receive some part of Your divine essence. Let the earth become the most honored of all the elements. Since I give all things to all beings, let me revere myself as the vessel of Your blessings."

After hearing the pleas of the elements, God filled the universe with His divine voice.

"Go forth," He said, "sacred children, worthy of your Father's greatness. Do not try to change anything, and do not deny your service to My creations. I will send a pure Being, an extension of Myself, who will examine all actions. He will be the feared and incorruptible Judge of the living, and His justice will reach even the shadows beneath the earth. In this way, each person will receive what they deserve." After this, the elements stopped their complaints and returned to their proper roles and duties.

"But how," asked Horos, "did the earth receive this gift from God?"

"I cannot reveal this birth," Isis replied. "I dare not speak of your origins, mighty Horos, for fear that future generations may discover how the Gods were created. I will only say that the Supreme God, Creator, and Builder of the world, allowed Osiris, your father, and me, the great Goddess Isis, to come to the earth for a time to bring the salvation that was promised. With our arrival, life reached its fullness.

Violent and bloody wars were brought to an end. We dedicated temples to the Gods who came before us and began the practice of offerings. We provided laws, food, and clothing to mortals."

"They will read my sacred writings," said Hermes, "and divide them into two parts. Some will be kept secret, while others will be engraved on columns and obelisks for the benefit of mankind." Osiris and Isis established the first courts of justice and brought order to the world. They introduced the practice of honoring treaties and the sacred duty of making oaths. They taught the proper rites for the burial of the dead, explored the mysteries of death, and explained how the soul longs to return to the body. If this return is blocked, life itself is disrupted.

Following the teachings of Hermes, they inscribed secret messages on hidden tablets, revealing that the air is filled with spirits. Through Hermes' guidance in divine law, they became humanity's first teachers and lawgivers, introducing people to knowledge, skills, and the advantages of civilized life. They also learned from Hermes about the connections between heaven and earth, which the Creator had established, and used this knowledge to create religious rituals and sacred ceremonies. Understanding that all physical bodies are subject to decay, they developed practices of prophetic initiation. This way, prophets who raise their hands in prayer to the Gods would gain full knowledge, allowing philosophy and magic to nourish the soul and medicine to heal the body.

After completing these tasks and seeing the world reach its peak, Osiris and I were summoned back to the heavens. But we could not return without first praising the Lord, ensuring that the celestial Vision would fill the skies and that the path for a joyful ascent would open before us, for God delights in hymns."

"O Mother," said Horos, "teach me this hymn so that I may learn it too."

"Listen carefully, my son," Isis replied.

PART 2

My honored son, if you wish to know anything more, ask me. Horos replied, Revered Mother, I would like to understand how royal souls are born. Isis responded: My son Horos, this is what makes royal souls different. There are four regions in the universe, each governed by unchanging laws: heaven, the ether, the air, and the sacred earth. In heaven live the Gods, who, like everything else, follow the commands of the Creator of the universe. The stars reside in the ether and are ruled by the great fire, the sun. The souls of spirits dwell in the air, ruled by the moon. On earth are humans and animals, led by a soul that serves as their king during its time on earth.

Even the Gods themselves create the souls that are meant to become kings in the earthly world. Kings give birth to princes, and the one who embodies the most kingly nature will rise to become a greater king than others. This isn't just about ordinary kings who rule nations, but about souls destined to lead humanity, whether spiritually, intellectually, or politically. The sun, being closer to God than the moon, is stronger and greater, and the moon follows the sun both in power and rank. A king is the lowest among the Gods, yet the highest among men. While he walks on earth, his divine nature remains hidden, but there is something within him that sets him apart from others and brings him closer to the divine. His soul comes from a higher place than those of ordinary people.

There are two reasons why souls are sent to reign on earth. Some souls, having lived pure and honorable lives before, are rewarded with a chance to become divine, with royalty serving as their preparation for this higher state. Others, who committed small mistakes against the inner divine law, receive royalty as a way to correct these faults. Through the challenges and burdens of being incarnated as royalty, they ease the hardships of their earthly existence and move closer to spiritual purification.

When these souls take on a body, their experience is different from others. They remain as blessed as when they were free. The differences in the nature of these kings are not in their souls, since all are royal. Instead, it comes from the qualities of the angels and spirits that guide them. Souls chosen for these roles are always accompanied by guardians and helpers. Even though they are sent away from the divine realms, they are still treated according to their true nature.

When the angels and spirits assigned to them are warriors, the soul adopts that nature, temporarily setting aside its own. If the angels are peaceful, the soul becomes calm. If the guardians value justice, the soul takes pleasure in judging fairly. If the spirits love music, the soul finds joy in singing. If they cherish truth, the soul becomes drawn to philosophy. In this way, souls take on the qualities of their guardians. When they enter human bodies, they lose their original state and become more like the beings that helped them take form.

Horos said, Mother, your explanation is clear, but you haven't told me how noble souls are born. On earth, just as there are different roles among people, souls also have different ranks. A soul that comes from a higher realm is nobler than the rest, just as a free person is nobler than a slave. Royal and noble souls are destined to be leaders over others.

How are souls born as male or female? Horos asked. Isis answered: All souls are the same by nature because they come from the same place, created by the Creator. There are no males or females among souls—those differences exist only in physical bodies, not in spiritual beings. Some souls are more active and others are gentler, and this reflects the air that surrounds them. Souls are wrapped in airy bodies made of earth, water, air, and fire. In women, there is more coldness and moisture than heat and dryness, making their souls softer. In men, the air around the soul has more heat and dryness, which makes them more energetic and lively.

And how, my mother, are the souls of wise people born? asked Horos. Isis replied: Think of vision, which is covered by layers of tissue. If the coverings are thick, the sight is weak; if they are thin and clear, the sight is sharp. The soul, too, has coverings made of invisible air. If these coverings are fine and light, the soul becomes clear and insightful. But when the coverings are heavy and dense, the soul can only see what is nearby, like trying to see through a cloudy day.

Why is it, my mother, that the minds of people outside our sacred land seem less open than the minds of those who belong to it? Horos asked. Isis answered: The earth is positioned in the center of the universe, like a person lying on their back and looking up at the sky. The different regions of the earth correspond to different parts of this body. The earth looks to the heavens like a child looking to a father, and its changes follow the movements of the sky.

The head of the earth lies to the south, the right shoulder to the east, and the left shoulder toward the winds of Libya. The feet rest under the stars of the Bear constellation, with the right foot beneath the tail and the left foot beneath the head of the Bear. The waist aligns with the sky closest to the Bear, and the middle of the body lies under the center of the heavens. You can see proof of these connections in the way people from different places look and behave. Those who live in the south have beautiful faces and thick hair. People from the east are skilled with their hands, good in battle, and quick with a bow, using their right hands with ease. Those from the west are strong and fight with their left hands, doing with their left what others do with their right. People living beneath the Bear constellation are known for the shape and beauty of their legs. Those from places beyond the Bear, such as Italy and Greece, are admired for the beauty of their waists, which is why they often favor male companionship. That part of the body, being lighter in color, produces men with fairer skin.

The sacred land of our ancestors lies at the center of the earth. Just as the heart sits in the middle of the human body and serves as the seat of the soul, the heart of the earth gives life and wisdom to the people born from it. This is why, my son, the people of this land possess not only the same qualities that all humans share but also a higher intelligence and deeper wisdom, for they are nourished by the heart of the earth. Additionally, my son, the southern region stores the clouds, gathering them until they release the river (Nile) when the cold grows intense. Wherever these clouds gather, the air becomes heavy with mist, which not only clouds vision but also dulls the mind.

The east, my son Horos, is restless with the rising sun, just as the west stirs with the setting sun. Those who live in these regions find it difficult to maintain clear thinking. In the north, the cold hardens both body and mind. Only the central land remains calm and bright, blessing its people with tranquility. From this peaceful place, life is created and perfected. The central land stands strong against others, triumphs over them, and, like a noble ruler, shares the rewards of victory with those it has defeated.

Horos asked, Tell me more, Mother. What causes people to lose clarity, reason, or even part of their soul during long illnesses? Isis replied: Every animal connects with one or more of the elements—fire, water, earth, or air. Some creatures are closely tied to a specific element, while others are connected to two, three, or even all four. In the same way, some animals avoid certain elements. For example, insects and locusts flee from fire. Eagles, hawks, and other birds avoid water. Fish fear both air and land. Snakes, like all creatures that crawl, love the ground but avoid open air. Fish thrive in deep waters, and birds enjoy life in the skies. Those birds that fly highest find joy in the heat of the sun and remain close to it. Some creatures, like salamanders, even live within fire.

The elements surround and bind the body, and every soul in a body feels the weight of these elements. As a result, every soul is drawn to certain elements and repelled by others, which keeps it from finding perfect happiness. Yet, since the soul is divine, it continues to seek and reflect, even while trapped in a physical form. However, the soul's thoughts are not as free as they would be without the body. If the body is troubled by illness or fear, the soul is thrown into confusion, just as a man is tossed around by stormy waves.

PART 3

You have given me wonderful knowledge, powerful Mother Isis, about how God creates souls, and I am amazed by it. But you have not yet explained where souls go when they leave their bodies. I deeply wish to understand this mystery and will be grateful for your guidance. Isis replied: Listen carefully, my son, for this is a very important question, and it must not be overlooked. I will answer you fully. Do not think that when souls leave their bodies, they get lost in the vastness of the universe, merging into a boundless spirit with no way to return to a body or retain their identity. Imagine water spilled from a vase—it cannot return to the vase, and instead, it mixes with all other water. But this is not what happens with souls, wise Horos. I have been initiated into the mysteries of the immortal soul, and I walk the path of truth. I will tell you everything, leaving nothing out.

Water is made up of countless fluid particles without reason or purpose, while the soul is an individual being, created by God's mind and hands, filled with intelligence. Souls are born from unity, not from many things, so they do not mix with other beings. To join the soul with a body, God enforces a union through divine necessity. Souls do not return to the same place by chance or in confusion but are sent to the place that matches their experience. What they go through while living in a body, which weighs them down and limits them, determines where they will go next.

Listen to this example, my beloved Horos. Imagine a prison filled with people, eagles, doves, swans, hawks, swallows, sparrows, flies, serpents, lions, leopards, wolves, dogs, hares, oxen, sheep, and amphibious animals like seals, turtles, hydras, and crocodiles. Now imagine all these creatures being set free at the same time. Each would go where it belongs—humans to cities and public places, eagles to the sky, doves to the lower air, hawks to the higher air, swallows to places where people gather, sparrows to orchards, and swans to places where they can sing. Flies would stay close to the ground, living off the smells and vapors they find there. Lions and leopards would run to the mountains, wolves to remote places, dogs would follow humans, hares would go to the woods, oxen to fields, and sheep to pastures. Serpents would seek caves in the earth. Seals and turtles would return to shallow waters and rivers, living as they are meant to, close to both land and water. Every creature knows where it belongs, guided by its nature. In the same way, every soul—whether it lived as a human or some other form—knows where it must go. It would be as foolish as saying a bull could live in water or a turtle could survive in the air to believe that souls would forget their place.

Even while they are trapped in flesh and blood, souls obey the laws of order, even though living in a body is a kind of punishment. How much more, then, will they follow these laws when they are free from the body! This sacred law applies to everything, even reaching up to the heavens. Now, my noble son, listen to how the hierarchy of souls is arranged. The space between the highest heaven, called the empyrean, and the moon is filled with gods, stars, and divine powers. Below the moon, between it and the earth, lies the home of souls.

The endless air, which we call wind, has its own paths to follow as it moves across the earth to give it life. But the movement of the wind does not block the path of souls. Souls travel freely through the air without mixing with it, much like water gliding over oil. This space between the earth and the heavens is divided into four main sections and sixty smaller regions. The first section starts from the earth and rises through four regions until it reaches certain high points, which it cannot go beyond.

The second province includes eight regions where the winds begin their movement. Pay close attention, my son, for you are hearing the hidden mysteries of the earth, the sky, and the sacred fluid that lies between them. Now, I will tell you, my glorious Horos, which souls inhabit each of these regions, starting with the highest. In the province of the winds, the birds fly, for beyond that point, there is no moving air, and no creatures can live there. However, the air spreads into every corner within its reach and fills all the boundaries of the four directions of the earth, even though the earth itself cannot rise into the homes of the air.

The third province contains sixteen regions filled with a pure and delicate element. The fourth province has thirty-two regions where the air becomes so thin and clear that fire can pass through it without resistance. This is the order that rules from the lowest point to the highest: four main divisions, twelve intervals, and sixty regions, where each soul lives according to its nature. Though all souls share the same essence, they are arranged in a hierarchy. The farther a region is from the earth, the greater the dignity of the souls living there.

The space between the earth and the heavens is divided into these regions with careful order and harmony, my son Horos. Different people have called them by many names—zones, firmaments, or spheres. These are the places where souls dwell—both those who have been freed from their bodies and those who have not yet taken one. The position each soul occupies reflects its worth. Divine and royal souls reside in the upper regions, while the less noble souls remain close to the surface of the earth. Souls of ordinary rank inhabit the middle areas.

The souls destined to rule descend from the higher zones. When these souls are freed from their bodies, they return to their original home, or even to a higher realm—unless, of course, they have acted in ways that go against their dignity and God's laws. If they have failed, divine Providence sends them to lower regions according to their mistakes. Similarly, souls of lower rank may be moved to higher places as they grow in strength and honor.

Two great ministers serve universal Providence. One guards the souls, and the other leads them, giving them bodies and guiding them through their paths. The first minister protects the souls, while the second binds or releases them according to God's will. This sacred law of fairness governs the changes above, just as it shapes and forms the physical bodies in which the souls are housed.

This law works alongside two forces: Memory and Experience. Memory ensures that all things in creation retain their original design, as determined in the heavens. Experience ensures that every soul receives a body that matches its nature. Passionate souls are given strong bodies, lazy souls weak ones, active souls energetic bodies, gentle souls peaceful ones, powerful souls robust forms, and cunning souls are given quick and nimble bodies. In short, every soul is provided with the right kind of body.

There is wisdom in the way all creatures are formed. Birds are covered with feathers, intelligent beings are given sharp senses, and animals in the wild are equipped with horns, tusks, claws, or other defenses. Reptiles, with their smooth and flexible bodies, are also given sharp teeth or scales to protect them from harm, since their moist nature could otherwise make them weak. Fish, being timid creatures, are given a home in water, where the power of fire is dulled, for it can neither shine nor burn in that element.

Each fish swims freely using its fins, moving wherever it chooses, and its weakness is hidden by the darkness of the deep water. In the same way, souls are placed in bodies that suit their nature: rational souls in human bodies, wild souls in flying creatures, and souls without reason in beasts, whose only rule is strength. Deceptive souls dwell in reptiles, for they do not attack openly but strike by hiding and waiting. Timid souls inhabit fish, as they are not fit to live in other elements. Yet in every kind of creature, there are some that act against their nature.

How does this happen, Mother? asked Horos. And Isis replied: A person might act without reason, a beast might escape the need for survival, a reptile may forget its cunning, a fish could lose its fear, and a bird might abandon its freedom. You have now heard about the hierarchy of souls, their descent, and how bodies are created. In each type of soul, there are some royal ones, with various qualities—some fiery, some cold, some proud, some gentle, some clever, some simple, some thoughtful, and others active. These differences reflect the regions from which the souls descend into bodies. Royal souls come from a royal realm, though there are many kinds of royalty—spiritual, physical, artistic, intellectual, and moral.

How do you describe these kinds of royalty? asked Horos. Isis answered: The king of souls is your father, Osiris. The king of bodies is the ruler of each nation. The king of wisdom is the Father of all things. The master of knowledge is Hermes Trismegistus, and Asclepius, the son of Hephaestus, presides over medicine. Power belongs to Osiris, and after him, to you, my son. Philosophy is guided by Arnebaskenis, and poetry by Asclepius, the son of Imhotep. So, as you reflect on this, you will see that there are many forms of kingship. The highest form of royalty belongs to the highest realm, while the lesser ones correspond to the different regions from which they originate. Souls born from the fiery realm handle fire; those from the watery realm thrive in water; those from the realms of art and knowledge pursue these paths; and those from the realm of idleness live in ease. Everything that happens on earth has its origin in the higher realms, where all things are measured and balanced. Nothing begins here that does not first come from above and eventually return there.

Explain this further, Mother, said Horos. And Isis replied: Nature has stamped this truth into every creature. We breathe in air from above, exhale it, and breathe it in again through our lungs, which are made for this purpose. When our lungs can no longer receive air, we leave this life. Other disruptions can also break the balance of our nature.

What do you mean by this balance, Mother? Horos asked. Isis answered: It is the mixing and union of the four elements, which produce a vapor that surrounds the soul and enters the body, giving both a certain nature. This combination explains the variety in both souls and bodies. If fire is the dominant element in the body, the soul—already fiery—becomes even more energetic, and the body more lively and active. If air is dominant, both body and soul become unstable and restless. When water is the strongest element, the soul becomes gentle, kind, and adaptable, as water mixes easily with other things. If there is too much water, the body becomes soft and weak, easily broken by illness. If earth is dominant, the soul becomes slow, as the body's dense structure prevents clear expression. Such a soul turns inward, burdened by the heavy body, which moves slowly and with effort. But when all elements are balanced, the entire nature becomes lively in action, quick in movement, sensitive in perception, and strong in health.

Birds are born from a mixture of air and fire, matching the nature of the elements that form them. Humans have a large amount of fire, with a little air, and equal parts of water and earth. This abundance of fire gives humans intelligence, for thought is like a flame—it burns through obstacles, not with destruction, but by insight.

When water and earth dominate, with a little air and very little fire, animals are born. Those that have more fire than others are braver. When water and earth are present in equal amounts, reptiles are formed. Lacking fire, these creatures have no courage or honesty. Too much water makes them cold, while too much earth makes them dull and heavy, and with little air, they struggle to move easily. Creatures like fish are born when water far exceeds the amount of earth. Without fire or air, they are timid and prefer to stay hidden. The heavy presence of water and earth in their nature makes them similar to the way soil dissolves in water.

The growth of the body happens through the balanced increase of these elements. When the right amount is reached, growth stops. As long as the original balance of fire, air, earth, and water stays the same, the creature stays healthy. But if these elements lose their balance—whether by too much or too little fire, air, water, or earth—illness will arise. I am not talking about changes in activity or shifts in order, but rather a disruption in the balance itself. If air and fire, which are closest to the soul's nature, become too strong, the creature loses its natural state, as these elements tend to weaken the body.

The body relies on earth to sustain it, while water helps bind it together. Air provides movement, and fire gives energy. When these elements combine, they create vapors that merge with the soul, influencing it with their own qualities, whether good or bad. As long as the soul stays in harmony with these elements, it maintains its current state. But if the balance shifts, the relationship between the body and soul also changes. Fire and air, which naturally rise upward, pull the soul with them, while water and earth, which are drawn toward the ground, weigh down the body, making it heavy and keeping it tied to the earth.

...

A Treatise on Initiations; or, Asclepios

PART 1

Hermes: It is by the will of a god that you have come to us, Asclepios, so that you may take part in a divine discussion. This will be the most sacred teaching we have ever shared or been inspired to deliver. If you understand it, you will gain every blessing—though, perhaps, it is more accurate to say that all blessings are really just one, since they are all connected. They come from the same source, forming a unity that cannot be separated. You will understand this if you listen carefully to what we are about to say. But first, Asclepios, step away for a moment and find someone to join us for this discussion.

[Asclepios suggests inviting Ammon.]

There is no reason why Ammon cannot join us, replied Trismegistus. I have written to him before on topics about nature and other teachings, as I would to a beloved son. But it is your name, Asclepios, that I will place at the beginning of this work. Do not invite anyone else except for Ammon, for a conversation about the holiest matters should not be shared with too many. It would be wrong to reveal these divine teachings to a large audience, just as it would be wrong to share sacred truths with those who cannot understand or respect them.

[Ammon enters, completing the group, which now has four members.]

The presence of four is essential for these teachings, for they reflect the four great aspects of existence, representing the entirety of the universe. As Nebuchadnezzar said in the allegory recorded by Daniel, "The form of the fourth is like the Son of God." This shows how, through transformation instead of destruction, the earthly elements of man are purified by suffering.

Hermes: Every human soul, Asclepios, is immortal. But not every soul's immortality is the same. The way they experience it and the length of their journey differ from soul to soul.

Asclepios: That must be because not all souls are of the same kind, Trismegistus.

Hermes: You understand quickly, Asclepios! I haven't yet mentioned that everything is one, and one is everything. All things existed within the Creator before they came into being, and we call Him "all" because everything belongs to Him. Throughout this discussion, remember that the Creator is both One and All, the source of everything. All things flow from above—down to the earth, into the waters, and through the air. Fire alone rises, giving life, while everything that descends becomes subject to it. What comes down from above creates, and what rises from below nourishes. The earth, which supports itself, receives and reshapes all that it takes in.

The universe contains everything and is everything. It moves the soul and the world and encompasses all that nature holds. Though life expresses itself in countless different forms, all these forms are connected, creating unity. Everything emerges from this oneness. The universe is made of four elements: fire, water, earth, and air. There is one world, one soul, and one God.

Now, focus your thoughts fully, for understanding the Divine requires divine help. This knowledge is like a powerful river rushing forward with great speed. It moves so quickly that it can easily escape the attention of those listening—and even the one who teaches it.

PART 2

Heaven, which reveals God, governs all things. The sun and moon determine the growth and decline of all bodies. But it is the true God—the Creator—who directs heaven, the soul, and everything that exists in the world. From His high place, countless influences flow down, spreading through the world into every soul, both in general and in specific ways, and into the nature of all things. God prepared the world to receive every individual form. Through Nature, He shapes these forms and draws the world upward toward heaven using the four elements. Everything follows God's plan, though the things that come from above are separated into individuals in a specific way.

Each type contains many individuals that share its nature. A type is whole, while each individual is a part of that whole. For example, gods make up one type, as do spirits, humans, birds, and all other beings in the world. These types create individual beings that resemble their original type. There is also a type without sensation but not without a soul—plants, which survive by rooting themselves in the earth. Individual plants can be found everywhere. Heaven is filled with God's presence. The types I mentioned extend all the way up to the beings whose individual souls are immortal. While types are eternal, not all individuals are. For example, humanity as a type is immortal, but individual humans are not.

Divine beings form a type where both the type and its individuals are as eternal as the divine itself. For other beings, only the type is eternal, while individual creatures die and are replaced through reproduction. Some individual beings are mortal. For example, man is mortal, but humanity as a whole is immortal. Yet, individual beings of all kinds can mix with those from other types. Some are original creations, while others are brought forth by gods, spirits, or humans. All of them resemble the type they come from. Bodies only take shape through divine will, individual beings take on their unique qualities with the help of spirits, and humans play a role in the care and training of animals.

Some spirits leave their original type and join with divine beings, becoming companions and allies of the gods. Those who keep their original character are called spirits and are drawn to things connected with humanity. Humans are similar to spirits, and in some ways, they even surpass them. Human individuality is complex and diverse because it results from the connections between different types. Humans serve as a vital link between many other kinds of beings. A person who aligns with the gods through intelligence and devotion becomes close to God. A person who aligns with spirits draws closer to them. Those who remain content with ordinary human life stay part of the human type. Other individuals will find themselves connected with the beings they are naturally drawn toward.

PART 3

Man, Asclepios, is a great wonder, a being worthy of admiration and respect. He moves within this divine world as though he were a god himself. He understands the nature of spirits and, knowing that he shares the same origin, he rises above his human side to focus on the divine within him. How fortunate and close to the gods mankind is! By connecting with the divine, man lets go of his earthly nature. Through love, he forms a bond with all other beings and feels his role is essential to the order of the universe. He looks toward the heavens and, from his place between the higher and lower realms, he loves everything beneath him and is loved by everything above him.

He works the land, harnesses the speed of the elements, and uses his sharp mind to explore the depths of the sea. Nothing is hidden from him. Heaven does not seem too distant, for knowledge lifts him up to it. His mind's brilliance is not dimmed by the thick air, the pull of the earth does not hold him back, and the depths of the ocean do not trouble him. He embraces everything and remains the same, no matter where he is.

All living beings seem to have roots that reach downward, but lifeless things have only one root that grows upward, supporting many branches like a tree. Some creatures live by feeding on two elements, while others need only one. There are also two kinds of nourishment—one for the soul and one for the body. The soul of the world is sustained by constant motion, while bodies grow through the nourishment provided by water and earth, the elements of the lower world. The spirit, which fills all things, mingles with everything and brings life to it. This spirit gives consciousness to intelligence, and through the fifth element—the ether—man receives the unique gift of awareness. In humans, this awareness becomes a deeper understanding of the divine order.

Since I am now speaking of consciousness, I will soon explain its purpose, which is as grand and sacred as divinity itself. But first, let us continue what we have already begun, speaking of humanity's union with the gods—a gift given only to mankind. Only a few people have the great fortune to understand the divine, a knowledge that exists only within God and the human mind.

Asclepios: Do all men have this awareness, Trismegistus?

Hermes: No, Asclepios, not everyone has true intelligence. Some people are deceived by the surface of things, following appearances without searching for their deeper meaning. This is where evil arises in man, causing the highest of creatures to lower himself to the level of animals. But I will explain more about consciousness and the mind later.

Man alone is made of two parts. One part is single and essential, as the Greeks say, formed in the image of the divine. The other part, which the Greeks call Kosmic, belongs to the material world and is made of four elements. This part makes up the body, which serves as a covering for the divine spirit within. The divine part, along with its pure perceptions and intelligence, hides behind the barrier of the physical body.

PART 4

Asclepios: Why, then, Trismegistus, was man placed in this world instead of with God, where he could live in perfect happiness?

Hermes: Your question is a reasonable one, Asclepios, and I ask God to help me answer it, for everything depends on His will—especially these great matters we are now discussing. Listen carefully, Asclepios. The Lord and Creator of all things, whom we call God, brought forth another God—one that can be seen and perceived by the senses. I call him sensible not because he possesses feelings, for this is not the place to discuss that, but because he is experienced through sight and touch. After bringing forth this being—who stands above all creatures and ranks second only to Himself—God saw that His creation was beautiful and filled with every kind of goodness. He loved it as His own child.

For God, to will something and to make it happen are one and the same. His will is instantly accomplished. Knowing that the essential part of man could not understand everything unless it was wrapped in the physical world, He gave man a body to dwell in. God wanted man to have two natures. He united and blended these natures perfectly. Through this, man could admire and worship the celestial and eternal things and also take care of and govern what is on earth.

Man was made with both spirit and body, with a nature that is partly eternal and partly mortal. This combination allows him to honor what is divine while managing the things of this world. I speak here of earthly things—not just the elements of earth and water that are under man's care, but also the things that come from him or depend on him. These include tending the land, raising livestock, building structures, creating ports, navigating the seas, engaging in trade, and carrying out exchanges that form the bonds between people.

Earth and water are part of the world, and this earthly part is supported by arts and sciences. Without these, the world would be incomplete in God's eyes. Whatever God wills must happen, and the result always accompanies His will. We cannot believe that anything which pleased Him at the beginning would stop pleasing Him, for from the very start He knew what would exist and what would bring Him joy.

PART 5

I see, Asclepios, that you are eager to understand how heaven and its inhabitants can become the focus of human aspiration and worship. Know then, Asclepios, that to seek after the God of heaven and all who dwell there is to offer them constant reverence, for man alone, among both divine and earthly beings, is capable of doing so. The admiration, worship, praise, and devotion of man bring joy to heaven and its celestial inhabitants. The Muses were sent to men by the supreme Divinity so that the earthly world would not lack the beauty of hymns, and so that the human voice might sing to the One who is All, the Father of everything. In this way, the gentle harmonies of earth are united with the choirs of heaven.

Only a few men, with minds pure and clear, are given the sacred task of seeing heaven clearly. Those whose minds are weighed down by the conflict between their earthly and divine natures are connected to the lower elements. Man is not lessened because he has a mortal part. In fact, his mortality increases his abilities and strength. His dual nature allows him to fulfill both earthly and divine roles. He is made in such a way that he can connect with both the physical world and the divine.

I hope, Asclepios, that you will give this teaching your full attention and focus, for many people lack faith in these things. Now I will explain the true principles for the benefit of the purest minds.

PART 6

The Master of Eternity is the first God, the world is the second, and man is the third. God, the Creator of the world and everything in it, governs the universe and places it under man's authority. In turn, man focuses his efforts on the world, making it his responsibility. The world and man are interconnected, each depending on the other, which is why the Greeks call the world Kosmos. Man understands both himself and the world, so he should know what aligns with his nature, what he can use, and what he should revere. As he offers praise and gratitude to God, he must also honor the world, which reflects God's image, just as man is also an image of God. God has two likenesses: the world and man.

Man's nature is complex. His soul, consciousness, mind, and reason are divine qualities, capable of reaching toward heaven. But his physical body, made of fire, water, earth, and air, is mortal and belongs to the earth, returning to it when life ends. In this way, man is made of both a divine part and a mortal part, with his body serving as the temporary vessel for the soul. The guiding principle of this dual nature is religion, and its result is goodness. Man reaches perfection when he frees himself from desires and rejects what is not truly part of him. The material things the body craves are external to the divine mind and can be called possessions only because they are not born with us but are acquired later. They are foreign to man's true nature, just as even the body itself is. For this reason, man must resist both the objects of desire and the part of him that makes him vulnerable to those desires.

It is man's duty to direct his soul through reason, allowing the contemplation of the divine to help him focus less on the mortal body that was given to him to care for the material world. For man to function fully, both his physical and spiritual aspects must work together. His body, with its two hands, two feet, and other organs, connects him to the lower, earthly world. At the same time, his inner nature is equipped with four essential faculties: sensibility, soul, memory, and foresight. These enable him to understand and perceive divine truths. With these abilities, man can explore differences, qualities, causes, and quantities. However, if the body weighs too heavily on him, it will prevent him from understanding the deeper truths of existence.

When man fulfills his purpose—governing the world and worshiping the Divine—what reward should he receive? If the world is the work of God, then the person who tends and enhances its beauty becomes a helper of God's will, using both his body and his daily efforts to serve what was created by God. What reward could be greater than the one given to our ancestors? May divine goodness grant us the same reward. All our hopes and prayers strive toward this goal: that we may be freed from the prison of the body and, released from the chains of mortality, return pure and sanctified to the divine inheritance of our nature.

Asclepios: What you say is just and true, Trismegistus. This is indeed the reward for honoring God and caring for the world. But those who live without piety are denied this return to the heavens. Instead, they must endure punishment, being sent into new bodies, a fate from which holy souls are spared.

The end of this teaching gives us the hope of an eternal future for the soul, a future earned through how we live in this world. Yet some find this idea hard to believe. To others, it is a mere story, and still others mock it. For many, the pleasures of the physical world are too sweet to resist. That is the problem—they become attached to their mortal part, forgetting their divine nature, and they lose sight of immortality.

I tell you this with prophetic insight: in the future, no one will choose the simple path of philosophy, which consists of studying divine things and practicing holy religion. Most people will complicate philosophy with all sorts of questions, adding subjects that do not belong to it. Why do they burden it with unnecessary sciences, and how do they mix it with so many irrelevant matters?

Hermes: Asclepios, they mix philosophy with all sorts of unnecessary subjects—like arithmetic, music, and geometry. But pure philosophy, which should focus on holy religion, should only touch on other sciences to admire the predictable movements of the stars, their positions, and their paths, as measured by calculation. It should explore the size of the earth, its qualities and quantities, the depths of the sea, and the power of fire. It should seek to understand the effects of these things and how Nature works, honoring both Art and the divine intelligence behind it. As for music, it is understood when one grasps reason and the divine order of the universe. This order arranges everything perfectly within the unity of the whole, creating a beautiful harmony and a divine melody.

Asclepios: What, then, will happen to men after us?

Hermes: Misled by the clever tricks of false teachers, they will stray from true, pure, and holy philosophy. To worship God with simple thoughts and a pure heart, to honor His works, and to bless His will—this alone is philosophy untouched by the distractions of idle curiosity. But that is enough on this subject.

PART 7

Let's begin by discussing Mind and related matters. In the beginning, there were God and Hylè—the Greek word for the first substance or matter of the universe. Spirit was present in the universe but not in the same way as with God. The things that make up the universe are not God; before they came into being, they did not exist, though they were contained in the source from which they would eventually emerge. Beyond created things is not only that which has yet to be born but also that which lacks the ability to create anything. Whatever has the power to create holds within it the seeds of all that can come into being, for it is natural that what exists can bring forth more existence.

God, however, is eternal and cannot be born. He always is, has been, and will be. His nature is to exist without a beginning. Matter, or the nature of the world, and mind both seem to have been brought forth at the beginning, possessing the ability to grow and create. The potential to generate life lies within Nature herself, and she acts as the source of creation without needing outside help. This is different from beings that can only create when they mix with something else. The universe holds within it all of Nature, acting as a womb for everything that exists. I call it a womb because nothing could come into being without a space to hold it. Everything that exists must occupy a place, for without a space to contain them, things could have no qualities, quantities, positions, or effects.

Although the world itself was not born, it holds within it the source of all creation, providing a fitting place for everything to be conceived. The universe contains the potential for both good and evil. This leads some to ask whether God could have prevented evil from existing. There is no need to answer them, but for you, Asclepios and Ammon, I will explain. Some say that God should have kept the world free from evil, but evil is an inherent part of creation. God has provided humanity with emotions, knowledge, and intelligence so that we can avoid evil. These gifts make humans superior to other animals, giving us the ability to recognize and escape evil before being trapped by it. True knowledge rests on supreme goodness.

Spirit animates and gives life to everything in the world. It acts as the tool through which the will of God is carried out. We must understand the supreme, invisible God through intelligence alone. This

God directs the secondary, visible God—the universe—containing all space, matter, and energy, along with everything that can create and produce. Spirit, or Mind, governs all individual beings in the world according to the nature assigned to them by God. Matter—called Hylè or the Kosmos—serves as the container, motion, and reflection of everything that God directs. It provides each thing with what it needs and fills it with spirit according to its nature.

The universe takes the shape of a hollow sphere, containing within itself the reason for its form, though the cause of this form remains invisible. If someone were to examine any point on its surface and try to see what lies at its center, they would find nothing visible. The sphere can only be seen through the forms that appear on its surface, but in itself, it remains invisible. The center of this sphere—if it can be called a place—is known as Hades in Greek, meaning "the unseen," since it cannot be observed from the outside. The Greeks called the forms that shape reality "Ideas" because they represent the unseen patterns that give shape to everything. This hidden center, known as Hades by the Greeks, is called Hell (Inferno) by the Latins because of its deep and concealed location. These are the fundamental principles from which all things arise. Everything exists in them, through them, or emerges from them.

Asclepios: Are these principles the foundation of all individual beings, Trismegistus?

Hermes: Yes, the world sustains bodies, and spirit sustains souls. Thought, which is a gift from heaven and a privilege of humanity, nourishes intelligence, though only a few people have minds capable of receiving this gift. Thought is like a light that illuminates the mind, just as the sun illuminates the world. But it is even greater than the sun's light, which can be blocked by the moon or hidden when night falls. Once thought has entered the human soul, it becomes part of her nature and can never again be darkened by ignorance. This is why it is rightly said that the souls of the gods are pure intelligences. As for me, I say not this of all of them, but of the great supernal Gods.

PART 8

Asclepios: What are the fundamental principles of everything, Trismegistus?

Hermes: I am about to reveal to you profound and divine mysteries. As we begin, I ask for the favor of heaven, for these truths are not ordinary. There are many levels of divine beings, and each of them contains an element of intelligence. Do not think they are beyond our perception. In fact, we can understand them more clearly than things that are merely visible, as you will soon discover. If you pay close attention to what I am about to say, you will grasp this truth. These ideas are lofty and sacred, far beyond human understanding, so you must remain focused. If not, these words will pass through your mind without taking root, only to return to their source and be lost again.

There are gods above all visible forms, followed by spiritual gods. These gods, because they have both spiritual and physical aspects, express their presence through their visible nature, with each one illuminating the others through their works. Everything is connected, from the center of creation to its farthest reaches, in accordance with the natural relationships between things. The supreme being of the heavens is called Zeus, for it is through the heavens that Zeus gives life to all things. The supreme being of the sun is light, which reaches us through the sun's disk. The thirty-six constellations are ruled by a being named Pantomorphos, meaning "one with all forms," because he gives divine shape to everything. The seven planets are governed by the spirits of Fortune and Destiny, who ensure the laws of Nature remain stable, even amid constant change. Ether serves as the medium through which everything is created.

Everything follows its kind: mortal beings are drawn to what is mortal, and visible things to what is visible. However, the ultimate guidance belongs to the highest master, so all diversity resolves back into unity. All things either emerge from unity or depend on it. Though things may appear separate, they are really parts of the same whole, which consists of two fundamental principles. These principles are the substance from which all things are made and the will of the One who shapes them.

Asclepios: What is the reason for this, Trismegistus?

Hermes: It is because God is the Father and ruler of everything. Though we may call Him by many names—each sacred in its own way—none of these names can fully describe His divine nature. Words are just sounds carried by air, expressing what a person's mind understands through the senses. Names, made of syllables and spoken aloud, are symbols that connect the voice to the ear. But no matter how complex a name may be, it cannot capture the essence of the One who is the source of all greatness. Yet, since He must be named, we must either call Him "All" or refer to Him by the names of everything that exists.

He is both one and all, containing the fullness of both masculine and feminine principles. Through His own will, He continuously creates everything He intends. His will is universal goodness, and this same goodness is present in everything. Nature is born from His divine essence, ensuring that all things are exactly as they should be and that Nature itself has the power to give birth to everything that will come into existence.

This, Asclepios, is why everything has both male and female aspects.

Asclepios: Do you say this is true even of God, Trismegistus?

Hermes: Yes, not just of God but of all things, whether they are alive or not. Nothing that exists can be without the ability to create. If things could not bring forth life, they could not remain as they are. This law of creation is present in Nature, in the mind, and throughout the universe, sustaining everything that is brought into existence. Both male and female are full of creative power, and their union—or rather, their perfect merging—can be known as Eros, or Aphrodite, or even by both names together.

If the mind can grasp one truth more clearly than any other, it is this: the duty to create life is a law that the God of Nature has placed on all beings. To this law, He has also attached the highest joy, delight, longing, and the purest love. There would be no need to explain the importance of this law, since everyone can sense it within themselves. Notice how, at the moment when the essence of life flows from the brain, the two natures blend into each other. One eagerly draws in and hides the seed of the other. Through this joining, the female receives the strength of the male, and the male rests on the embrace of the female.

This sacred union is performed in secret, for if it were openly displayed, the divine nature of both would risk being mocked by those who do not understand. True piety is rare in this world, and it would not take long to count the few who possess it. Most people are filled with malice because they lack wisdom and knowledge of how the universe works. Understanding divine religion is the foundation of all things, leading to the rejection of vices and providing the remedy for them. But when ignorance takes hold, vice grows and wounds the soul in ways that are difficult to heal. A soul poisoned by vice swells with sickness, and only knowledge and understanding can restore it.

Let us continue this teaching, even if only a few will benefit from it. Now, Asclepios, listen carefully as I explain why God gave part of His intelligence and knowledge to humanity alone.

God the Father, the Ruler above all gods, gave man reason and intelligence to help him avoid or overcome the weaknesses of the body and to hold on to the hope of immortality. Man was created good, capable of living forever, and formed from two natures: one divine and one mortal. This dual nature makes man superior to both the gods, who possess only immortality, and mortal beings, who lack divinity. Because of this, man is closely connected to the gods, honoring them with religious devotion, and the gods, in turn, care for human affairs with affection. But I speak only of pious men. As for the wicked, I will not mention them here, for discussing them would spoil the holiness of this teaching.

PART 9

And since we are now speaking of the connection and similarity between humans and gods, consider the power and ability of man, Asclepios. Just as the Ruler and Father—whom we call God—created the celestial gods, man creates the gods that dwell in temples. These gods enjoy being close to humans, for they not only receive light but also give it in return. This connection benefits both mankind and the gods, strengthening them.

Does this surprise you, Asclepios? Do you doubt it, as many others do?

Asclepios: I am amazed, Trismegistus, but I accept your words. I see that man is truly fortunate to have such a gift.

Hermes: Yes, he is indeed worthy of admiration, for he is the greatest of all gods. The celestial gods are made from the purest part of Nature, without any mixture of other elements, and their visible forms are like heads only.

Asclepios: But the gods made by humans have two aspects—one divine, which is their purest nature, and the other human, formed from earthly matter. These gods not only have heads but also full bodies, with all their limbs. This means that humans, remembering their own nature and origins, imitate the divine by creating these gods. Just as the Father and Lord shaped the eternal gods to reflect Himself, so mankind creates gods in its own image. Are you referring to statues, Trismegistus?

Hermes: Yes, I am speaking of statues, Asclepios. How little faith you have! What else could I mean but these statues, which are so full of life, emotion, and purpose? They perform many amazing acts—

some offer prophecies by sending dreams or other signs, while others bring illness or healing according to what people deserve.

Do you not understand, Asclepios, that Egypt is a reflection of heaven, a mirror of the divine order on earth? In truth, this land is the temple of the world. Yet, as wise men must foresee what is to come, there is something you should know. A time will come when it will seem that all the Egyptians' devotion to the gods was for nothing and that their prayers have gone unanswered. The divine presence will leave the earth and return to the heavens, abandoning Egypt, which was once its sacred home. Religion will fade, and the gods will no longer be found here. Foreigners will overrun the land, and not only will sacred practices be neglected, but religion, worship, and reverence for the gods will be outlawed and punished by law.

The land, once filled with temples, will become full of tombs and the dead. O Egypt, Egypt, all that will remain of your religion will be legends that future generations will not believe. Only the words carved into stone will bear witness to your devotion. Barbarians—whether from Scythia, India, or other neighboring lands—will take control of Egypt. The gods will return to the heavens, and mankind, abandoned, will be lost. Egypt will be left empty, deserted by both men and gods.

I call upon you, O sacred River, to bear witness to what is to come! Waves of blood will stain your waters, overflowing your banks. The dead will outnumber the living, and if any Egyptians survive, they will no longer act as Egyptians but as foreigners in their own land.

You weep, Asclepios, but even sadder things will come to pass. Egypt will fall into apostasy, the worst of all evils. Once the sacred land loved by the gods, Egypt will become a place of corruption, a school of impiety, and a home to all forms of violence. People will grow tired of everything. They will no longer admire or love the world. They will turn away from this beautiful creation, which is the most perfect work of all time—past, present, and future. The weariness of their souls will leave them with nothing but contempt for the universe, this magnificent creation of God. They will reject this masterpiece, in which God's will united everything in perfect harmony, worthy of eternal reverence, praise, and love.

Darkness will be preferred to light, and death will seem better than life. No one will look toward heaven. Those who remain faithful to religion will be seen as fools, while the wicked will be praised as wise. The violent will be honored as heroes, and the evil-hearted will be celebrated as the best of men. Everything related to the soul—whether mortal or capable of eternal life—will be mocked and dismissed as foolishness. Faithful people will even face death for their beliefs. Believe me, Asclepios, those who remain true to religion and wisdom will face great danger.

New laws and customs will arise, and not a single sacred word or belief will remain—nothing religious or worthy of heaven will endure. What a tragic separation there will be between gods and humans! Evil spirits will be all that remain, and they will mix with the suffering human race, driving people toward wickedness, war, greed, lies, and everything that goes against the nature of the soul. The earth will lose its balance, the seas will become impossible to navigate, and even the stars will stray from their usual paths. Every holy voice will be silenced, crops will rot, and the land will no longer be fruitful. Even the air will become heavy with gloom. This will be the world's old age, a time marked by irreligion, disorder, lawlessness, and the confusion of good people.

When all of these things come to pass, Asclepios, the Lord and Father—sovereign God over all the world—will see the evil ways and actions of men. Then, through His divine will and goodness, He will put an end to these misfortunes. To stop the errors and corruption, He may flood the world, burn it with fire, or destroy it with wars and plagues. Afterward, He will restore the world to its original beauty, making it once more a place worthy of admiration and worship. Songs of praise and blessing will again celebrate Him, the One who created and redeemed this marvelous work.

This rebirth of the world, the restoration of all good things, and the renewal of Nature will happen at the appointed time, according to the eternal and unchanging will of God.

Asclepios: Truly, Trismegistus, God's nature reflects His will, which is absolute goodness and wisdom.

Hermes: Yes, Asclepios, will arises from reflection, and to will is itself an act of choice. God, who contains everything and has everything He desires, wills nothing out of whim. Everything He wills is good, and He possesses all that He wills. Whatever is good, He thinks and wills, for such is His nature. The world reflects His righteousness.

Asclepios: Then the world is good, Trismegistus?

Hermes: Yes, Asclepios, the world is good, as I will now explain. Just as God grants all beings various gifts—such as thought, soul, and life—the world distributes good things to mortals. These include the changing seasons, the fruits of the earth, birth, growth, maturity, and other blessings.

Though God is beyond the highest heavens, He is also present everywhere, watching over all things. Beyond the heavens lies a starless sphere, which surpasses all physical existence. Between the heavens and the earth rules the giver of life, whom we call Zeus (Jupiter). Over the earth and sea reigns the one who nourishes all living creatures, as well as the plants and fruit-bearing trees—this is Zeus Sarapis (Jupiter Plutonius).

Those who are destined to rule the earth will be sent to the farthest reaches of Egypt, to a city built toward the west, where people from every part of the world will gather by land and sea.

Asclepios: And where are they now, Trismegistus?

Hermes: They are already established in a great city on the mountain of Libya. But enough of this.

PART 10

Let us now discuss what is mortal and what is immortal. People who do not understand the nature of things are troubled by the thought and fear of death. Death happens when the body, exhausted by its work, falls apart. When the force that holds the body together reaches its limit, the body can no longer carry the burdens of life, and so it dies. Death is simply the breaking down of the body and the end of physical sensations. There is no need to trouble ourselves over it. However, there is another law that people often ignore or refuse to believe.

Asclepios: What is this law that people overlook?

Hermes: Listen carefully, Asclepios. When the soul leaves the body, it comes under the power of God, who judges it according to its deeds. If the soul is found to be pious and just, it is allowed to dwell in the divine realms. But if it is stained with vice, it is cast down, tossed between the forces of air, fire, and water. Such a soul is caught in endless storms, drifting between heaven and earth, condemned to eternal punishment. Its immortality only ensures that it suffers the consequences of its actions without end.

We should fear such a terrible fate. Those who now doubt the truth of these things will be forced to believe—not through words, but by the suffering they will endure.

Asclepios: So human laws alone are not enough to punish wrongdoing?

Hermes: Everything on earth is mortal, Asclepios. Those who live according to the desires of the body, without obeying the laws that guide human life, face even greater punishment after death. The punishment will be especially harsh for those whose sins were hidden, for God knows everything and ensures the punishment fits the crime.

Asclepios: Who suffers the greatest punishment, Trismegistus?

Hermes: Those who die violent deaths for their crimes seem to escape the debt they owe to Nature. Their earthly punishment might appear to be the result of their actions, but they still owe a debt. Because they could not pay this debt while alive, they must suffer greatly after death. Without the chance to correct their actions or seek forgiveness, they are delivered into torment until their debt is fully paid.

The Father and Lord of all things, who is everything and rules over all, reveals Himself willingly to everyone. However, He does not show His dwelling place, His glory, or His greatness. Instead, He grants people understanding through intelligence, which clears away ignorance and reveals the truth.

A just person finds strength in religion and piety, and God protects him from harm. Through this connection with divine intelligence, man rises above his mortal nature and hopes for eternal life. This is the difference between the good and the wicked. The person who is guided by piety, wisdom, and devotion to God gains true understanding, as if seeing with open eyes. This faith gives him confidence and allows him to rise above others, just as the sun shines brighter than the other lights in the sky.

If the sun gives light to the other stars, it is not only because of its size and strength, but because of its divine nature and holiness. You must see the sun, Asclepios, as a secondary god that governs the rest of the world, giving light to everything, both living and non-living. If the world is a living being—one that exists, has always existed, and will always exist—then nothing within it is truly mortal. Every part of it is alive, for in something that lives forever, death has no place. In the same way, God is the fullness of life and eternity, for He must live forever. The sun, which endures as long as the universe, continuously sustains all living beings, acting as the source and provider of life.

God is the eternal ruler of everything that both gives life and receives it. He is the one who gave life to all living creatures through an unchanging law, which I will explain to you. The movement of the universe is what makes eternity alive, and the endless motion of life is what keeps the universe eternal. The universe will never stop moving, nor will it ever decay. Eternal life surrounds and protects it like a fortress, giving life to everything inside it and keeping everything connected under the sun's rule.

This movement has two effects: the universe is kept alive by the eternity that encircles it, and in turn, it gives life to all that it holds. This life spreads through everything, following specific patterns, numbers, and seasons. All things follow their appointed times according to the sun and the stars, under divine law. Earthly cycles are marked by changes in the atmosphere, through the shifts between heat and cold. Celestial cycles are measured by the movement of the stars, which return to the same places in the sky at regular intervals.

The universe is the stage on which time plays out, and its constant motion sustains life. Time and order ensure the renewal of all things through the recurring seasons.

PART 11

Since the universe is as it is, nothing in nature—whether in the heavens or on the earth—remains unchanged or stable. Only God is complete, perfect, and unchanging in Himself. He is firm in His stability and cannot be moved by anything, for everything exists within Him, and He alone is everything. If we say that God moves, it can only be within eternity. Yet eternity itself does not move, because time, with all its motion, exists within eternity and draws its meaning from it.

God has always been and will always remain unchanging. Together with God exists eternal stability, containing within it an unmanifest universe—an image of the eternal world that has yet to appear. The created universe mirrors this eternal one. Time, though constantly moving, has its own kind of stability because it repeats its cycles endlessly. So, while eternity is fixed and unchanging, time flows within it, and this flow is essential to the nature of time. It may seem as though eternity moves because of the motion within time, and in the same way, it might seem that God Himself moves within His unchanging nature.

Even in the vast balance of existence, there is a kind of movement within what does not change. The law of God's immensity remains unaltered. The Infinite, the Unknowable, and the Immeasurable cannot be grasped or carried by anything. We cannot know where it comes from, where it is going, where it exists, or what it truly is. It rests within its own perfect stability, just as its stability rests within it. Whether God exists within eternity or eternity exists within God—or both exist within each other—remains a mystery beyond understanding.

Eternity cannot be measured by time, and time—defined by cycles, numbers, and repeating patterns—shares in eternity. Both time and eternity appear endless. Stability, as the foundation of all movement, holds the highest place because everything relies on stability. Thus, God and eternity are the source of all things, while the changing world cannot be considered their source. The changing nature of the world outweighs its stability, following the law of eternal movement within balance.

The divine consciousness is unchanging, moving only within perfect equilibrium. It is holy, incorruptible, and eternal. Or, to say it more clearly, it is the essence of eternity itself—rooted in the absolute truth of the Supreme God, filled with all understanding and knowledge, or, simply put, in God Himself. The consciousness of the natural world includes everything that can be sensed, while human consciousness holds memory, which allows us to recall what we have done. The divine consciousness reaches even to human beings, though God did not extend this supreme awareness to all creatures, for if every living thing shared it, the divine glory would be lessened.

The intelligence of the human mind depends entirely on memory, and it is through memory that humans have become masters of the earth. The intelligence of nature and the essence of the universe can be understood through the things we can see and experience. Eternity reveals its nature through the physical world. However, the consciousness of the Divine Being, the awareness of the Supreme God, is the only true reality. This truth cannot be found—even as a shadow—within the ever-changing world, which is full of illusions, shifting appearances, and errors. In this world, everything is understood only in terms of time.

Do you see, Asclepios, how profound these matters are? I thank the Most High God for granting me the light of His grace. And to you, Tat, Asclepios, and Ammon, I say: keep these divine mysteries within your hearts, and speak of them only in silence.

There is a difference between perception and intellect. The intellect, through study, can understand the nature of the universe. The universal mind connects to the awareness of eternity and the divine beings beyond this world. Yet, as humans, we can only glimpse these heavenly things as if through a mist, because the limits of our senses allow us to see them only dimly. Our strength is too small to fully grasp such divine truths, but when we do manage to reach them, we are blessed with the joy of knowing them deep within ourselves.

PART 12

Regarding the concept of the void, to which many people give great importance, I believe it does not exist, has never existed, and never will. Every part of the universe is filled, just as the earth is full of bodies of different shapes and qualities. Some bodies are larger, others smaller; some are solid, others light or thin. The larger, more solid things are easy to see, while the smaller, more delicate ones are harder to notice or even invisible. We can only recognize them through touch. Many people believe these things are not real bodies but just empty spaces. However, true emptiness cannot exist.

If there were something beyond the universe—though I do not believe this—it would still be filled with divine beings suited to the nature of such a place. The world we see is filled with bodies appropriate to its qualities. We do not perceive everything within the world. Some things are vast, others small. Some seem tiny only because they are far away, or our vision is too weak to notice them. Other things may be so fine and subtle that we are entirely unaware of them. I am referring to the spirits and heroes that dwell between us and the higher skies, where there are no clouds or storms.

It is incorrect to say that any space is truly empty unless we specify what it is empty of—whether fire, water, or something else. Even if a space lacks one of these elements, it is never without spirit or air. The same is true of the idea of "place." A place only makes sense when it refers to something within it. Saying "place" without naming what belongs there makes no sense. For example, we say "the place of water" or "the place of fire." Just as there can be no space completely empty of everything, there is no such thing as place on its own. If a place were entirely empty, it would not exist. For this reason, in my view, no such empty place exists within the universe.

If nothing is truly empty, then space cannot exist on its own unless it has dimensions like length, width, and depth, just as human bodies have their own defining characteristics. If this is true, then we must understand that the higher world—what we call God, who is only known through intelligence—is incorporeal. Nothing material can mix with His nature or be described by qualities, quantities, or measurements. None of these things belong to Him.

This world that we call the physical world holds all things that can be seen, touched, or measured. But even this universe cannot exist without God. God is everything, and everything comes from Him and depends on His will. He contains all that is good, orderly, wise, and perfect. Only He can fully know and understand these things. Nothing exists without Him. Everything that was, is, or will be originates from Him, is contained within Him, and relies on Him—whether it be qualities, sizes, or countless forms.

If you understand this, Asclepios, give thanks to God. When you observe the universe, recognize that everything in this world, with all it contains, is wrapped like a garment by the higher, divine world. All beings—whether mortal or immortal, rational or irrational, living or non-living—carry the nature of the class to which they belong. Although each creature shares the general characteristics of its kind, there are also differences within every kind. Humanity, too, has a common type, though individual people differ from one another.

The essence that comes from God is without a body, as is everything that belongs to intelligence. Since there are two sources of form—one material and the other immaterial—it is impossible for anything created to be an exact copy of something else, no matter how much time or space separates them. Forms are constantly changing, just like the passing moments of an hour. Yet the world, which moves in endless cycles, reflects the nature of God, who contains all forms within Himself. Each form continues to exist, creating countless versions of itself as time moves forward. The world changes as it revolves, but the essence of each kind remains the same. While individual forms within a species may vary, the essence of the species does not change.

Asclepios: Does the world also change in its form, Trismegistus?

Hermes: Asclepios, have you not been paying attention? The world consists of everything that is created within it. Are you asking about the heavens, the earth, and the elements? These things also change in their appearance. The sky, for example, is sometimes rainy, sometimes dry; sometimes hot, sometimes cold. It may be bright or covered with clouds. Though it seems to remain the same, it constantly shifts.

The earth, too, changes. At times, it brings forth fruit, and at other times, it hides it away. It produces many different kinds of plants, trees, flowers, and seeds, each with unique properties, colors, scents, and shapes. Fire also transforms in many ways. The sun and moon show us different phases and appearances, like the reflections we see in mirrors.

We have now said enough on these matters.

PART 13

Let us turn our attention back to people and explore the gift of reason, which gives humans the right to be called rational beings. Among all the amazing things about humanity, one stands out the most: humans have discovered the divine force within nature and learned how to use it for their purposes. Long ago, our ancestors, confused about their beliefs in the gods and unable to reach an understanding of divine truth and religion, developed the art of making gods. Once they learned this art, they gave their creations special powers taken from the natural world. But since they couldn't create souls, they called on the spirits of beings like angels and genii to fill their sacred images and ceremonies with life. This gave these idols the ability to bring about good or bad outcomes.

In this way, Asclepios, the founder of medicine, has a temple on a mountain in Libya, near a river known for its crocodiles. There, his earthly body rests. As for his spirit—the better part of him—it resides elsewhere. The idea behind this is explored further in earlier sections. Understanding these thoughts requires some knowledge of occult teachings, especially about spirits connected to the world and nature. In ancient times, people believed that the idols representing their gods had powers, just as many today believe that certain statues of saints have special abilities. For example, we hear stories of how a particular statue of the Virgin Mary in one town grants prayers, while another in a different place does not. Even now, sacred images are said to heal the sick, stop plagues, uncover hidden water sources, and bless worshippers.

Hermes explains that these abilities come from the divine power in nature, which humans shape to suit their needs. Humanity, he argues, must first go through the stage of worshipping nature before it can fully understand the divine order and recognize the existence of heavenly gods. Before human intelligence can reach the highest spiritual realms, it must pass through the levels between earth and heaven. This is why people first worship the images of gods before they come to know the gods themselves. These images are not always made of wood or stone. In fact, every personality is like an idol, reflecting deeper truths and holding a part of the divine essence. Though these images seem powerful and worthy of worship to those who don't understand true divine religion, Hermetists see them as symbols of essential truths that exist beyond any physical form and remain unchanged by it.

There are three signs of true divinity: it goes beyond physical form, beyond time, and beyond individual personalities. Instead of physical form, there is pure essence. Instead of time, there is eternity. Instead of individual people, there are universal principles. Events turn into continuous processes, and what we think of as physical occurrences become inner realities.

As long as any idea of the divine is tied to a physical event or historical fact, it shows that the heavenly realm has not been reached. Symbols, once recognized as symbols, are no longer misleading or harmful. They act like veils of light, revealing glimpses of the "Divine Darkness," which is the ultimate goal of the true Hermetist. Even the most refined or abstract way of expressing supreme truth is still only a symbol or metaphor. The real truth is something beyond words, only known from God to God. It is pure essence, silence, and darkness.

The person who understands this truth—because consciousness and life are one with the whole person—returns to the divine realm. Through his divinity, he offers help to the sick, just as he once taught people the art of healing. Likewise, Hermes, my ancestor whose name I carry, now rests in the land named after him. People from all over come to his shrine to seek health and guidance through their prayers. We also see how Isis, the wife of Osiris, brings blessings to people when she is pleased, and misfortune when she is angry. These earthly gods can feel both kindness and anger, as they are shaped from nature by humans. This explains why in Egypt, people worship animals, and cities honor the souls of those who gave them laws and whose names they still remember. For this reason, Asclepios, gods worshipped in one place might be ignored elsewhere, which often causes conflicts between cities in Egypt.

Asclepios: What kind of divinity do these earthly gods possess, O Trismegistus?

Hermes: Their divinity lies in the spiritual essence found in plants, stones, and fragrant substances. This is why these gods are drawn to sacrifices, songs of praise, and sweet music that echoes the harmony of the heavens. These rituals attract them to their shrines, where they remain among humans for long periods. This is how people create gods. But do not think, Asclepios, that the actions of these earthly gods are random. While the gods in the heavens maintain their order and position above, these earthly gods also have their own roles. Some predict the future through signs and divination, while others assist with different aspects of life, acting as helpers, family, or friends to those who call upon them.

PART 14

Asclepios: O Trismegistos, what role does Destiny or Fate play in how things work? If the heavenly gods rule the universe and the earthly gods control specific events, where does Destiny fit in?

Hermes: O Asclepios, Destiny is the force that makes everything happen. It's like a chain connecting all events together. It's the reason behind everything and can be seen as the highest power—or rather, the second god, created by God Himself. It's the law governing everything in both heaven and earth, based on divine rules. Destiny and Necessity are inseparable: Destiny starts everything, and Necessity makes sure things unfold as they were meant to. From this process, Order arises—it's the way things follow one another in Time, for nothing can happen without Order. This is how the world becomes complete. The world is built on Order, and the universe holds together because of it.

These three forces—Destiny (or Fate), Necessity, and Order—completely depend on God's will. He governs the world through divine reason and law. These forces have no will of their own; they are unmoved by anger or kindness. They are simply the tools of eternal Reason, which never changes, never wavers, and never breaks.

Destiny comes first, carrying within it the seeds of future events, just like freshly planted soil contains seeds waiting to grow. Next is Necessity, which pushes these events to happen. Lastly, Order keeps everything in place, ensuring that what Destiny and Necessity create holds together. This entire process is a never-ending cycle, with no clear beginning or end. It continues forever, governed by an unchanging law that flows through eternity. As time moves on, things that once disappeared rise again, and what was on top sinks back down. This is how the circular movement works. Everything is so connected that it's impossible to tell where one thing begins or ends. They follow and lead each other endlessly.

However, chance and luck still influence earthly events.

PART 15

Now that we have spoken of all things within our reach, as much as God has allowed, it is time to offer our blessings and prayers to Him and return to our earthly responsibilities. After filling our minds with sacred knowledge, which nourishes the soul, we leave the sanctuary and lift our prayers to God. Turning toward the south, they began their orations, for it is proper to look toward the sun's descent when offering praise, just as one should face the east at sunrise to honor the new day. While they prayed, Asclepios spoke quietly: "O Tatius, let us ask our Father to allow our prayers to rise with the fragrance of incense and perfumes."

Trismegistos overheard him and responded with emotion: "May the omen be favorable, O Asclepios. But to burn incense or perfume during prayer is almost a sacrilege. He who is all things and contains all things needs nothing from us. We should offer Him only our praise and devotion. The purest offering is the grace we give in worship."

They prayed: "We thank You, O Most High, for through Your grace, we have received the light of knowledge. May Your name be praised and honored, for it is the name through which divinity is worshipped in the tradition of our ancestors! You grant us the gifts of faith, love, and devotion, and above all, You bless us with awareness, reason, and understanding. Through awareness, we recognize You; through reason, we seek You; and through understanding, we rejoice in knowing You.

"By Your divine power, we are saved, and we take joy in seeing Your presence revealed. We are grateful that from the time we came into this body, You have chosen to prepare us for eternity. Our only true joy is the knowledge of Your greatness. We have come to know You, O magnificent Light, grasped only through understanding. We have known You, O true Path of Life, inexhaustible Source of all creation! We have known You, O abundant Spirit of Nature, unchanging and eternal!

"In this prayer, we honor Your holy sanctity and ask only that You allow us to continue loving Your truth, so we may never stray from this way of life. Filled with this hope, we now go forth to enjoy a pure meal, free from the flesh of animals."

The Definitions of Asclepios

PART 1

Asclepios to the King Ammon. I send you, O King, an important message. I will begin by calling upon God, the Master of the Universe, the Creator and Father of everything. He contains all things, is everything in one, and is one in everything. Everything that exists comes from unity and remains in unity. These two are not separate, for they are one. Keep this in mind, O King, throughout my entire message.

It is pointless to try and separate the All from the One by calling everything "the All" and ignoring their unity. This distinction cannot be made because the All cannot exist without unity, just as unity cannot exist without the All. Unity always exists and never stops being one; otherwise, all things would fall apart.

What I am saying goes against common beliefs and may even seem different from some of my other teachings. My teacher Hermes often spoke with me, either alone or with Tatios present. He used to say that those who read my writings would think they are simple and clear, but in truth, they contain deeper, hidden meanings. This hidden meaning has become harder to understand because the Greeks translated our words into their language, which caused misunderstandings. The Egyptian language has a special power that makes the meaning clear to the mind. As much as you can, O King—and you have great power—do not allow this message to be translated, or these mysteries may fall into Greek hands. Their polished way of speaking could weaken the seriousness and strength of these teachings. The Greeks love new ways of talking and are very wordy in their philosophy, while we focus more on actions and facts rather than many words.

In the earth, there are powerful springs of water and fire. These represent the three elements—fire, water, and earth—which all come from the same source. It shows that all matter comes from one great origin, filled with abundance, receiving its existence from above. This is how the Creator, through the sun, governs heaven and earth. The sun sends down essence and draws up matter, holding the universe together and giving everything life through its light. The sun spreads its energy not only in the heavens and air but also on earth and deep into the abyss. If there is an essence beyond what we can see, it must belong to the sun, and light is its messenger. Only the sun knows its true nature and origin.

To fully understand these hidden things, we would need to be close to the sun and share its nature. However, what the sun reveals to us is not guesswork—it is the brilliant vision that lights up both the heavens and the world. The sun stands at the center of the universe like a crown-bearer, guiding the world like a skilled charioteer. It controls the reins of life, soul, spirit, immortality, and birth, carrying everything along with it. Through this process, the sun forms everything and grants immortality to eternal beings.

The light that radiates outward nourishes the eternal spaces of the universe. The light that spreads across the waters, earth, and air becomes a fertile place where life begins. Here, all kinds of births and transformations take place, as things change from one form to another in a continuous spiral movement. This transformation allows creatures to move through different parts of the world, shifting between forms and appearances while keeping the balance of all these changes, just like in the creation of larger beings. The stability of physical forms comes from constant change, but immortal forms never break down, while mortal bodies do. This is the difference between what is immortal and what is mortal.

The sun creates life as constantly as it shines, without ever stopping. Surrounding it are countless groups of spiritual beings. These spirits stay close to the immortal gods and watch over human affairs. They carry out the will of the gods through storms, fires, earthquakes, wars, and famines to punish those who act against the divine. The greatest sin people can commit is disrespecting the gods. The gods are meant to do good, humans are meant to honor them, and the spirits are there to discipline those who stray.

The gods do not hold people accountable for mistakes made by accident, bold actions taken because of fate, or through ignorance. Only true wrongdoing falls under their judgment. The sun supports and sustains all living things, just as the Ideal World surrounds the physical world and fills it with countless forms. Similarly, the sun wraps everything in its light, bringing life and helping all creatures grow. When they become tired and weak, the sun gathers them back to itself. The sun commands the Genii—actually, many groups of Genii—whose numbers match the stars. Every star has its own Genii, some naturally good, some bad, and others mixed, depending on what they do. A Genie's actions define its essence.

Some Genii perform both good and harmful deeds. All of these Genii oversee what happens on Earth. They disrupt governments and individual lives, shaping our souls. They are present in our nerves, marrow, veins, arteries, and even our brains and internal organs. When a person is born, they are assigned to Genii responsible for overseeing births, who operate under the influence of the stars. These Genii are constantly changing, moving in cycles, never staying the same. They act through the body to affect two parts of the soul, leaving their unique influence on each. However, the rational part of the soul is beyond the reach of the Genii, as it is meant to receive God's light, which shines like a ray from the sun.

Only a few people receive this divine light, and for those who do, the Genii have no power over them. Neither gods nor Genii can interfere when even a single ray from God touches someone. For all other people, both their souls and bodies are guided by Genii, and they become connected to these spiritual forces, mirroring their actions. Desire, which often misleads, is not the same as reason, which remains steady. The Genii control earthly matters and use our bodies as their tools. This influence is what Hermes refers to as Destiny.

The Intelligible World is linked to God, while the physical world is connected to the Intelligible World. Through these two realms, the sun transmits God's energy, which is creative in nature. Surrounding the sun are eight spheres: the sphere of the fixed stars, the six planetary spheres, and the sphere that encircles the Earth. The Genii are tied to these spheres, and humans are connected to the Genii, creating a chain that binds all beings to God, the universal Father. The sun is the source of creation, and the world is like a crucible where creation takes shape. The Intelligible Essence governs the heavens, the heavens guide the gods, the gods oversee the Genii, and the Genii direct human beings. This is the divine order, and through this hierarchy, God works through both gods and Genii to carry out His will.

Since everything is a part of God, God is present in all things. By creating everything, God is continually extending Himself without pause. God's energy exists only in the present, for it has no past, and because God has no limits, His creation has neither a beginning nor an end.

PART 2

If you think about it, O King, you'll realize that some things are both physical and non-physical. "Which things are those?" asked the King. Things like the images you see in mirrors—aren't they non-physical, even though they appear to be real? "That's true, Tat," the King replied. "You have quite an interesting way of thinking!" There are other non-physical things too, such as abstract ideas. Wouldn't you agree that these ideas are not physical themselves, but they still appear through living and non-living things? "That's true again, Tat," said the King. So, it seems that non-physical things reflect onto physical things, and physical things reflect back onto the non-physical. In other words, the physical world and the world of ideas mirror each other. Therefore, O King, honor the sacred images, for they are reflections of the physical world. The King then stood up and said, "I think it's time to take care of our guests, prophet. We can continue this theological discussion tomorrow."

PART 3

When a musician tries to play a melody but can't get the instruments to work together in harmony, his efforts end in failure, and the audience laughs. No matter how skilled he is or how hard he tries, he cannot blame the instrument for his inability to create music. The great musician of Nature, the God who oversees all harmony and controls how every instrument plays in perfect rhythm, never tires. Fatigue doesn't touch the gods. If a conductor leads a concert with trumpeters playing their parts, flute players performing the soft melodies, and lyres and violins accompanying the song, no one would blame the composer if one instrument plays out of tune. Instead, we honor the composer's talent, even if the music is disturbed by a single instrument.

In the same way, it would be disrespectful to blame Humanity for the failures of our physical bodies. God, the untiring Artist, is always perfect in His craft, working flawlessly and providing equal gifts to all. If Phidias, the great sculptor, struggled with material that was difficult to shape, we should not blame him for doing his best. Likewise, we shouldn't fault a musician for the mistakes of a faulty instrument. Instead, we should recognize that a musician deserves even more praise if he can still draw beautiful music from an instrument with broken strings or faulty notes. When the music is flawed, it is the instrument's fault, not the artist's. Those who listen will respect the musician even more for overcoming such difficulties.

Just like that, my noble audience, we must adjust the strings of our inner selves to match the intentions of the musician. Imagine a musician, without his usual instrument, being asked to create beautiful music. He might find a new way to make the sound, using unfamiliar tools, and amaze his listeners even more. There is a story about a cithara player who had Apollo's favor. While playing a melody, one of the strings on his instrument snapped, but a cicada stepped in with its song to fill the missing notes. Thanks to this divine help, the musician continued his performance without fear and won great praise.

I feel the same, noble listeners, as though when I doubt my own strength, the power of the Supreme Being steps in and fills the melody in my place, giving me the ability to honor the king. The purpose of this speech is to glorify royalty and celebrate their achievements. So let us proceed! The musician has begun, and the lyre is ready. May the beauty and sweetness of the music match the message of our song! Since we are here to praise kings and honor their greatness, let us first give thanks to the good God, the supreme King of the universe. After Him, we will honor the rulers who reflect His image and hold the royal scepter.

Even kings welcome songs that descend from the heavens, step by step, knowing that it is Heaven that grants them victory. So let the singer praise the mighty God of the universe, who is eternal and whose power has no end. He is the greatest of all victors, the source of all triumphs, one after another. Let us now finish this speech so we can honor the kings—those who protect peace and keep everyone safe, who hold their ancient power from the Lord above and receive victory from His hand. These rulers hold shining scepters that signal the trials of war, with triumph already in sight. They are not only given the right to rule but also the power to conquer. Even their march into battle strikes fear into their enemies before the fight begins.

PART 4

This discourse ends where it began, with praise for the Supreme Being and the most holy kings who bring us peace. Just as we started by honoring the Almighty, we now end by returning to that same greatness. Just as the sun nurtures seeds and gathers the fruits with its rays, like divine hands collecting gifts for God, so too do we gather within ourselves the beauty of divine wisdom. After breathing in the sweetness of these heavenly gifts, we must now collect the blessings of this sacred harvest, which God will enrich with His nourishing rains. Even if we had ten thousand mouths and ten thousand voices to glorify the pure God, the Father of Souls, we would still fall short of offering Him the praise He deserves. Just like infants who cannot properly honor their father, but are still forgiven for their efforts, we too receive His mercy.

The greatness of God shines in His ability to rise above all creatures. He is the Beginning, the End, the Center, and the Continuation of all praise. In Him, all beings recognize their source—He is all-powerful and limitless. The same is true of our king. As his children, we love to praise him and ask for his forgiveness, knowing that he has already granted it to us. Just as a father is pleased when his children recognize him, even in their weakness, so too does our king rejoice when we acknowledge him. The universal wisdom that gives life to everything and allows us to honor God is itself a gift from God. Since God is good, He holds within Himself all perfection. Being immortal, He possesses endless peace, and His eternal power brings blessings to the world.

In God's divine order, there is no division or change. All beings in Him are filled with wisdom, and the same divine care governs them all. They are guided by the same intelligence, moved by the same kindness, and united by the same love, creating harmony throughout the universe. Therefore, let us bless God and honor the kings who receive their authority from Him. And since we have begun to praise the kings, let us also glorify the reverence they show toward the Supreme. May God teach us how to honor Him properly, and may He help us in this pursuit. Our highest aim must be to revere God and celebrate the kings, for they bring us the peace we enjoy.

The virtue of the king lies in his power to create peace, and his very name carries the meaning of peace. He is called king because he leads with reason and calm authority. He surpasses all other rulers, and even his name becomes a symbol of peace. Just the mention of his name can often drive away enemies. His image acts as a beacon of safety in troubled times. The sight of the king alone brings victory, ensures security, and makes us feel invincible.

Some scholars argue that this text, "Asclepios to King Ammon," might not have been written by one of Hermes' disciples, believing it unworthy of someone taught by such a great master. Dr. Menard notes that despite the criticism of the Greeks in the earlier part of the text, it was likely written in Greek, as suggested by the reference to the Greek word for king, "basileus," and the discussion of its meaning from the Greek verb "bainein," meaning "to advance." The text also mentions Phidias and Eunomios, a musician from Locris, showing Greek influence. The description of the sun as a charioteer, along with the reference to the one who "bears the crowns," reflects Greek customs.

In Egypt, the sun was usually depicted as traveling across the Nile on a barge.

Because of these points, Dr. Menard suggests that the negative remarks about the Greeks may have been added later to mislead readers about the text's true origin. He also believes that the kings mentioned in this passage might refer to the Roman emperors Valens and Valentinian. However, I respectfully disagree. Whether or not Asclepios wrote these words, I believe the references to "kings" and "royalties" carry a deeper, mystical meaning. If the intention was simply to flatter a ruler, as Dr. Menard suggests, then why would the writer emphasize that the message contains hidden meanings? Everything said about kingship here fits the symbolic nature of Osiris, the divine ruler whose essence lives within all people.

Osiris reflects the supreme Lord of the Universe and represents the ideal form of humanity. That is why, in the Egyptian Book of the Dead, the soul of the deceased is described as "an Osiris." This symbolizes that the higher part of our nature, the true divine self within us, is like Osiris. It is to this inner king—our higher reason and the divine word of God—that we owe our loyalty, devotion, and eternal service.

Fragments of The Book of Hermes to His Son Tatios

PART 1

Trismegistus: Out of love for humanity and respect for God, my son, I begin writing this. There is no higher religion than to reflect on the universe and express gratitude to the Creator, and this is something I will always do.

Tatios: Father, if nothing here on Earth is real, how can we use our lives wisely?

Trismegistus: Be religious, my son. Religion is elevated philosophy, and without philosophy, there is no true religion. The person who understands the universe—its laws, principles, and purpose—offers thanks to the Creator, who is like a loving father, a wise teacher, and a faithful protector. This is the essence of religion, for through it, we discover what truth is and where to find it. The more we learn, the deeper our connection to religion becomes. Once the soul, trapped within the body, reaches an understanding of the true Good and Truth, it can never return to ignorance. The power of Love and the forgetting of all evil bind the soul to the Good and prevent it from separating from the Creator.

This is the goal of religion, my son. If you can reach it, your life will be pure, your death will be peaceful, and your soul will know where to go. This is the path that leads to Truth, the same path our ancestors followed to discover the Good. It is a beautiful and steady path, but it is hard for the soul to walk it while trapped in the body. The soul must first struggle with itself, dividing into parts and submitting to its highest aspect. The higher part of the soul fights to rise, while the lower parts—desire and passion—try to drag it down.

If the higher part wins, it builds a defense for itself and its master. But if the lower parts overpower the higher one, the soul is led astray and punished in this life. It is the higher part, my son, that must be your guide. Prepare yourself for the struggle, fight to keep your soul strong, and aim for victory. Now, let me summarize the principles we have discussed. Everything that exists moves, except for things that do not exist. All bodies change, though some only break apart. Not all beings are mortal, nor are all immortal. Things that can break down are corruptible, while those that remain unchanged are eternal.

God comes first, then the universe, and finally humanity. The universe exists for humanity, and humanity exists for God. The emotional part of the soul is mortal, but the rational part is eternal. Every substance is subject to change, yet all true essence is immortal. Everything has two aspects; nothing stays the same forever. Not all things have a soul, but anything that exists is alive through a soul. What is passive can feel, and everything that feels is temporary. All creatures that feel pain and pleasure are mortal, but those that only experience joy without pain are immortal.

Not every body suffers from disease, but anything that can suffer from illness will eventually be destroyed. Intelligence resides in God, and reason in humanity. Reason belongs to intelligence, and intelligence never changes. Nothing physical is fully real, and nothing non-physical is false. Everything that is born undergoes change, though not everything that changes becomes corrupted. There is no perfection on Earth, and no evil in Heaven. God is perfect, while humanity is flawed. Goodness arises through choice, while evil goes against the will. The gods always choose good.

Time belongs to the divine, but law belongs to humanity. Evil feeds the world, while time destroys humans. Everything in Heaven stays the same, while nothing on Earth is unchanging. In Heaven, there is no servitude; on Earth, there is no true freedom. In Heaven, nothing is unknown, while on Earth, nothing is fully understood. There is no connection between celestial things and earthly things. All is perfect in Heaven, and nothing on Earth is free from fault. The immortal knows nothing of death, just as the mortal cannot comprehend immortality. Not everything that is planted will grow, but everything that grows has been planted.

Mortal bodies have two stages of existence: from conception to birth, and from birth to death. Eternal beings, however, exist in a single, unchanging state from the moment they come into being. Mortal bodies increase and decrease. Perishable matter moves between destruction and creation, while immortal essence either remains within itself or transforms into something similar. The birth of one thing brings about the end of another, and every ending is also a beginning.

Some beings exist in physical form, some in pure form, and others in energy. The body contains forms, and forms contain energy. The immortal receives nothing from the mortal, but the mortal can receive from the immortal. Mortal things do not enter immortal forms, but the immortal can dwell in mortal bodies. Energy always moves downward, not upward. What exists on Earth does not benefit what is in Heaven, but everything in Heaven benefits what exists on Earth.

Heaven is filled with immortal beings, while earth holds perishable bodies. The earth is irrational, but heaven is guided by reason. Heavenly things are governed by celestial forces, while earthly things remain on earth. Heaven is the original source of all. Divine providence creates order, and necessity is the tool that providence uses. Chance brings disorder—it is a false image of real energy, only an illusion. God is unchanging Goodness, while man is constantly entangled in evil. If you remember these principles, you will also recall everything I've explained to you in more detail. But be careful about sharing these ideas with the masses. It is not that I want to keep these truths from them, but because exposing them may cause you to become a target for ridicule. Like attracts like, but opposites find no harmony. These teachings should be shared with only a few, or else they might be ignored completely.

There is also a danger in these ideas—if wicked people misuse them, they could become even worse. Stay away from the crowd, for they cannot grasp the value of these teachings.

Tatios: What do you mean, Father?

Trismegistos: Listen closely, my son. Humans are naturally drawn toward evil—it is part of their nature, and they find it pleasing. If people understood that the world was created through divine order and that everything happens because of providence and necessity, they might misuse this knowledge. They could begin to look down on everything that is created, blame destiny for their vices, and indulge in all kinds of wrongdoing. This is why it is wise to avoid sharing these truths with the crowd. Sometimes, ignorance helps keep people within limits, as fear of the unknown can prevent them from acting out.

PART 2

Tatios: You have explained these things clearly, my father, but I still have more questions. You told me that knowledge and skill are activities of reason, and now you say that animals are called "brute" because they lack reason. So does that mean animals cannot possess knowledge or skill?

Trismegistus: Yes, my son, that is correct.

Tatios: But, father, how do you explain animals that seem to display knowledge and skill? For example, ants store food for the winter, birds build nests, and cattle recognize their stables and return to them.

Trismegistus: These actions are not guided by knowledge or skill, my son, but by nature. Knowledge and skill are things we acquire, but these creatures have learned nothing. What they do comes from universal nature. Knowledge and skill belong only to those who acquire them. Actions that are shared by all creatures are natural, not learned. For example, all people can see with their eyes, but not everyone becomes a musician, an archer, or a hunter. Only a few people learn a specific skill or craft and put it to use. If only some ants stored food while others didn't, then you could say those ants possessed the skill of gathering provisions. But since they all behave the same way without deliberate thought, it is clear that neither knowledge nor skill directs them.

Activities, my son, are not physical; they exist within the body and are carried out through the body. Because they are not physical, they are immortal in a sense. But since they must be expressed through a body, they always appear within a body. Anything that has a purpose, determined by divine will and necessity, cannot remain idle. What exists will continue to exist, and that is its life and purpose. This is why bodies will always exist, for the creation of bodies is an eternal function. Even though earthly bodies are corruptible, they are necessary as vessels and tools for the energies that flow through them. Energies are immortal, and because they are immortal, they are always active.

The creation of bodies is ongoing and endless. The abilities of the soul do not all appear at once. Some abilities are present from birth, within the nonrational part of the soul, while the higher abilities emerge as the soul grows in wisdom over time. These abilities are linked to the body, but they come from divine forms and flow into mortal forms, creating bodies. Each ability serves a function, either of the body or the soul, but these abilities remain within the soul even when not connected to a body. The energies are eternal, but the soul is not always confined within a mortal body. The soul can exist without the body, but the abilities cannot manifest unless they have a body to work through.

This is a deep truth, my son. The body cannot exist without the soul, but being itself can.

Tatios: What do you mean by that, father?

Trismegistus: Listen carefully, Tatios. When the soul leaves the body, the body remains, but it begins to break down from within until it completely dissolves. Such a process requires an active force, so even after the soul departs, some energy remains in the body. The difference between an immortal being and a mortal being is this: the immortal being is made of pure, simple essence, while the mortal being is not. One is active and governs, while the other is passive and obeys. One is free, while the other is ruled. Energies are present not only in living beings but also in lifeless things like wood, stone, and similar objects. Through energy, these things grow, ripen, decay, decompose, and change. Energy is what causes transformation, and all becoming is part of the universal process.

There will never be a time when the universe lacks new life, for it constantly produces and destroys beings. Energy itself can never be destroyed, no matter what form it takes or where it manifests. Some energies work through divine beings, others through mortal beings. Some energies are universal, affecting many, while others are specific, working on individual beings. Divine energies operate within eternal beings and are as perfect as those beings themselves.

Partial energies act through living beings, while specific energies operate within everything that exists. This means, my son, that the entire universe is filled with energies. Since energies need bodies to manifest, and there are many bodies in the universe, we can see how abundant these energies are. However, there are even more energies than bodies because one body can hold multiple energies—sometimes one, two, or three—on top of those energies that exist everywhere. I call these universal energies the ones that cannot be separated from bodies, which show themselves through sensations and movements. Without these universal energies, no body could exist.

In contrast, specific energies appear in the minds of humans through art, science, and labor. Sensations come with energies or result from them. Understand, my son, the difference between energy and sensation. Energy comes from a higher place, while sensation belongs to the body and depends on it. The body serves as a seat or vehicle for energy, allowing the energy to express itself through it. For this reason, I say that sensations are tied to the body and are mortal. Their existence begins and ends with the body. On the other hand, immortal energies do not have sensations because of their nature. Sensations can only arise from some good or bad experience affecting the body, and immortal beings are not subject to these changes.

Tatios: So, does every body experience sensation?

Trismegistus: Yes, my son, every body experiences sensation, and energies act in all bodies.

Tatios: Even in lifeless things, father?

Trismegistus: Yes, even in lifeless things. Sensations vary by type. In beings with reason, sensations are accompanied by thought. In beings without reason, sensations are purely physical. In lifeless things, sensations take the form of passive processes, such as growth and decay. Both passion and sensation are the result of energies, coming from a single source and leading to a single outcome.

In living beings, two more energies accompany passion and sensation: joy and sorrow. Without these, no living being—and especially no reasonable being—would be able to feel anything. Therefore, joy and sorrow can be seen as forms of emotion in all living beings. They appear through sensations, as movements within the body, driven by the irrational parts of the soul. Both joy and sorrow are forms of suffering. Joy, which is the feeling of pleasure, often brings about greater troubles. Sorrow leads to pain and punishment, making it equally harmful.

Tatios: Is sensation the same thing in both the soul and the body, father?

Trismegistus: What do you mean by the sensation of the soul, my son?

Tatios: The soul is not physical, father. But sensation seems to be tied to the body, since it exists within it.

Trismegistus: If we say that sensation belongs to the body, then we must compare it either to the soul or to the energies, which are not physical, even though they exist within the body. However, sensation is neither an energy nor a soul, nor is it separate from the body. Therefore, it cannot be something non-physical. If it isn't non-physical, it must be physical, because nothing exists that is neither physical nor non-physical.

PART 3

The Lord, the Creator of immortal forms, Tatios, completed His work and made nothing more. He does not create anything new now either. Once these eternal forms were given life and connected to one another, they began to move on their own, needing nothing to sustain them. Even if they rely on each other in some ways, they do not need anything outside themselves because they are immortal. This is how the creations of the supreme God are meant to be.

However, our immediate creator, the one who made us, has a body. He created us and continues to create mortal bodies that are subject to change and decay. Unlike the supreme Creator, he cannot create immortal beings, nor should he try to imitate Him. The supreme God created eternal forms from His own essence, which is incorporeal. But our creator formed us from material substances, giving us physical bodies that are naturally weak and dependent on external support.

Because we are made of physical matter, we need constant nourishment and renewal to survive. The earth, water, fire, and air flow into us, restoring and sustaining our bodies. Without these elements replenishing us, the combination of substances that make up our bodies would fall apart. We are so fragile that we cannot even remain active for a full day without rest. You know well, my son, that without the night's rest, our bodies could not endure the strain of the day's work.

In His wisdom, our good creator has provided for our survival by creating sleep, which restores movement and strength. He made sure that the time spent resting is equal to or even longer than the time spent working. Think, my son, about how sleep serves the body and how important it is, even though it contrasts with the soul's constant activity. If the soul's function is to keep moving, the body relies on sleep to loosen the tension within and restore what it needs. Sleep provides the body with water to nourish the blood, earth for the bones, air for the nerves and vessels, and fire for the eyes. This is why the body finds such pleasure in sleep.

The teachings of Hermetic philosophy reflect the idea that divine energy flows constantly into the universe, even though the forms through which it flows remain unchanged and self-sustaining. The natural order was set from the beginning and cannot be altered. The soul's journey into physical life is an ongoing process and will only end when the creative cycle is complete. The flow of divine energy has never stopped since the beginning of creation. Life continues to emerge because of this constant outpouring of being into existence, and without it, the process of creation and evolution would halt. The creator mentioned here is the Demiurge, the one responsible for shaping the physical universe.

PART 4

A great and divine power, my son, is placed at the center of the universe, observing everything that people do on earth. In the divine order, everything is guided by providential Necessity, while among people, this role is fulfilled by Justice. The first order governs heavenly things, for the Gods neither wish to, nor are able to, break any laws. They cannot make mistakes, and because mistakes lead to sin, they are free from sin.

The second order, Justice, is responsible for correcting the wrongs that happen among people on earth. Since humans are mortal and made of corruptible matter, they are prone to losing their way when they no longer focus on divine things to guide them toward virtue. This is where Justice steps in to act.

Through the energies he draws from Nature, man is subject to Destiny. But through the mistakes he makes in life, man is subject to Justice.

PART 5

Here, then, is what can be said about the three aspects of time. They do not exist independently, and they are not completely separate from each other. Yet, in another way, they are both connected and distinct. Can we imagine the present without the past? One cannot exist without the other, because the present is created by the past, and the future emerges from the present.

If we want to fully understand this, we need to reason like this: The past has already moved into what no longer exists. The future does not exist until it becomes the present. And the present, in turn, stops being itself the moment it passes. How can we call something present when it doesn't stay for even an instant and has no fixed point? If it vanishes as soon as it appears, can it really be said to exist?

Moreover, since the past is closely tied to the present, and the present connects directly to the future, they blend into one. They share an identity, unity, and continuity. Time flows without interruption, constantly moving and changing, even though it remains one and the same.

PART 6

My son, matter is always in the process of becoming. It has existed before, and it continues to change, for matter serves as the vehicle for transformation. Becoming is how the uncreated and all-knowing God expresses His activity. Matter carries within it the seed of change, and through this seed, it is brought into existence. The creative force shapes matter according to ideal forms, giving it structure. Before it is formed, matter has no shape or identity. It only takes on form when it is put into motion through creation.

PART 7

It is impossible for a human, who is imperfect and made up of many flawed parts, to speak with certainty about what is truly real, my son Tatios. Our bodies are formed from different elements that are not originally part of us. Still, as much as I can, I say that reality only exists in eternal beings, for their forms are truly real. Fire is simply fire, earth is only earth, and air is only air. But our bodies are made of a combination of these elements—fire, earth, water, and air—yet our bodies are not really fire, earth, water, or air, nor anything truly real.

Since reality has never been a part of us from the start, how could we ever see it, speak of it, or even understand it unless God allows us to? The things of this world are not truly real but only copies of reality. In fact, not all things are even proper copies; some are nothing more than illusions and errors, mere tricks of the mind. When something receives a spark of higher truth, it can become a reflection of the real. Without this divine influence, it stays an illusion. It is like a portrait: a painting of a person, but not the person it represents. It may have eyes, but it cannot see; it may have ears, but it cannot hear. A portrait only gives the appearance of a person but is nothing more than an image that fools the eye. It seems real but is only a shadow. Those who avoid being deceived by false appearances see what is true. If we can see things as they are, we understand the real, but if we only see what is false, we cannot understand or know the real at all.

Tatios: So, is there anything truly real on earth, my father?

Trismegistus: Reality does not exist on earth, my son, and it cannot be found here. However, a few people may grasp it if God grants them the gift of divine vision. What exists on earth is only made up of appearances and opinions, not reality itself. And yet, reality can be found through intelligence and reason. To think and speak the truth is as close as we come to what is real.

Tatios: But how can that be? How can we think and speak truthfully if nothing on earth is real?

Trismegistus: It is true, my son, that we know nothing of absolute Truth. How could it be otherwise? Truth is the highest virtue, the ultimate Good. It is not clouded by matter or trapped in physical form. It is pure, unchanging, and eternal. But the things here on earth, as you see, are not compatible with the Good. They are temporary, always changing, and constantly shifting from one form to another. How can something be real if it cannot even remain the same as itself? Anything that is always changing is not just an illusion in itself, but it also deceives us by appearing in different ways at different times.

Tatios: Does this mean that even man is not real, father?

Trismegistus: No, my son. Man is not real in the truest sense. Reality only belongs to something that remains the same and stays true to itself. Man, on the other hand, is made up of many different parts and never stays the same. As long as he lives in a body, he changes from one age to another, from one state to the next. Sometimes, after only a short while, parents no longer recognize their children, and children no longer recognize their parents. Can something that changes so much that it is no longer recognizable be considered real? Should we not see these ever-changing forms as illusions? Only what is eternal and good can be considered real. Man is temporary, and therefore not real; he is just an appearance, and appearances are the ultimate illusion.

Tatios: So even the stars and celestial bodies are not real, since they also change?

Trismegistus: Anything that is born and subject to change cannot be real. However, the works of the great Creator can receive a kind of reality from Him. Still, even they contain an element of falsehood because they change, and nothing can be truly real unless it remains the same.

Tatios: Then what can we call truly real, my father?

Trismegistus: The sun is the only being among all creatures that does not change and remains constant. This is why it is given the task of overseeing the universe. It is the leader and creator of all things. I honor the sun and bow before its truth. After the One, it is the second creator I recognize.

Tatios: What, then, is the original Reality, father?

Trismegistus: He is the One and only, Tatios, who is not made of matter, who does not exist within any body. He has no color, no shape, and He never changes. He simply is. Anything that is an illusion will perish, my son. The order of the Real ensures that everything in this world will end through dissolution, for the cycle of birth depends on things breaking apart. Everything that is created must eventually dissolve, only to be born again. From dissolution, life emerges, and life must also decay, so that creation can continue without end.

See, then, the Creator who existed before everything. The things born from dissolution are just shadows; they shift and change, becoming one thing today and another tomorrow. They can never remain the same, and how can something that is always changing be truly real? Such things are mere appearances, my son. Man, too, is only an appearance of Humanity, just as a child represents childhood, a youth represents adolescence, a grown man represents adulthood, and an old man represents old age. How can we say that a child remains a child, or a man remains the same man, when constant changes hide what they were and what they have become?

So understand, my son, that all these things are only illusions reflecting a higher Reality. Since this is the case, I define illusion as a reflection of what is truly Real.

It is difficult to understand God, and it is impossible to describe Him. The physical world cannot express the non-physical, and something imperfect cannot fully grasp what is perfect. How can the eternal be connected with the temporary? The eternal remains forever, while the temporary quickly passes away. What is eternal is Real, while what is temporary is only a faint reflection. The difference between the mortal and the divine is as great as the difference between weakness and strength, or smallness and greatness. This distance between them clouds our understanding of true beauty.

We can see physical things with our eyes, and what the eyes perceive, the tongue can describe. But what has no body, no appearance, no shape, and no form cannot be understood by the senses. I know, Tatios, that God cannot be fully described. He is beyond anything we can define or explain.

Fragments of The Writings of Hermes to Ammon

PART 1

The force that governs the universe is Providence. What holds the universe together and sets its boundaries is Necessity. Destiny drives and controls everything with the power it possesses. It is Destiny that causes both the beginning of life and its end. Providence comes first and gives order to the universe. It reaches to the heavens, where the gods move in endless, tireless motion. Destiny exists because Necessity exists. Providence sees what is to come, and Destiny decides the arrangement of the stars. This is the universal law.

PART 2

Everything is brought into existence by Nature and Destiny, and no place is beyond the reach of Providence. Providence is the free will of the Supreme God, from which two natural forces arise: Necessity and Destiny. Destiny follows the guidance of both Providence and Necessity, while the stars follow the path set by Destiny. No one can escape from Destiny or defend themselves against the influence of the stars, as they act as tools of Destiny. Through them, the will of Destiny is carried out across all of Nature and in the lives of human beings.

PART 3

The soul is an essence that has no physical form, and even when it is within a body, it does not lose its true nature. Its essence lies in constant movement—the free movement of thought. Yet the soul does not move through anything, towards anything, or for any specific purpose. It is a primal force, and what is primary does not rely on anything secondary.

The phrase "in anything" refers to place, time, and nature. "Towards anything" refers to harmony, shape, or structure. "For anything" refers to the body, since time, place, nature, and form are connected to the body. All these elements are tied together in a cycle of mutual dependence. A body requires a place, because it cannot exist without occupying space. A body changes its nature, and such change must happen over time, through movement in nature. The parts of a body cannot come together without harmony in form.

Space exists because of physical bodies. It holds their changes and prevents them from being lost as they transform. A body shifts from one state to another, but even when it leaves one state, it remains a body; it just takes on a new condition. It is still a body—only its state has changed. This means that what shifts in a body is not its essence, but its qualities and way of being.

Place, time, and natural movement are not physical things, but each has its own unique role. The role of space is to contain. The role of time is to mark intervals and measure change. The role of nature is movement. The role of harmony is connection. The role of the body is to change. And the role of the soul is to think.

PART 4

The soul is an essence without a physical form. If it had a body, it could not preserve itself, because every body needs breath and life, which depend on order. Wherever something is born, it is always changing. To "become" implies growth, and growth brings increase, but every increase eventually leads to decrease, which brings about destruction. Anything that receives the form of life can only exist through the soul. For something to exist, it must already be part of life. I define existence as the process of becoming reasonable and participating in intelligent life. Life creates the creature, intelligence makes it reasonable, and the body makes it mortal.

The soul has no physical form and holds an unchanging power. Can a being be intelligent without a living soul? Can it be rational if there is no intelligent force guiding its rational life? Intelligence does not show itself equally in all creatures because the way their bodies are formed affects their harmony. If a body contains too much heat, the creature becomes restless and energetic. If cold dominates, the creature becomes sluggish and heavy. Nature arranges the elements of the body according to a balance or harmony. This balance comes in three forms: hot, cold, and balanced or temperate.

The way these elements combine in a body depends on the influence of the stars. The soul takes the body that is destined for it and gives it life through the work of nature. Nature matches the harmony within the body to the arrangement of the stars, aligning the elements in the body with the harmony of the heavens. This creates a mutual connection, where the stars and the body reflect each other. The purpose of this stellar harmony is to create sympathies that align with destiny.

PART 5

The soul, Ammon, is an essence that exists for its own purpose, receiving the life it was given from the start. It draws to itself a certain kind of reason mixed with passion and desire. Passion is like a raw material; when it aligns with the intelligent part of the soul, it becomes courage, standing firm against fear. Desire, too, is a raw material; when it works alongside the rational part of the soul, it turns into aspiration and resists indulgence. Reason acts like a light, guiding and correcting the blindness of desire. When the soul's different abilities are balanced under the control of reason, they create justice.

The management of the soul's abilities belongs to the Intellectual Principle, which functions with its own thoughtful reason. It governs everything like a judge, with its reason acting as its advisor. This Principle understands how reason can guide even the irrational parts, giving them a form of rationality. Though this rationality is weaker than true reason, it still surpasses the irrational—much like how an echo reflects a voice or how the moon reflects the sun's light. Passion and desire follow their own patterns of reason, attracting each other and creating a flow of thought between them.

Every soul is immortal and always in motion. Movement either comes from energy or from the body. Since the soul is without a physical form, it does not come from matter but from an essence that is also non-material. Everything that is born must come from something else. All things that are born and eventually decay involve two kinds of movement: the soul moves the being to life, while the body grows, shrinks, and decomposes as it breaks down. This is the cycle of perishable bodies. But the soul itself is in constant motion, never stopping. It moves by its own nature, creating movement from within. Every soul, therefore, is immortal because it is always in motion.

There are three kinds of souls: divine, human, and irrational. The divine soul exists in a divine form, which gives it the energy to move and act. When this soul leaves mortal beings, it abandons its irrational parts and returns to its divine form. Because the divine soul is always in motion, it flows along with the universal movement. The human soul also contains something divine, but it is bound to irrational elements like desire and passion. These irrational parts are energies, and although they are tied to mortal bodies, they do not die. However, they are separate from the divine part of the soul, which belongs to the divine form. When the divine part enters a mortal body and meets these irrational elements, it becomes a human soul.

The soul of animals is made up of passion and desire, which is why animals are called brutes—they lack reason. The fourth type of soul is the one connected to lifeless things. This soul exists outside the bodies it influences. It moves within the divine form and passively directs the objects it touches.

PART 6

The soul is an eternal and intelligent essence, guided by its own reason. It aligns itself with the concept of harmony. Even when it is separated from the physical body, the soul continues to exist on its own, independent in the world of ideals. It governs its reason and gives life a movement similar to its own thought—this is the essence of being, for the soul's nature is to shape other things according to its own character.

There are two types of life movements: one that matches the essence of the soul, and one that follows the nature of the body. The first type is universal and free, while the second is specific and bound by necessity. Everything that moves must follow the laws of whatever causes its movement. However, the soul's movement is connected by its nature to the principle of intelligence. The soul must be without a physical form and entirely distinct from the body because, if it had a body, it could not have reason or thought. All bodies lack intelligence, but when they receive the spirit, they become alive and breathe.

Breath belongs to the body, while reason focuses on the beauty of what is essential. The spirit connected to the senses interprets appearances. This spirit is divided among the different senses, such as sight, hearing, smell, taste, and touch. It interacts with thought to make sense of sensations; without thought, it only produces illusions because it belongs to the body and passively receives everything. Judgment belongs to reason, which understands higher things, while opinion belongs to the sensory spirit. The sensory spirit draws its energy from the outside world, while reason finds its energy within itself.

Various Hermetic Fragments

PART 1

There are essential spirit, reason, intelligence, and perception. Opinion and sensation lean toward perception, while reason aligns with the essential spirit. Thought moves independently but is also connected to perception. When combined, these elements form the soul. Opinion and sensation aim for perfection but do not stay consistent. They can shift between excess, deficiency, or change. Without perception, they decline, but when they follow perception closely, they connect with intellectual reason through learning and knowledge.

We have the power to choose, and it is up to us whether we select the best or the worst path by our will. Choosing what is harmful ties us to the physical world and places us under the control of Destiny. However, the intellectual spirit within us is free, and because of that, our reason is also free, unchanging, and beyond the reach of Destiny. When we follow this higher, intelligent reason, which is guided by the will of the supreme God, the spirit rises above the natural order of created things. But when the soul becomes attached to these created things, it becomes connected to their destiny, even though it is not truly part of their nature.

PART 2

There is a state of Being that is higher than all other beings and everything that exists. This Being is what gives universal essence to everything that is real and intelligible. Nature is the essence we can sense, containing within itself all physical objects. Between these two realms are the intellectual gods and the gods of the senses. The thoughts of intelligence connect with the intellectual gods, while opinions align with the gods of the senses, who reflect the higher intelligences. For example, the sun is a reflection of the creative and celestial God. Just as God created the universe, the sun brings animals to life, causes plants to grow, and controls the movement of water and other fluids.

PART 3

Thus, the soul's formless vision rises beyond the body to gaze upon true beauty. It lifts itself up in reverence, not for shape, body, or appearance, but for what lies beyond them all—something serene, still, essential, and unchanging. It is everything, complete in itself, singular and whole, existing by and through itself, always the same, without change or variation.

PART 4

If you understand this one and only Good, nothing will be beyond your reach, for all virtue is contained within it. Do not think this Good exists inside anyone or outside of anyone—it has no boundaries, yet it is the boundary of all things. Nothing holds it, but it holds everything within itself. What difference is there between the physical and the non-physical, the created and the uncreated, the things bound by necessity and those that are free, or between earthly things and heavenly things, between what can decay and what is eternal? The difference lies in this: some things exist freely, while others are bound by necessity. What belongs to the lower realm is incomplete and will pass away.

PART 5

Beneath nature and the ideal world stands the pyramid. At its peak is the cornerstone, the Creative Word of the universal Lord. This Word is the first power after Him—uncreated, infinite, and existing before everything He made. It is the child of the Most Perfect, the true and fruitful Son. The nature of this intelligent Word is to generate and create. You may call it generation, nature, or character, but know this: it is perfect in the Perfect, it comes from the Perfect, and all its works are perfectly good. It is the source of both creation and life.

Because this is its nature, it is rightly named. If not for the care and guidance of the universal Lord, who has caused me to share these truths, you would not have such a strong desire to explore these matters. Now, listen to the conclusion of this message. The Spirit I have spoken of so often is essential to all things. It sustains everything, gives life to all beings, and nourishes them. Flowing endlessly from the holy Source, it continually provides support to spirits and all living creatures.

PART 6

The Ideal Light existed before any other light, and the pure Intelligence of Intelligence has always been. Its unity is nothing other than the Spirit that surrounds the entire universe. From this Spirit comes neither gods, nor angels, nor anything else essential, for He is the Lord of all things, the source of power and light. Everything depends on Him and exists within Him. His perfect Word, both generative and creative, descended into the forces of nature and into the waters that bring forth life, making them fruitful.

After saying this, he stood and declared: "I call upon you, Heaven, sacred work of the great God. I call upon you, Voice of the Father, spoken at the beginning when the universe was created. I call upon you, Word, the only Son of the Father, who holds all things together. Be kind, be kind!"

PART 7

Seven planets move along the paths of Olympus, and through them, Eternity is measured: the Moon that lights the night, the dark Kronos, the gentle Sun, the Paphian Goddess who protects marriage, the bold Ares, the fertile Hermes, and Zeus, the source of life and nature's foundation. These planets have also been connected to humanity, for within each of us are the Moon, Zeus, Ares, Aphrodite, Kronos, Phoebus, and Hermes.

From the heavenly essence, we draw our tears, laughter, anger, speech, creation, sleep, and desire. Tears come from Kronos, creation from Zeus, speech from Hermes, courage from Ares, sleep from Artemis, desire from Kytheraea (Aphrodite), and laughter from Apollo, who brings joy to human thoughts and fills the endless world with delight.

PART 8

Hermes teaches that those who know God are protected from the attacks of evil and are no longer bound by Destiny. Knowing God is what true religion means.

Thank You for Reading

Dear Reader,

We hope this timeless classic has sparked your imagination and enriched your literary journey. Now that you've turned the final page, we want to share a vision for the future of reading—one where every classic you've ever wanted to explore is at your fingertips, in a format that best suits your life.

We'd like to invite you to gain immediate, unlimited digital & audiobook access to hundreds of the most treasured literary classics ever written—along with the option to secure deluxe paperback, hardcover & box set editions at printing cost. Together, we can spark a new global literary renaissance alongside our small, independent publishing house called "The Library of Alexandria."

Thousands of years ago, the Library of Alexandria stood as a beacon of knowledge—until it was lost to history. We aim to reignite that spirit of preservation and discovery right now, in the modern age—only this time, it's accessible to all, in every language and every format.

Picture a world where every timeless classic, novel, poem, or philosophical treatise is not only available to read but also updated for today's readers—modernized, translated into any language or dialect, and ready to enjoy in any format you choose, whether that is in an eBook, audiobook, paperback, or deluxe hardcover & box set version a printing cost.

By joining our movement to rebuild the modern Library of Alexandria, you become part of an unprecedented mission to offer:

- **Unlimited Audiobook & eBook Access to the Greatest Classics of All Time**

  Instantly explore thousands of legendary works, from Plato and Shakespeare to Jane Austen and Leo Tolstoy. All are instantly ready to read or listen to, giving you a complete literary universe at your fingertips.

- **Paperback & Deluxe Editions at Printing Costs:**

  Purchase any title in a paperback, deluxe hardbound, or deluxe boxset edition at printing costs, shipped right to your doorstep. Curate your personal library of Alexandria with editions worthy of display—crafted to last, designed to captivate, and delivered straight to your door.

- **Modern translations for Contemporary Readers in all languages and dialects**

  Discover a vast selection of classics reimagined in clear, current language—no more struggling with outdated phrases or obscure references. Next to the original versions, we aim to offer translations in as many languages and dialects as possible.

  As we continue our translation efforts and add new languages, readers everywhere can connect with these works as if they were written today. By bridging linguistic divides, you're contributing to ensuring that these timeless stories become more meaningful, accessible, and inspiring for people across the globe.

- **Your Personal Library of Alexandria:**

  Over the months and years, you'll curate a unique physical archive of classics—each volume a testament to your taste, curiosity, and love of knowledge. It's not just about owning books—it's about curating a cultural legacy you'll cherish and pass down for generations to come.

- **Join a Global Literary Renaissance:**

  Your support fuels an ongoing mission: allowing us to reinvest in offering deluxe print editions (including special boxsets) at their true cost, broaden the range of available formats and translations, and extend the reach of these works to new audiences worldwide. By joining today, you're not just preserving a legacy of masterpieces; you set in motion a powerful wave of literary accessibility.

  We are more than a publisher—we're a movement, and we can't do it alone. Your support lets us scale our mission, preserving and reimagining history's greatest works for tomorrow's readers.

Become a Torchbearer of knowledge.

Thank you for picking up this book and allowing us into your literary journey. As you turn the pages, know that you're part of something larger: a global effort to keep these stories alive, share their wisdom across borders and generations, and spark a true cultural revival for the modern era.

If this resonates with you—please consider taking the next step by visiting:

www.libraryofalexandria.com

With gratitude and a shared love of knowledge,

The Modern Library of Alexandria Team

Visit:

www.libraryofalexandria.com

Or scan the code below: